"So you're in?" Cheff asked. "We can't do it without you, Sable."

She looked Cheff in the eye. "I'm in."

Mid looked incredulously at Sable, then at Cheff, then threw up his hands. "Great. She's *in*. *She's* in. That takes care of getting up to the loading dock. Now all we have to do is"—he counted on his fingers again—"sneak out of the Labor Compound, steal a boat, sail across the bay in the dead of night without drowning or getting caught by patrols—"

"—or crushed by a freighter—" Sable added.

"—get Sable onto the loading platform, knock our secret knock, hope our new friend Lery opens the door, find Uncle Karf in the basement of the *Iron Fortress*, no less, and steal him out from under the noses of a bunch of Sephs up to who knows what? Is that all? Did I miss anything?"

"No, Old Son," Cheff said, "I think you got it all."

Buttons held Starry Stargazer up to her ear and listened intently for a few seconds. "Starry says, 'Piece of cake.'"

Mid buried his face in his hands. "Great."

OPERATION BREAK IRON

Book One

by

Liam Kincaid

with illustrations by

Daniel Wood

LBME Publishing

Operation Break Iron—Fellstone Tales Book One
LBME Publishing: http://LBMEPublishing.com/
ISBN: 978-1-64676-010-7 (trade paperback)
ISBN: 978-1-64676-011-4 (ebook)

Second Edition

Printed in the United States of America.

This book is a work of fiction. Names, characters, places, and
incidents either are products of the author's imagination or are
used fictitiously. Any resemblance to actual persons, living or
dead, events, or locales is entirely coincidental.

This book is lovingly dedicated to

R. L. G.

Best Friend, Mentor, Brother, and Master World Builder

Acknowledgments

Thank you to all who helped create this book, including:

Robert L. Graham, Creator of the Continent of Andaran.

Jason Wood, Editor Extraordinaire, who began my education as a writer.

Sarah J, Topnotch Beta Reader and dear friend who offered unlimited encouragement.

And my Twitch Crew:
  J. T. "Jack" Shennaghy
  FemaleWriter
  Dear Alisa
  EmperorOfFinland
  Mayah Robinson
  NightWriter
  Charlie Stone

And, as always, my heartfelt thanks to Lon Böder and Penney Knightly for the many hours of brainstorming and all the encouragement and support, without which this book would never have come to be.

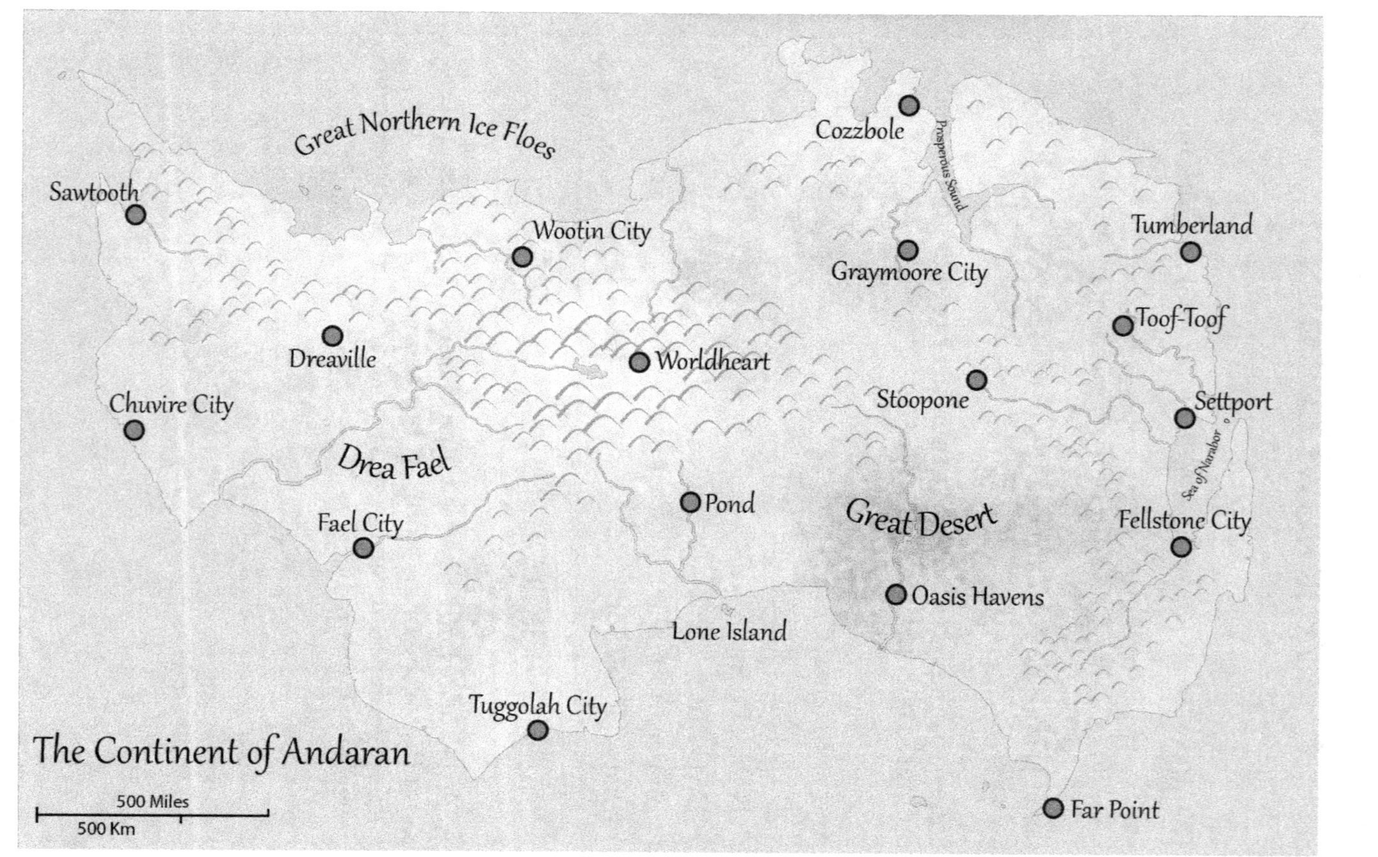

Great Northern Ice Floes
Sawtooth
Cozzbole
Prosperous Sound
Wootin City
Tumberland
Graymoore City
Toof-Toof
Dreaville
Worldheart
Stoopone
Settport
Chuvire City
Sea of Narabor
Drea Fael
Pond
Great Desert
Fellstone City
Fael City
Oasis Havens
Lone Island
Tuggolah City
The Continent of Andaran
500 Miles
500 Km
Far Point

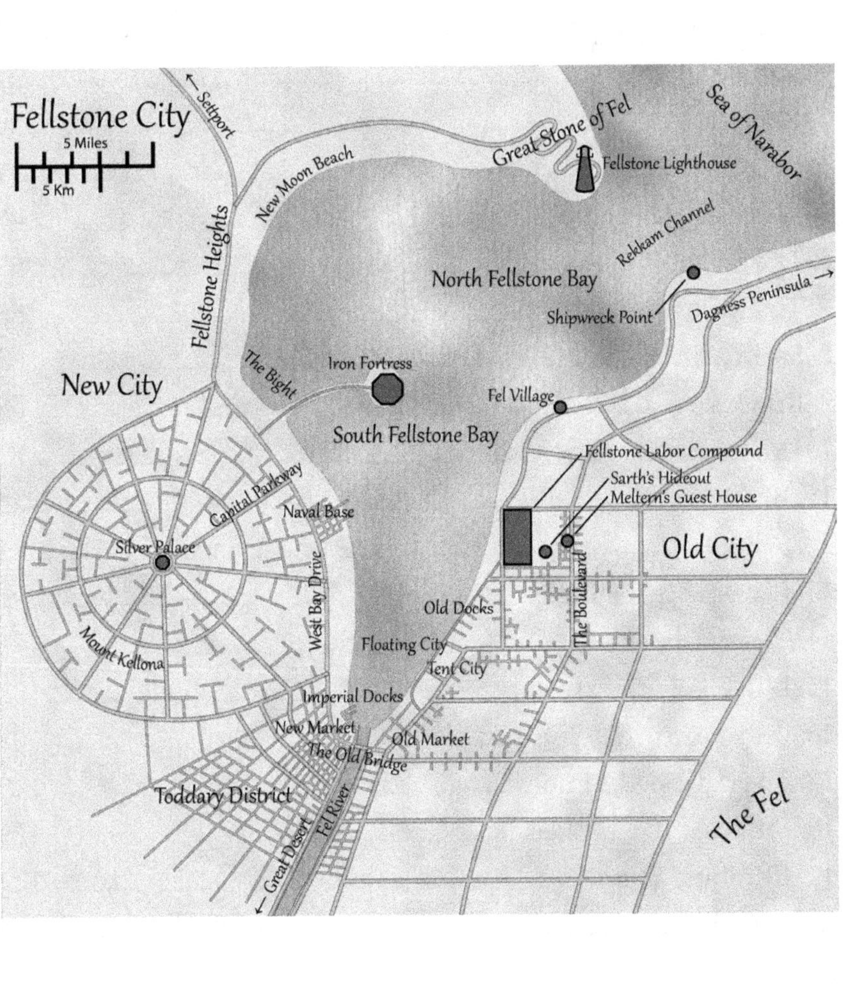

Fellstone City
5 Miles
5 Km
Sealport
Great Stone of Fel
Sea of Narabor
New Moon Beach
Fellstone Lighthouse
Fellstone Heights
Rekkam Channel
North Fellstone Bay
Shipwreck Point
Dagness Peninsula →
The Bight
Iron Fortress
New City
Fel Village
South Fellstone Bay
Fellstone Labor Compound
Sarth's Hideout
Meltern's Guest House
Capital Parkway
Naval Base
Old City
Silver Palace
West Bay Drive
Mount Kellona
Old Docks
The Boulevard
Floating City
Tent City
Imperial Docks
New Market
Old Market
The Old Bridge
Toddary District
Fel River
The Fel
Great Desert

Table of Contents

— 1 —

THE LABOR COMPOUND

MY FIRST VIEW of the Iron Fortress was from the deck of the rusty old freighter the Imperium used for transporting political prisoners.

At twilight, we rounded the rocky point that marked the entrance to Fellstone Bay. "Is that the Fellstone Light?" I asked the first officer, who was standing by me at the rail.

He pointed to the northwest. "No, the Fellstone Lighthouse is behind us now. This light you see is the Iron Fortress. It warns ships to steer clear of the Caudon Peninsula."

I peered into the foggy gloom. "All I see is the light—I can't see the Iron Fortress itself."

"Let's hope you never do, lad, let's hope you never do." He shivered. "Best go find your mother now. We'll be docking in a few minutes."

Two armed marines escorted us down the gangplank and onto the wooden pier. I carried Mother's suitcase along with my own. Mother slumped onto the rough planking, heedless of the creosote that stained what had once been an elegant travel coat. The sooty, black autumn rain matted her hair and made greasy black streaks down her pale face.

"Wait by the road," a marine instructed. "There'll be a bus for you and the other prisoners before long."

I helped Mother to her feet, but she was almost too wobbly to stand. I put her arm around my shoulders and carried both suitcases with my other hand. We followed the rest of the prisoners to the bus stop, where Mother collapsed again.

Soon, amidst a great clattering and clanking and clouds of steam, an ancient bus shuddered to a stop. A fellow prisoner kindly helped Mother and me aboard and handed up our luggage. We found a vacant seat. I put the suitcases on the overhead rack. Mother leaned against the window and promptly fell asleep.

The prisoner who had helped us took the seat across the aisle. "Is she your mother?"

"Yes, sir. She… she's not doing so well. She's been poorly since they shot Father. Mother was seasick the entire voyage. She wasn't able to keep anything down, not even thin soup."

"It was a rough trip," the prisoner agreed. "That old transport ship is a hazard. Should have been scrapped ages ago. The passage is worse in winter, I've heard."

When all the passengers were aboard, the steam bus strained and grunted and finally lurched forward, then wheezed its way up the steep hill to the Fellstone Labor Compound. The bus came to a stop a few dozen yards (40m) from the massive iron gates.

Mother awoke when the bus stopped, but I waited until the other passengers had gotten off before I coaxed her to her feet. Of course, that put us at the end of the line. Mother had rallied a little after her rest on the bus. The view from the top of the hill was amazing—the sky had cleared partially. High above, the Great Fisherman Nebula was coming to life for the night. To the west, a dense gray fog rolled into the bay. As the line slowly shuffled forward, it clouded over and rained again, this time in earnest.

A massive concrete wall, twelve feet high with a huge, sol- id-iron gate, surrounded the Fellstone Labor Compound. On each side of the gate stood a tall tower with an armed guard keeping watch. To our left sat a small, squat guardhouse, its paint peeling off in long, gray strips.

When it was our turn, I gathered my courage and stepped up to the window. A guard stuck his head out and looked us over. I knew him for a Fessal by his long nose and prominent front teeth. "One moment." His head disappeared, a door opened, and he stepped out, a dark rain cloak over his uniform. He consulted his clipboard, then extended his hand. "Papers!"

Mother searched her handbag, then handed me a packet of papers, which I handed to the guard.

He examined them and checked his list. "Let's see, Lildur species... Lildurs... Lildurs... Ah, here we are. Family name, Tylandine?"

"Yes, sir," Mother replied.

"Rose Tylandine, widow of the condemned. Is that you?"

Mother whispered, "Yes."

"Birn Tylandine, son of the condemned. That you?"

"Yes, sir."

"Small for your age. Says here you wear glasses. Where are they? Did you lose them? Fall overboard, maybe, when you were seasick?"

I took my glasses from my shirt pocket. Greasy black smears obscured the lenses. "I have them, sir. I took them off because they weren't working anymore."

He noted the grimy lenses, grunted, and went back to his list. "Wen Tylandine, father, condemned, deceased. Shot like the traitor he was, no doubt."

Mother opened her mouth to answer, but nothing came out. She gave a tiny nod.

"Right, in you go." He scribbled an address on a scrap of paper and gave it to me. "Get moving. I'll give you twenty minutes to get there, not a second longer."

The guard opened the gate and let us pass through. I wondered how we would ever find the address in the dark. Our friend from the bus was long gone, so we were on our own. As we started down the central avenue, we strained to make sense of the building numbers.

Back in Tumberland, I'd heard plenty of stories about the Fellstone Labor Compound—who hadn't? But nothing I'd heard could have prepared me for what I saw. Dozens of tall factory chimneys belched clouds of black smoke. The buildings, the walls, the towers, and even the people, were all coated with a layer of grimy black soot. The rain had turned the soot on the cobblestones into slippery black mud. Light from a few bare windows reflected bleakly on the wet pavement, but most of the windows were dark. Boards covered many of them. From a puddle near a tenement, a ragged cloth doll stared up at me with her single remaining eye. Somewhere inside, a young child wept disconsolately, and I wondered if the doll was hers. From another building came the sound of a man coughing in long racking spasms, no doubt because of the soot and dust. Would I be coughing like that before long?

We steered around the deeper puddles as we wound our way through a maze of narrow passages. We passed blocks and blocks of factories, and more blocks of grim, dreary, brick tenements, all constructed in the same cheerless, boxlike design. As we went along, the tenements showed more and more signs of life—fewer were boarded up and tattered curtains in some of the windows ruffled as people peeked out at us.

At last, we splashed to a halt in front of a huge red-brick building and checked the house number. "Well, here we are, Mother. Building 12, Unit 54. Home, sweet home!" I set the suitcases down in front of our door.

Mother wiped her face with her soot-blackened hands, then tried to pick up a suitcase, but she staggered and dropped it.

I caught her by the elbow. "Let's get you inside first, Mother. After that, I'll get the bags." I guided her into our new home. I groped for a light switch and found one by the door. A dim bulb in a lone light fixture barely lit the shabby room. From the look of the place, the previous tenants must have been a family of diseased marsh pigs. Moldy wallpaper peeled in strips. A broken window pane had let the rain in, which had formed a puddle of black mud beneath the windowsill. Dirt and soot covered every surface inside, the same as they did outside.

A lone battered chair in the main room sported several springs jutting through its torn upholstery. I threw an abandoned blanket over the broken springs and helped Mother settle into it, then wrapped my coat around her legs. She sagged, her chin on her chest, and closed her eyes.

"Are you okay, Mother?" I couldn't hear her breathing.

After a long interval, she took a deep breath. "Yes, Birn, I'm fine. I'm just tired. Go see about the bags, won't you please?"

I was about to take the two suitcases into the house when a tall Coastal Lora boy, with typical brown-and-white facial markings, strode up. "Hello, there. My name's Cheff. I live three doors down in Unit 51." We shook hands. "Here, let me help you with your—"

A long, shiny, black car roared around the corner toward us, fishtailing on the slimy black cobblestones, followed by a military truck belching clouds of angry, black smoke from its steam boiler. They skidded to a halt in front of Unit 51. A grim man in a dark civilian business suit stepped out of the car and stood by the cab of the truck. He consulted an official-looking document and checked the house number. He rapped the side of the truck three times. Four Fessal soldiers in dark green army uniforms jumped out of the back of the truck, rifles at the ready. They stormed up to the front door of Unit 51, kicked it open, and disappeared inside. We heard yelling and screaming. They came back out, dragging a man by his shirt collar. The soldiers clubbed the man on the back of his head with a rifle butt and dropped him onto the street behind the truck, then turned away and fussed with the tailgate.

Cheff dashed to the fallen man and dropped to his knees. "Uncle Karf! Uncle Karf!"

The man stirred, clutched Cheff's sleeve, and whispered something into his ear. A soldier kicked Cheff in the chest, which sent him sprawling.

"Hey!" I yelled as I ran to where Cheff lay. "You can't—"

The soldier stabbed the barrel of his rifle into my face. I felt a searing pain and clutched at my left eye. My hand came away covered in blood.

"Interfere again, you die, Lildur brat." The soldier smashed his rifle butt into Uncle Karf's face. Uncle Karf collapsed.

Cheff stood up, covered in filth, his fists clenched. "Where are you taking him?"

"Why, do you want to come along? They got plenty of cells in the Iron Fortress."

Cheff glared, jaw muscles twitching, nostrils flared, until the tears welled up, then he lowered his eyes.

The soldier laughed. "No? Then go on, get out of here! MOVE!"

The four soldiers flung Uncle Karf into the back of the truck, slammed the tailgate shut, jumped in, and roared off, sending the thick street slime flying everywhere. The man in the dark clothes gazed at Cheff, then smiled grimly. He got back into the car, which roared after the army truck.

Cheff stood in the street, stunned, then knelt over me. "Are you all right? That was a dumb thing to do. But nervy, too. Let me see your face."

He examined the gash under my eye. "You came awfully close to wearing an eye patch for the rest of your life. Your eye looks okay, but you're going to have a fine scar on your cheekbone."

From inside Cheff's house, someone called in a shrill voice, "Cheff! Cheff! Come quickly!"

Cheff's face turned bone-white. He leaped to his feet and screamed, "AUNT DEE! BUTTONS!" then ran off and disappeared into Unit 51.

The sudden silence was deafening. I waited to see if something else bad was going to happen, but nothing did. The streets were quiet. The nosy neighbors had vanished from the windows. There was no sound from Cheff's house. I hoped the rest of my time in the Labor Compound wasn't going to be like this.

I struggled to my feet and went to see about patching up my face.

"...the soldiers clubbed the man on the back of the head..."

— 2 —

SUPPER

MOTHER WAS STILL asleep in the chair. When I came in, she stirred a little. "Birn! What did you do to your face?"

"Slipped, cut it on a loose stone. No big deal. I'll see to it. You rest." I didn't see any point in adding to her concerns.

Carefully, so as not to disturb Mother, I looked around the tiny apartment. The main room, where Mother was sleeping, faced the street. A ragged sofa occupied the space in front of the window, accompanied by an equally ragged chair and a couple of small tables. A tiny kitchen with a small table and four chairs made up the back wall of the main room. Next came a bathroom, then a small bedroom with an ancient narrow bed, a small writing table, and a chair. Last came the main bedroom. It contained a larger bed, sagging severely in the center, a chest of drawers, and an old armchair like the one in the main room. A hallway ran down the left side, connecting the kitchen, bathroom, and bedrooms.

I figured the smaller bedroom would be mine, so I took my bag, put it on the chair, and opened it. There was my father's old camera right on top. He'd given it to me when I was a boy, and I couldn't bear to leave it behind. I found a handkerchief in my bag, dusted the old camera off, and put it in a place of honor on the little dresser. Then I took the handkerchief to the bathroom sink. I turned the handle and a grudging dribble of rust-colored water oozed out. I wet the handkerchief and used it to wipe the dried blood from around my wound. It wasn't nearly as bad as it looked. I wished I had something to use for a bandage, but that would have to wait. While I was at it, I cleaned my glasses. It took a while to get the greasy black grime off, but it was a relief to see clearly again.

I heard Mother in the kitchen, so I went to see if I could help. She had wiped the grime off the kitchen table and was setting out the last of the stale bread and cheese we'd brought with us.

"Well, Birn," she said, "this is what we have come to. Still, I suppose it could be worse. We must make do with what there is."

Mother ate a few bites of the bread and cheese, washing them down with the foul-smelling tap water. "I'll have to clean up tomorrow. I'm too tired tonight. And I'm supposed to work in the morning." A large tear ran down her cheek. "I don't know how I'll be able to work, Birn. Maybe I'll feel better after I get some sleep."

I walked her down the hallway, waited while she used the bathroom, then helped her get into bed. She was too tired to undress—she slipped out of her coat and shoes and collapsed onto the dusty mattress. I got the old blanket from the chair in the main room and covered her.

When I was sure she was sleeping soundly, I slipped out, went up the street, and knocked on the door of Unit 51. Cheff stuck his head out and glanced up and down the street. "Oh, it's you, uh…"

"Birn."

"Right, Birn. Come inside before the Bluebands spot you. I'm glad you came over, Birn. How's the eye?"

"It's okay," I said. "I washed the blood off and you can hardly see the cut."

"Faces are like that," Cheff said. "Knuckles, too. They bleed like crazy, but the actual cut or scrape is nearly invisible." He examined the skin below my eye. "You're right—it's not as bad as I thought it was. I still think you'll have a scar. That's okay, though—girls like men with scars."

I didn't know what to say. I blushed and stepped into the main room, curious how it compared with ours. It was just as old and dilapidated, but it was clean—spotless. And it had an upstairs. A multicolored oval rag rug covered the worn wooden floor. White curtains framed the single window next to the door—old and tattered, but real curtains with remnants of a lace border still visible in places. They, like the area rug, had been recently washed. And the enticing aroma of newly prepared soup and fresh bread made the place feel homey.

"I wasn't sure you'd want company, after what happened," I said. "I can go if that would be better."

"No, it's okay. I wanted to meet you." Cheff turned and called out, "Aunt Dee? We have a visitor."

A Lora woman with long, graying hair appeared from the kitchen, anxiously wringing her hands. "Who is it, Cheff?" When she saw me, she relaxed a little and managed a smile. "Oh. You're the new family, just moved into Unit 54." She looked me over. "I saw you talking with Cheff when they came and—" She began to cry.

Cheff put his hand on her shoulder. "This is my Aunt Deelia. She's still shaken—we all are."

I took her hand. "My name's Birn, Birn Tylandine. This is a bad time. Maybe I should come back later."

She patted my hand. "It is a bad time, but it is kind of you to look in on us. Please come in." She sat down and motioned for me to do the same. "How's your mother doing? I saw her when you arrived. She didn't look well."

"Her name is Rose. She's sleeping now. When we arrived, she collapsed into a chair in the main room. She didn't see what happened with Uncle Karf. I'm glad. I'm afraid it would have reminded her of when my father..."

She pulled the bottom of her apron up and dabbed at her eyes. "Of course it would have. Everyone here in the Labor Compound has had something like this happen. It's sad to say, but one gets used to it, after a fashion. In any case, life goes on."

She touched my face. "Here, look up at the light. I want to see your eye." She tenderly inspected the wound, which made me wince.

"It's sore," I said, "but I don't think it's too serious."

"You did a good job cleaning it," Aunt Deelia said, "but I think we should cover it to keep it clean. The air's dirty here, as I'm sure you've noticed. No point in letting it get infected. Mellabee! Bring the first-aid kit, please."

A young Lora girl stepped in from the kitchen and handed Aunt Deelia a small first-aid kit. While Aunt Deelia applied the bandage, I looked the little girl over. Oddly, she was a Mountain Lora, with black-and-white facial markings, unlike Cheff's and Aunt Deelia's brown-and-white markings, and I wondered why. She wore a baggy cream-colored shirt and what I guessed were her brother's hand-me-down purple pants, with patches on both knees. Her jet-black hair was tied in twin ponytails. She held two small stuffed ponies in one hand, one dark brown, one golden-tan.

When she saw me looking at them, she held up the golden one. "This is Starry Stargazer. I usually call her Starry. This other one is her sister, Moka. They're glad to have new neighbors." She held Starry out, right forehoof extended.

I reached out to take Starry, but Mellabee pulled her back, then slowly extended her again. This time I got it. I took the little pony's forehoof between my thumb and forefinger and shook it gently. "Pleased to meet you, Miss Stargazer."

Mellabee glowed and extended Moka in the same manner.

I solemnly shook Moka's hoof. "Pleased to meet you, too, Miss Moka."

"It's Miss Mokacheena," Mellabee said. She held Mokacheena to her ear. "She says it's okay for you to call her Moka if you like."

She held Starry to her ear the same way. "And Starry says she'd be pleased if you called her Starry. Except on formal occasions, of course."

"Of course," I said. "Thank you, Starry and Moka. You've made me feel most welcome. And you can call me Birn."

"You can call *me* Buttons," Mellabee said.

"Okay," I said. "Thank you. Nice to meet you, too, Buttons." I shook her forehoof, er, *hand*, formally.

Aunt Deelia said, "You can call me Aunt Dee. Most everyone does."

"Thank you for the bandage, Aunt Dee."

"You're most welcome. Let's hope you don't need too many of those. Now, come sit down. I'm about to put supper on the table."

I started to object, but there were already four plates on the table, so I said, "Yes, Aunt Dee. Thank you." Cheff indicated a chair, and I settled into it.

Buttons and Aunt Dee brought in steaming, fragrant bowls of soup. A platter of sliced warm bread sat in the center. Without comment, Aunt Dee placed a small bowl of soup in front of the ponies. Buttons carefully arranged Starry and Moka so they could sip from their soup bowl.

The soup and bread were absolutely wonderful. I tried to eat slowly and use my best table manners, but aside from a few scraps of hard bread and cheese, I had barely eaten for days. Before I knew it, I had emptied the bowl.

Aunt Dee didn't say a word. She took the bowl and filled it up again, then gave me another slice of bread. She asked me, "When was the last time you and your mother ate anything substantial?"

"I don't know. A couple of days, maybe. I think that's partly why she's so weak. She couldn't eat on the transport ship—sea-sickness."

"Well, when we're done, I'll fix up a tray and take it to her."

"Thank you, but I… I wouldn't feel right taking what little food you have. I've already eaten more than my share."

Buttons grinned mischievously. "Oh, don't even think about it. It's no trouble at all. We have more than enough. Aunt Dee can always toss another mouse into the soup."

I gagged, which made soup come squirting out my nose. Buttons and Cheff were laughing so hard that even Aunt Dee giggled behind her hand. I swallowed and laughed, too.

Cheff slapped my shoulder. "She's only kidding, Birn—about the mouse, I mean. Yes, food is scarce, but—"

Buttons blurted out, "Cheff has ways of getting us extra—"

"Mel, stop."

"But—"

"No! Don't say another word!" Cheff turned to me. "What Buttons means is that sometimes we're surprised to find some extra food, meat mostly, that mysteriously appears in our cupboards." He smiled and added, "I'll tell you more about it, sometime. Maybe." He frowned at Buttons. "Some *other* time."

After I wiped my face, the table around my bowl, and the front of my shirt, I said, "I'm sorry for laughing. I didn't mean to be disrespectful. I'm sure it's not appropriate in view of what happened today with Uncle Karf."

"Not at all, Birn," Aunt Dee said. "The Labor Compound is full of tragedy, one after another, day after day. Any chance we have to laugh a little, we take it."

Cheff added, "If Uncle Karf were here, he would have laughed the hardest. He had a working philosophy that 'A Fact Is a Joke.'"

Aunt Dee said, "Different folks react to tragedy in different ways. Some get depressed. Others go crazy. Some buy into the rotten system completely. Others reject it and become criminals of one sort or another. While Karf was with us, he taught us to maintain our hope and optimism in the face of the worst possible circumstances. We're no strangers to hardship. Everyone in the Labor Compound has lost a loved one. Some have lost more than one." She hesitated. "You mentioned your father?"

"They shot him." My voice choked up.

"Easy, Birn. What I'm saying is, we all know that it could happen to any one of us at any time. That makes it extra important to keep a balanced outlook."

"Which includes our sense of humor," Cheff said. "Never miss a chance for a good laugh."

"I see. Thank you. That helps."

Aunt Dee filled my bowl a third time and cut me another slice of bread. "Does your mother have her work assignment yet?"

"Yes, she'll be working as a seamstress in a uniform factory. She got the assignment before we boarded the transport ship. She's supposed to start work tomorrow morning, but I'm not sure she's well enough. If she can't work, I'm afraid things will get worse, a lot worse."

Cheff frowned. "Excuse me for asking, but do you have any money left after your trip?"

My face flushed, but I reluctantly pulled the coins out of my pocket and showed them.

Aunt Dee threw her napkin on the table. She patted my hand again. "Don't worry, Birn. I worked in the uniform factory myself, when we first came to the Compound. The manager there is a decent man, for a Fessal. He figured out that people work better on a full belly, so he got permission to serve lunch every day. It's only bread and soup, but it will keep her going."

Cheff said, "She'll get her ration stamps and a few coins at the end of the week. Meanwhile, I'm sure we can rustle up enough to share."

"Thank you," I said. "You're very kind." We ate in silence for a while, then I asked Buttons, "How did you get your nickname?"

"Because," Cheff explained, "when she was little, she couldn't fasten her buttons by herself, and she wouldn't let anybody help her with them except me. She'd toddle after me, calling, 'Buttons! Buttons!' until I'd button them for her. So, I started calling her Buttons, and it stuck."

"And you like that better than Mellabee?" I asked. "Mellabee is such a nice name."

"Never call me Mellabee. I hate that name. It's too *girly*. I don't mind Mel as much. That's what most people call me. 'Buttons' is what my friends call me, and I'm pretty sure we're going to be friends. The ponies think so, anyway. Also, 'Buttons' is what I call myself in my head."

Cheff drained the last drops from his bowl and wiped his mouth with his sleeve. "You done, Birn? Great! Come on, let's go upstairs. I've got some stuff I want to show you."

Buttons gathered Starry and Moka. "We're coming, too!"

Aunt Dee took her by the arm. "No, you are not, Miss Mellabee! You and I are going to pay a social call on Birn's mother."

— 3 —

FATHERS

CHEFF'S BEDROOM WAS in the front of the house with a single window overlooking the street. A small table and chair stood by the window. A rumpled bed and a wardrobe lined the interior walls. Cheff pointed at the chair. "Have a seat."

On the table, a handful of sharpened pencils, along with several kinds of rulers and protractors, surrounded a stack of large drawings. A cracked saucer held several sticks of charcoal. One of the drawings, a map, lay on the top of the pile. "Did you draw this?"

"I did. It's a map of the entire Fellstone Labor Compound, our home, sweet, sooty home. For the next few years, anyway."

I picked up a charcoal stick. "What are these for?"

"They come in handy for shading." He showed me some gray areas in the drawings. "See? The pencils are for fine lines, and the charcoal is for shading big areas."

"I see. Where'd you get the charcoal?"

"I make it. It's pretty easy. I put a bunch of willow sticks in a tin can, poke a few holes in the lid, and put it inside the coal stove while Aunt Dee is cooking."

"That's it?"

"That's it. They come out ready to use. They make your fingers all black, though. You'd better wipe your hand off before you get black marks everywhere."

I wiped my fingers on my shirt while I looked at the map. "The Labor Compound is bigger than I thought."

"It's a mile across, east to west, and two miles north to south. We're allowed to walk around the compound in the daytime when we're not at work or in school." He held the map up to catch the light from the bare bulb hanging from the ceiling. "I think I've got nearly every building in the place. I've been working on it for over a year. It's good practice."

"Is it legal to have a map like this? It wasn't in Tumberland."

"It is for me because I'm on the Civilian Leadership Track at school. I'm going to be a Factory Manager. Managers are supposed to draw maps and plans and diagrams and things like that. This map is officially part of my homework. I don't exactly go waving it around, though. Those backstabbing Bluebands are always looking for an excuse."

He peeked out the window, then spread the map on the table and pointed at a building in the southeast quadrant. "See? Our building here, Building 12. This is my house, in the middle of the block, Unit 51. Yours is this one, Unit 54. This entire area is housing for families with children. In fact, you're fortunate to have gotten the house you did. Apartments that size are usually assigned to families with a minimum of three people. Don't be surprised if they move you to a smaller unit or move someone in with you." He thought about it. "They might even move us, now that we're down to three people. I hope not. I'm kind of attached to this place, such as it is."

I raised my eyebrows. "Seriously? They move us around whenever they like?"

"I'm afraid so," Cheff said. "It happens all the time here in the Compound. One day, you're getting on with what little family you have left, and the next, someone you love is taken, and everything changes. You can't afford to get attached to anything—not your house, not your job, not your friends, not even your schoolwork." He composed himself. "But this place, well, after my mother and father were taken, Aunt Dee and Uncle Karf made us feel like a family again. We made some wonderful memories here in spite of everything. But now—" He stared out the dark window, then sat back down heavily on the bed.

"Don't worry," Cheff said, "they probably won't move either of us. Not for a while, anyway. Quite a few housing units are empty right now. Every so often, a few families disappear altogether, usually about the time the Labor Compound starts getting crowded. No one knows where they go, but they are never seen or heard from again. I suppose they're moved to some other city, maybe out west. Afterward, everyone gets shuffled around to make room for new people.

"Anyway, it is what it is—you can't afford to worry about things you can't control. Let's change the subject, okay?" He reclined on his bed with his back to the headboard, his hands interlocked behind his head. "So, you're from Tumberland? How'd you wind up in this place?"

"Actually, we lived right outside Tumberland City, but it was more country than city. We lived in a house, not an apartment. It wasn't a very good house, but it was a lot better than this place. My father worked in the train yards. He was a mechanic. He could fix anything. He planned to get me a job with him when I turned fifteen, but I'm not mechanically inclined like he is. Was."

"What happened to your father?"

"Well…"

"It's okay if you don't want to talk about it."

"No," I said, "it's all right, I don't mind."

"Keep your voice low," Cheff said. "There are microphones in every room. They can't possibly be listening to every room at every moment, but it's best not to take any chances."

I lowered my voice. "It was bad, with my father, like with Uncle Karf today. The soldiers broke our door down about an hour before the sun came up, as were sitting down to breakfast. They grabbed my father and shot him dead, right there in the kitchen in front of my mother and me. Then they ripped up everything—the furniture, the beds, even the floors and the ceiling and the walls—looking for something they could use against us. But they couldn't find anything, and that made them even angrier. The officer in charge pulled some papers from his pocket and read a bunch of words so loud and fast that we couldn't make out what he was saying. All I remember are 'FRM' and 'collaborating with the enemy.' That's it."

"Was it true? *Was* he FRM?"

"I don't know. If he was, he never said anything to me about it. But then he wouldn't, would he? I've heard of the FRM of course, but I don't know much about it other than they're against Emperor Pallador. I never saw my father collaborating with anyone. He went to work and came home, every day the same. Anyway, I don't believe a word those Fessals said."

"What happened next?"

"They left without a word." I stared at the floor. "My father… I felt so helpless… I should have done something, but it all happened so fast." I looked at Cheff. "It was horrible, like a nightmare that I couldn't wake up from."

"I get it," Cheff said. "Today was the third time for me. First my father, then my mother, and now Uncle Karf. I keep wondering how long it'll be before they come for Aunt Dee, and my sister and I will be left alone." He took a deep breath. "No point in dwelling on that, either. How's your mother coping?"

"Not well. I'm not sure she'll ever recover. She barely speaks anymore. I'm… I'm afraid she's going to give up."

Cheff said kindly, "I wouldn't worry too much about that, now that she's in Aunt Dee's care. Aunt Dee has a remarkable effect on people. It's something about her. If anyone can bring your mother around, it'll be Aunt Dee."

"You think so? I hope you're right."

"I am. You'll see. So, how'd you and your mom get from Tumberland to here?"

"The next morning, the soldiers came back and kicked the door in again. We were terrified, but they only told us to pack one suitcase each. They gave us ten minutes. Except for a few clothes, some books, and my dad's old camera, we had to leave everything else behind. Then they took us to a prison camp in the mountains north of Tumberland. It was a tiny little camp, not like this place. Someone told us they only use it to hold prisoners until they have a full boatload to ship to Fellstone. We were in that camp for eleven days with hardly any food. We slept on the ground in our clothes. It was filthy. And I don't even want to tell you about the sanitary facilities, if you can call them that."

I went to the window. The rain had lightened, but it was still leaving dirty streaks down the glass. "How about you? How'd your family get here? Where are you from, anyway?"

"We're from right here in Fellstone City. Buttons and I lived with our mother and father in a pretty nice house across town, in the Toddary District, about ten miles southwest of here, across the river. It's south of New City, near the market district. The houses there are a lot nicer than these dumps—they're bigger and newer, and much easier to keep clean because most of the factories near the Toddary District use water power instead of coal. My mother and father both had decent jobs, so we could afford nicer things, like furniture without any holes in it. We had nice clothes and pretty good food."

He sighed. "I miss the food. We always had plenty to eat. In fact, we had so much food that my mother helped the poorer families whenever she could. She used to take us with her every night after supper, with all the food we had left. She helped everyone no matter what species they were, even Torphs."

I sat on the chair by the worktable. "Your mother sounds like a kind person. Where did your father work?"

"At the oil refinery—he was supervisor over half the plant. It was hard work. He was always exhausted when he came home, but he hardly ever talked about what he did there. Mom told Buttons and me he was protecting us from the snoops."

"Snoops?"

Cheff scooted to the edge of the bed, leaned close, and said quietly, "'Snoops' is what Mom called nosy people, like the Bluebands. There are plenty of them here in the Labor Compound, too. They're always trying to find someone to report. There's a reward for turning in traitors."

"We had Bluebands in Tumberland, too," I whispered. "I remember when I was a little boy and my mother would take me into Tumberland City. She made me be silent and not talk at all. She was worried about Bluebands overhearing something. When I was little, I used to like the Bluebands. They were friendly and always stopped to talk to me. But when I got older, I realized they try to trick little kids into saying something incriminating about their parents, or something negative about the Imperium or the Emperor."

Cheff said softly, "Here in the Labor Compound, kids join the Bluebands to prove that they're not like their parents."

"What do you mean?"

"Don't you get it? Everyone here in the Fellstone Labor Compound is a family member of a 'traitor.' Everyone. Just like you and me. We're supposed to be 're-educated' and to have an opportunity to 'remove the stain of disloyalty' from ourselves and our families. Joining the Bluebands is one way to prove one's loyalty. Also, Bluebands get certain privileges. But you have to be careful about what you say, every minute of the day. The Bluebands are everywhere. They're vicious bullies and they'll hurt you if they get a chance."

"Was it the Bluebands who turned your father in?" I asked.

"We never found out who it was. It happened fast, with no warning. One day he went to work and didn't come home. My mother was frantic, of course, because we'd heard the stories of people disappearing, snatched up by Pallador's soldiers. Anyway, the next morning there was a loud knock at the door. Five Fessal soldiers, led by a tall, fat, Lildur magistrate, pushed their way into our home. The magistrate pulled some papers from his coat pocket and read, 'Fennel Karfendek has been accused of disloyal acts against the Emperor and of collusion with the Fellstone Resistance Movement. He is being detained in the Imperial Hall of Justice pending further investigation by the Imperial Intelligence Division. You, Marela Karfendek, and your children, Mellabee Karfendek and Cheff Karfendek, are hereby declared Suspicious Persons. You are to be sent to The Fellstone Labor Compound and remain there until further notice.'"

I jumped to my feet. "'The Fellstone Resistance Movement?' That has to be the FRM, the same group my father was accused of supporting! I asked my mother about it on the boat, but she said she didn't know anything, and that I shouldn't even ask about such matters. What do *you* know about it?"

Cheff pointed at the ceiling again, then said loudly, "Nothing!" He swung his legs off the bed and whispered, "Remember to keep your voice down. Also, it's not safe to know too much about anything. Grown-ups don't speak of it to children, but everybody in Fellstone City knows the FRM is working to overthrow Emperor Pallador. Have you heard of the IID, the Imperial Intelligence Division? Their entire job is to find and eliminate FRM members. When they took Uncle Karf, did you see the man in black clothes, the one who came in the car? He was almost certainly IID." He took a long, deep breath. "Anyway, we never saw my father again."

"Is he still in the—what was the name of the place? Imperial Hall of…?"

"Its official name is The Caudon Fortress and Imperial Hall of Justice because it's located on the Caudon Peninsula, but everybody calls it the Iron Fortress. When you came in on the boat, did you notice the huge, dark-gray building on the peninsula that sticks out into the west side of the bay?"

"No, it was raining pretty hard. I couldn't see much of anything. I saw the beacon on it from the transport ship."

"You'll see it soon enough. Your 're-education' requires an annual tour of the place. There's a museum there, designed to scare you out of ever being disloyal."

"Do you think you and your sister will ever see your parents again?"

Cheff remained silent for a long time. When he finally spoke, his voice quavered a little. "No, I'm pretty sure they're dead. We were told that they were sent West for re-education, but I think they're dead. My birth mother is dead, too. Buttons and I are alone, except for Aunt Dee and Uncle—well, only Aunt Dee, now."

"Your birth mother?"

"Yeah. Buttons and I had the same father, but we each had a different mother. My birth mother died when I was born. She was a Coastal Lora, brown-and-white, like me. When I was about five, my father married again, a beautiful Mountain Lora. She was Buttons' mother, and the only mother I ever knew." He sighed. "I still miss her, every day."

"So, Uncle Karf was...?"

"My father's brother. That's why he and Aunt Dee ended up in the Labor Compound. That's the way the IID does it. If you're even suspected of being FRM, they'll not only kill you, but they'll hurt or even kill your family, too. I'm sure that's all that keeps a lot of people 'loyal' to our benevolent Emperor."

"Was your father really in the FRM?"

Cheff put a finger to his lips, pointed at the ceiling again, and said loudly, "If the Emperor, in his wisdom, says he was, then he must have been. I know nothing of such matters." He whispered, "He never said so, but I'm pretty sure he was. I hope he was, or he died for nothing. I think my mother was, too. And when I'm old enough, I'm going to join. What about your father?"

"I don't know. Like I said, he never mentioned the FRM to me. But I hope he was, too."

Cheff continued, "Anyway, they stuck us in an apartment like this one, about half a mile from here, on the other side of the Compound. A week later our mother didn't come home from work one night. We never saw her again, either. For two weeks, Buttons and I lived alone, except for the rats and the roaches. Then another fat magistrate showed up. He read from some more papers ordering us to move into our uncle's apartment—this one. We didn't even know that Uncle Karf and Aunt Dee were in the Labor Compound, too. That all happened years ago." He sighed heavily. "Let's change the subject again."

Cheff Karfendek

— **4** —

Books

A SMALL BOOKSHELF MOUNTED on Cheff's wall prominently displayed several brightly colored books. I read the titles aloud for the benefit of anyone who might be listening:

"Pallador's blue book: *Your Labor and Your Emperor.* Pallador's green book: *Loyalty and Livelihood: Prosperity through Pallador.* Pallador's yellow book: *Pallador, Our Father—the Origin of All Life.* Pallador's red book: *Emperor Pallador—the Source of All True Knowledge.*

"Hmm... and here's the highly recommended booklet: *Greetings, Well-Wishing, and Other Authorized Rules of Conversation among the Peoples of the Imperium.*" I sat next to Cheff on the edge of his bed and whispered, "I think you're missing a few of our Beloved Emperor's books."

Cheff glowered. His whisper was barely audible. "I hate his books. I only have the ones required by law, and someday, I'm going to burn every one of *them.*" He got up and looked for Bluebands out the window, being careful not to disturb the curtains, then went back to the bed and spoke loudly for the benefit of the snoops, "Those are most of the required volumes. I'm working after school to earn enough to buy the others." He shook his head emphatically, poked his finger in his mouth, and made a gagging motion.

I laughed silently and whispered, "I have some books, too, but nothing the Emperor would approve. My books are old. They belonged to my father, and his father, and his father, and so on. They were written during the Sixth Kingdom, well over a hundred years ago, before The Fall."

Cheff blinked. "Sorry, you *what*, now?"

"I have three extremely old books: *Worldheart — A History*, *Adventures in Science*, and *The Voyages of Captain Amer — The Quest for Other Lands*."

Cheff's eyebrows shot up. "You're telling me that you don't keep the Emperor's books, even the required minimum, but you do have three highly outlawed Forbidden Books?"

"I used to have more, but I left them back in Tumberland. I hid them before we left. If I ever get back there, I know exactly where to find them. I would have brought them, too, but we were only allowed one suitcase each. And books are heavy. I guess I'll have to see about getting the required ones again."

"But how could you possibly get through so many checkpoints and inspections with forbidden books? And without the required books?"

"Easy. I tore the covers off of my books, and the covers off of the Emperor's books. Then all I had to do was glue the Emperor's covers onto my books. During inspections, all the soldiers see are the Emperor's books. No one ever makes me show the pages inside. Besides, most of the soldiers are stupid Fessal grunts. Have you ever heard of any Fessal who could read?"

"Birn, you're begging to get caught and killed. And yes, here in Fellstone, there are Fessals who can read. What if someone who can read tests you? Like, maybe, one of the teachers? Or a Blueband? Or a soldier?"

"I'll show you." I went to Cheff's bookshelf, selected the thickest one, Pallador's green book, and handed it to him. "Let's say someone wants me to read from '*Loyalty and Livelihood: Prosperity through Pallador.'* I'd ask him to choose a page in the book, any page. Then I'd hold my disguised book up as though I were reading from it, and tell him exactly what's on that page—word for word."

"Impossible! No one can do that!"

"Oh? Pick a page, any page."

Cheff thumbed through the green book. "Okay, wise guy, page 91."

I stood up, adjusted my glasses, cleared my throat, then held an imaginary book in front of me. "Right. I'll start from paragraph three." I 'read' in a loud, clear voice:

"The Loyal Torph

"Loyalty, my beloved people, can be found in the least expected places. One winter, many years ago, I traveled to the edge of the Great Desert. As I was basking in the hot sun, one of my Facilitators spied an elderly Torph gentleman in the distance. When the Torph saw my caravan, he turned from his path and made his way toward us. He approached bravely and fell to his knees before me, warmly demonstrating his obeisance.

"Do you see the point, my dear ones? This man, although a lowly Torph, deliberately approached his benevolent Emperor far out in the desert, when he could have run off at the first sight of my caravan. That, my dearest children, is true loyalty. Learn from it. Live for it. Fear me not. Love me, as I love you."

Cheff stared at me. "How did you do that? That's amazing! Let me try another one."

He flipped to a new page, and I recited the passage just as accurately. Then he went to his bookshelf, got Pallador's red book, and opened it at random. That page had a picture on it. I described the picture, then quoted from the page. After a few more repetitions, Cheff was satisfied. "That's fantastic! You say you have all the Emperor's books memorized?"

"Every one of them. And others, too. Some textbooks, some of my father's technical manuals."

"But—how do you do it?"

"I don't mean to—I don't even try. It's just something that happens." I tapped my head. "I only ever have to read a book once, and then it's in here forever."

"Incredible! You don't merely *read* books, you *are* books!" He shook his head, then grinned. "Well, good for you, Books. What else can you do?"

I laughed. "Isn't that enough?" We put our heads together and I whispered, "Wanna hear some stories from *before* The Fall?"

Birn "Books" Tylandine

— 5 —

MID

AFTER A KNOCK on the bedroom door, a short, round Troh boy with a big, gap-toothed smile entered. He had all the typical Troh features: short, stocky body, thick hair on his head, broad reddish nose, sticky-outy ears, and hands that seemed too large for his arms. He wore a tan shirt with a lace-up collar, brown trousers tied with a rope, and sandals. A bulging leather bag hung at his waist.

"Hi, Cheff. I came as soon as I heard about your uncle." He squinted at me and offered his hand. "Hello. My name's Mid. I'm Cheff's friend. I live a block from here. Who are you?"

I shook his hand.

"He's a new friend," Cheff said. "His name is Books."

"Friend?" Mid looked skeptical. "How can we be sure? Friends aren't that easy to come by in the Labor Compound. Not *true* friends. I've known Cheff for years. How do we know you're not a spy? Sounds like the perfect spy setup to me. No offense, Books, but how do we know you're telling the truth?"

"None taken," I said.

"He got here today," Cheff said. "He's from Tumberland. He and his mother were assigned to Unit 54." He gestured for Mid to come close and lowered his voice to a whisper. "But get this: when they came for Uncle Karf this afternoon, Books, here, jumped one of the soldiers."

Mid's thick eyebrows lifted. "He *what*?"

"I didn't exactly—"

"That's not all, Old Son," Cheff continued. "The soldier nearly poked Books' eye out with his rifle."

Mid stared at my bandage.

"Well, it's not as bad as—"

"And if that's not enough," Cheff added, "the FRM killed his father right in front of him and his mother. *Bang!* Poor man was shot dead. Fell right at Books' feet."

Mid said, "Andaran's bones, Old Man, that's horrible!"

"There's more," Cheff said. "Books' father was an FRM operative, like our fathers, and Books is going to be one, too, when he grows up. I think we can trust him, don't you?"

"I suppose, but it *is* the perfect setup for a spy."

"He might be a spy," Cheff said. "You're right—the whole thing could be a setup, including kidnapping Uncle Karf."

Mid looked startled. "I hadn't considered it that far."

"I know, Old Son, and you could be right. But if we start suspecting everybody, we'll end up like everyone else in this place: dark, depressed, and suspicious. And that's no way to live. I'm willing to take a chance on Books. How about you?"

Mid looked me over, top to bottom. "Well, it does seem that we may have a lot in common. But I'll be keeping an eye on him." He came over and shook my hand warmly. "Nice to meet you, Books. Is Books your real name?"

"No. You see—"

"I'll tell you later," Cheff said. "We have work to do."

I sat on the edge of Cheff's bed and Mid pulled up the chair. Cheff went to the door, checked the hallway, then closed the door and sat next to me. Cheff whispered, "I don't want Buttons or Aunt Dee or anyone else"—he pointed at the ceiling—"to hear this. Before they took Uncle Karf away, he said something to me. He said 'Contact Meltern. Tell him what happened.'"

"Who's Meltern?" Mid asked.

"I'm not sure. I kind of remember visiting someone years ago. His name might have been Meltern. When I was little, my father and Uncle Karf used to go to a guest house in Old City. It had rooms for travelers to stay in. I liked to go there because they had toys for little kids. The grown-ups would sit and talk and drink cider. Sometimes there would be music, and I liked that, too. After they took my father, of course, I never went there again. That's all I remember. It was a long time ago, and I was small."

Mid frowned. "Do you think you could find it again?"

"I don't know. Maybe. How many places like that can there be? Not many people are allowed to travel, but when they do, they need a place to stay."

I said, "I think I might have seen a place like that down by the docks when we got off the boat."

"That makes sense," Cheff said. "Some travelers do come in by boat, but the place I remember wasn't near the bay. My father took me to the docks sometimes. He'd bring old bread to feed the sea birds… that was back when we still had plenty of bread. No, I think it was on the main road that went through Old City."

Cheff rummaged through the papers on his worktable. He selected a roll, which he spread out on the bed. "Look, this map shows all I know about Old City. Here's the main road running north to south. I've seen it from a distance. It's well-lit, even at night. I stay away from there. These areas with the hatch marks are ruins. That's where I hunt."

"Hunt?" I asked. "What do you mean?"

Mid laughed. "He means 'sleepwalks.'"

"I don't get it," I said.

"Never mind," Cheff said. "Pretend you didn't hear that part. See? This is the Labor Compound, over here. And this"—he indicated an area south of the Compound — "is populated, too. It used to be ruins, but much of it has been rebuilt. We'll have to avoid it."

I picked up one side of the map. It looked new. "Did you draw this one, too?"

"Yes."

"But how could you possibly know where all these streets and buildings are? Did you get special permission to go outside the Compound to map the place?"

Mid laughed again. "There's no way around it, Old Man. It's time to tell Books about your terrible sleepwalking problem, don't you think?" He turned to me. "Cheff's afflicted, Books, with a horrible affliction."

"What kind of affliction?"

"Oh, it's fierce," Mid continued. "Several times a month, in the middle of the night, Cheff sleepwalks. He sleepwalks right on out of the Labor Compound. The strange thing is that he usually comes back with fresh meat."

"So *that's* what Buttons was on about at supper. How do you get out of the Compound? Isn't it dangerous?"

Cheff's smile faded. "Extremely. But then, so is starving to death. They don't feed us too well here, as you'll soon find out. Even if you have money, there isn't always food to buy. Fresh meat is always welcome, and not only by our fellow prisoners. The guards like fresh game, too, and they don't ask questions about where I found it."

"Uh… what sort of game?"

"There's a lot of small game living in the ruins of Old City. Sometimes I get a nice fat possum, a tola rabbit, or a raccoon, or even a wild dog or coyote, but mostly I get rats. And a few squirrels, too. But mostly just rats."

"*Rats?*" I shuddered.

Mid stifled a laugh and put his finger to his lips. "You'll be surprised at how good a fat, juicy rat can be. Aunt Dee knows how to spice them perfectly."

Cheff laughed, too. "What did you think was in the soup we had for supper?"

"But you said Buttons was kidding about the soup!"

"I said she was kidding about the *mouse*." He laughed again.

My stomach turned, but I fought to keep it down. Mid and Cheff were both laughing at me now. Mid said, "It's better than eating the roaches. A lot of people here do. If it weren't for Cheff's 'sleepwalking,' we'd be eating roaches, too."

"Which is still better than dying of starvation," Cheff added.

"I suppose it is." I swallowed hard. "But I sure hope it doesn't come down to that." I turned to Cheff. "Can you teach me to, um, sleepwalk, too?"

"All in good time, all in good time. First, we need to see about this Meltern fellow." He returned to the map and tapped a spot on the main road directly north of the big crossroads in Old City. "This is only about a mile and a half from the eastern wall of the Compound. I normally stay away from this area because there are always a lot of people around, even late at night. It might be a good place to start looking for Meltern. I'll do a little 'sleepwalking' tonight and see what I can find out."

"Sounds like fun," I said. "How are we going to get out of the Compound?"

"We?" Cheff rolled up his map and put it back on his worktable. "Thanks for the offer, Books, but it's my problem, not yours. You've already risked enough for me today."

"Hey, wait a minute, Cheff," Mid said. "You don't think we're going to let you ramble off and have all the fun without us, do you?"

"I appreciate the sentiment, Mid, Old Man, but you've never been hunting with me. It's not a picnic. It's dangerous out there. The guards, and even the Bluebands, are authorized to kill curfew violators, and they'd love to get the chance. I've spent the last few years learning how to move silently and avoid the patrols. I'll be faster and safer alone. Not to mention years of practice with my hunting sling. Do you even know how to use a sling? Thanks anyway, though."

I stood up and joined Cheff at his worktable. "Look, Cheff, I know I'm the new kid here, and you don't know me yet, but I grew up in the country and spent a lot of time in the woods that surrounded our house. I can move pretty quietly. I'll bet Mid can, too, can't you, Mid?"

"Cheff already knows how I can move." Mid danced a few steps across the floor, snapping his fingers above his head. "See? That's what I call movin'! Seriously, though, Books is right, Cheff. When I came over here tonight, I didn't expect you'd run off and leave me alone. Uncle Karf was always good to me, as though he were my own uncle. I have as much right to help him as anyone. And if we run into trouble, three of us are better than one, right?" His smile widened into a full grin. "Anyway, how do you propose to stop us? Tie us to the bed?" He looked around the room. "Where's your rope? I don't see any rope. Do you see any rope, Books? I don't think he has any rope. Gonna be hard to tie us up without any rope, Cheff. Maybe I can help you find some rope. You want me to help you find some rope, Cheff?"

Cheff laughed and threw up his hands. "Okay, okay, enough with the rope already. But if I let you go with me, you'll have to *promise* to do exactly what I say." He shook his head. "I have a feeling that I'm going to regret this."

We heard the front door open, then Buttons yelled up the stairs, "We're baa-aack!"

Aunt Dee stuck her head in the bedroom doorway. "Your mother was awake when I got there. She seemed to enjoy the soup. She even got some color back in her cheeks. As soon as she finished, she got sleepy, so we put her back to bed. I'll check on her again in the morning and take her breakfast. She asked me if I would mind keeping you here for the night. She wants to rest. I told her that would be fine." She turned to Mid and smiled. "Hello, Mid. Are you staying over, too?"

"Yes, Aunt Dee. My mother gave me permission if it's all right with you."

"Of course. It isn't safe to be walking around the Labor Compound after dark. Well, enjoy yourselves, boys. Don't stay up all night." She turned to Buttons, who was trying to push past her into the room. "Come along, Buttons, it's your bedtime."

"But I wanna—"

Aunt Dee took Buttons by the arm and closed the door behind her.

"So," I asked Cheff again, "how are we going to get out of the Labor Compound?"

Cheff grinned. "After Aunt Dee goes to bed, I'll show you. But whatever you do, don't say anything to Buttons, or she'll want to come, too."

Mid Persil

— 6 —
THE SECRET ROOM

WE TALKED FOR a couple of hours while the house grew quiet. After making sure that Buttons was sound asleep, Cheff led us downstairs into the dim hallway. Aunt Dee's bedroom door was closed. He held his finger up to his lips and opened the closet beneath the stairs. He pushed some coats aside and moved several pairs of old shoes away from the narrow end. He felt around the closet floor, then there was a soft *clunk* and a trapdoor swung gently upward. Cheff descended a wooden ladder into utter blackness. His voice came from below. "Well, how about it? Do you two still want to go 'sleepwalking?' Or are you scared of the dark?"

I gulped. "I'm still going."

Mid flashed me a wicked grin as he pushed past me into the dark hole. I closed the trapdoor behind me and followed Mid down the ladder. At the bottom, I heard Cheff moving about in the dark: a hissing sound, followed by a couple of flashes and a popping sound, and a dim light began to glow.

I jumped back. "What in Andaran is that?"

"It's an old miner's lamp Mid found in the scrapyard a while back. He cleaned it up and got it working, and gave it to me to help with the sleepwalking. I keep it down here." Cheff turned a knob and the light grew brighter. He handed it to me. "Here, hold this."

I held the light high and looked around. We stood in a little room about nine feet high and four feet on each side. Old, cracked boards nailed to a few vertical beams lined the walls. I could see all the way up to the closed trapdoor. "What is this place?" I asked Cheff.

"Somebody who lived here before us must have dug this out. I'm not sure why, but it was probably for hiding contraband from the Bluebands and the guards, or maybe black-market stuff. I found the trapdoor while I was helping Aunt Dee clean up when we first moved into this place. There was nothing down here except a few old boxes and this little barrel." He kicked the barrel gently with the toe of his worn leather shoe. "I never mentioned it to her. After I discovered the trapdoor, I piled some stuff on top of it. As far as I know, neither she nor Buttons has the faintest clue that it exists."

"So, now what?" I asked.

Cheff rolled the old barrel aside and removed a few loose boards from the wall, revealing a narrow dirt passage. "It's a tight squeeze, but if Mid can make it, you'll fit, too." He took the miner's lamp from me, got down on his belly, and disappeared into the tiny tunnel.

"Did he just imply that I'm fat?" Mid asked. "Me, fat?" He patted his ample belly. "I'll have you know, Old Man, I am *not* fat. I'm just a well-rounded individual."

At the far end of the tunnel, Cheff held the miner's lamp to light the way for us.

Mid crawled in, and I followed him. We crawled for what seemed like a long way, although later Mid told me that it was only about twenty-five feet (8m). When we got close to the end, Mid disappeared. I crawled forward a few feet more until the dirt passage ended, then dropped down to find myself standing in a tall, brick-lined tunnel with Cheff and Mid. A substantial stream of dirty water flowed down the middle of it.

Cheff held the miner's light high above his head and gestured broadly. "Welcome to our secret underground kingdom! How do you like it, Books?"

"Where are we?" I asked. "What is this place?"

"Storm drains." Mid kicked at the water. "Ancient storm drains. I'll bet they go back to when the Old City was built, hundreds of years ago, or even more."

Cheff picked up a square of wood, covered with fake bricks and moss, and camouflaged the end of the dirt passage we had come through. "If you weren't looking for it, you'd never see it, would you?"

I shook my head. "Who else comes down here? Workers? Other 'sleepwalkers'?"

Mid shrugged. "We've never seen anybody, but we camouflage it anyway, just in case."

Cheff said, "Imagine the fuss if some poor maintenance man crawled out from under Aunt Dee's stairs with his muddy boots on! She'd scold him until his ears caught fire!" He walked upstream. "Come on, let's get moving. South is this way."

Cheff aimed the light up a vertical shaft. "Here, take a look at this." At the top of the shaft was a round metal cover plate. "There are access hatches like this everywhere, but they're all paved over. This one would have been right in the middle of the street in front of your house, Books. They sealed all the hatches when they built the Labor Compound. Can't have people sneaking about in the drains, now, can we?" He grinned.

"There are still drain slits on all the street corners," Mid said. "You'll see them on the way to school tomorrow. It rains a lot here in the Fellstone region, all year round, but especially now during the rainy season. The water has to go somewhere, right? A couple of years ago, we worked out that there had to be some sort of drains under the streets. So, one day when Aunt Dee and Buttons weren't around, we started digging our little tunnel. And sure enough, we found this place. It's a lot bigger than we expected."

"What'd you do with all the dirt?"

Cheff said, "At first, we piled it up around the walls in the secret room. After we broke through, we used those old boxes to drag it out here to the drains. Whenever it rained, the dirt washed away, little by little. Took a while."

Mid added, "Right now there's only a small stream, but when it's raining, there's a regular torrent. These pipes fill right up. That's why we don't go sleepwalking when it's raining."

"Which is most of the time, this part of the year," Cheff said. "Autumn is the rainy season here in Fellstone City."

I asked Mid, "I thought Cheff said you hadn't gone sleepwalking with him before?"

"I haven't—not outside the Compound, anyway. This is as far as I've been." He shivered. "As far as I ever wanted to go. Until now."

As we continued down the dank, dark storm drain, Cheff kept the lamp pointed at the floor, which was littered with all sorts of debris: dirt, leaves, an occasional lost toy, a few small tree branches. Once we passed a soggy pair of pants. Every so often, Cheff would cover the lamp with his hand briefly. I asked, "Why are you doing that?"

He pointed up at one of the drain slits in the street above. "It wouldn't do for the Bluebands to get a glimpse of light from underground, now, would it? I cover the light every time we pass beneath one."

From time to time, Cheff pointed out a rusty grate or an old iron door with a corroded padlock. I asked him, "Where do all those doors go?"

"I don't know. Usually, when I'm down here, I'm in a hurry to get some meat and get back home. But, you know, that's a good question. Someday, we ought to pry some of those locks off and find out what's inside. You never know, it could be chests full of gold, ancient gold from before The Fall."

"Rats and roaches, more likely." Mid stopped to examine one of the rusty padlocks. "I don't think these are ever going to open again, even if we had the right keys. But I have an idea for an invention that will help us."

Cheff grabbed me by the shirt. "Shhh! Did you hear that?" We held still and strained to hear noises from the dark recesses of the tunnel. Cheff covered his miner's lamp. "I thought I heard a splash." We held our breath but heard nothing more. "I guess not. It was probably only a rat, but stay quiet and let's keep moving."

After another ten minutes or so, we came to a pile of rubble where Cheff said that the street above had caved in. At first, it looked like a dead end, but Cheff directed the lamp upward to reveal a narrow opening. "Another tight squeeze, but no worse than the last one. Just follow the light." Cheff turned his lamp off, then reached up and pushed the lamp through first. He pulled himself up after it. His face appeared at the top of the opening. "Well, what are you waiting for? Come on!"

He was right—it was a tight squeeze.

Operation Break Iron

$$-\ 7\ -$$

THE RUINS

WE WEDGED OURSELVES up through the debris until we came out on top of a collapsed roadway. Cheff hid the lamp in some bushes nearby. The rain had stopped, and the sky was clearing. I stared up at the full moon, shining brightly high overhead in the midnight sky, making glittering reflections on the wet pavement.

Cheff ran out from the shadows and grabbed me by my shirt. "Get out of the street!" He dragged me into the cover of a tight clump of trees that had grown in the remains of what once might have been someone's house. "You're not in Tumberland anymore, Books. This is Fellstone, and it's crawling with army patrols and Bluebands. Look!" He pointed down the street. Not fifty feet (15m) from our hiding place, a group of six Bluebands was crossing the intersection, illuminated by the ivory moonlight. We held our position until they were out of sight. "Good, they're heading west, but don't take it for granted that we won't see them again, or others like them. To the south and west is the area I showed you on the map, the area that's being rebuilt. There are hundreds of homes and businesses there now. It would be a lot faster if we could take the road the Bluebands are on, but we don't dare. The moon is too bright, and it won't be setting anytime soon. We're going to have to be extra careful."

"Why not find another way into the storm-drain system and bypass the cave-in?" I asked. "Surely one of the tunnels must go right past Meltern's place."

"Good point, Books, and I expect that someday we'll do exactly that, but not tonight. Lots of the storm drains have collapsed, and I haven't had time to explore them all. Been too busy hunting. Our best bet is to stay in the shadows like I do when I hunt."

He gripped my arm hard. "Remember: one mistake out here, Books, and you're dead. The same goes for you, Mid. I've been doing this for a while, now, and I'm telling you, it's all about being invisible. So, both of you be quiet and make yourselves small. Watch me and do what I do."

Cheff led us eastward along the south wall of the Labor Compound, crouching and darting in and out of the darkest shadows. A few minutes later, we reached the southeast corner of the Compound. Now that we were out from behind the wall, we saw the full glory of the Great Fisherman Nebula to the north. Its cloud of stars added red, green, and indigo highlights to the moonlight's reflection on the glassy streets.

Cheff led us up a small rise where we crouched near another cracked and crumbling stone wall, heavily overgrown with tangles of hanging vines. "See that area way over there that's all lit up? That's the edge of Old City. It's about a mile (.6 km) or so from here. That's where we're going. If my memory is correct, Meltern's place will be somewhere along the main road. The dark area between here and there is all brush-covered debris."

I looked out across the blocks and blocks of destruction. "Back in Tumberland, we have a few ruins from The Fall, but nothing like this. What happened here?"

"Didn't you read about this in one of your books?" Cheff asked. "That's Old Fellstone City, where the last battle of the 'Glorious Liberation' was fought, several years after The Fall of Worldheart. Pallador had decided to make Fellstone City his capital. All the forces of the Ten Peoples gathered here to make their last stand.

Pallador won, of course, but not before he'd devastated the place. Afterward, he didn't even try to rebuild Old City. Instead, he went across the river and built New City, starting with the Iron Fortress out on the peninsula. Some people say he wants Old City left like this as a reminder of what happens to those who oppose him." His mouth twisted into a grim, mocking smile. "In school, they call it the 'Battle for the Liberation of Fellstone City.' Doesn't it look like liberation to you, Books? Sure it does. The people who lived here were liberated, all right. Liberated from their houses, their jobs, and their families. A good many of them were liberated from their lives." He sneered. "If that's Pallador's idea of liberty, I wish he'd go liberate himself."

Cheff looked at the nebula, then at the moon. "I'd be a lot happier crossing these ruins if we weren't lit up from both sides. But it's the only way—stay in the shadows as much as you can and keep low."

Cheff led us through the crumbling remains of ancient buildings, once again darting and crouching in the few shadows we could find. We zigzagged through the cracked streets. Several times we heard the skittering of tiny feet scrambling through the crumbled buildings. Cheff laughed softly. "Hear that? Tola rabbits. Any other night, they'd be tomorrow's supper. Tola rabbits are good eating—kind of bland, but much nicer than rat."

Twice along the way, Cheff stopped, motioned for silence, and cupped his hands around his ears. "I keep thinking there's something following us, but I can't tell what it is. I don't see anything. It might be someone hunting. I've run into other hunters before, but they don't usually come this far."

"Other hunters from the Labor Compound?" I asked.

"No," Cheff said, "they're mostly from the squatters' tent city down the hill." He pointed toward the harbor.

"Do you think a Blueband patrol could have spotted us?" Mid asked.

"Not likely," Cheff said. "For one thing, if they did, they'd have tried to stop us by now. For another thing, they don't usually leave the lighted areas. Lots of folks don't like the Bluebands too much. There are stories about Bluebands venturing into the ruins, never to be seen or heard from again. I've heard some of the guards in the Compound talking about it. Let's be extra careful now. Whatever it is that the guards and the Bluebands are afraid of, I don't want to stumble across it, either."

After we'd gone a half-dozen blocks or so, Cheff stopped to get his bearings. He climbed a little way up a tree that was growing along a low wall. "It's not a good idea to poke your head up, but if you stay next to a tree or a wall, you're not likely to be spotted." He climbed back down. "We're not even halfway there. This is about as close to Old City as I usually go. Mostly, I catch some quick meat, whatever I spot first, then head back home. From here on, we'll be in unfamiliar territory, so watch yourselves. Let's move."

We hadn't gone ten steps when a tall, shaggy Fruen—no, a Frae, no white head stripe—swathed in dark rags loomed out from behind an old wall and clapped a filthy hand over Mid's mouth. A hoarse voice roared, "WHAT ARE YOU A-DOIN' IN MY RUINS?"

$$-\ 8\ -$$

SARTH

THE CREATURE SPUN Mid around and examined his face. "Who are you? I don't know you. Are you hunting? Who said you could hunt out here? This is *my* hunting ground."

I tried to run, but my legs wouldn't move. Mid was struggling against the powerful grip, but couldn't break free. The gigantic figure gave Mid a shake. "Well, what are you waiting for? Did you find anything? Give me your catch before I decide to eat *you* instead!"

"Hold on, Sarth," Cheff said, "they're with me." He patted the huge, hairy figure on the shoulder. "How've you been?"

"Oh, it's you, Cheff. I didn't see you at first. How's the hunting?"

"We're not hunting tonight. We're on an errand."

"Oh?"

Cheff pointed his thumb at Mid. "I think you'd better let him go, now, Sarth. He's having trouble breathing."

Sarth let Mid fall to the ground, gasping and coughing. "Sorry, Cheff, I didn't mean to hurt your friend. I don't *think* he's hurt."

He poked Mid's rib cage with the toe of his boot, causing Mid to yelp in pain. "Nah, he's not hurt. He's fine." He squatted down in the dirt next to Mid, who was still gasping for air, and shook him by the front of his shirt. "Hey, you're okay, right? You look like you're okay to me." He stood up again. "He's okay, Cheff."

Mid sat up, glared at the rag-covered man, then tried to spit the taste of Sarth's hand out of his mouth. He rose slowly to his feet, brushing the dirt off his clothes.

"See? I knew he was okay." Sarth was slapping Mid on the back, much too hard, trying to help brush him off. "What kind of errand are you on?"

"We're looking for a man named Meltern. You ever heard of him?"

"Sure," Sarth said. "He runs a Guest House on the old Boulevard. He buys meat from me, sometimes, when I have extra. You're going the right way. Go three more blocks to the north, then east for another mile or so. Don't go on the Boulevard, though—it's too busy, even at night. The street before you get to the Boulevard will take you to the alley behind Meltern's place."

"The old Boulevard," Cheff said. "That's the main north/south road through Old City, right?"

"Yup, that's the one."

"Say, Sarth," Cheff asked, "have you seen anyone else out hunting tonight? I keep having this feeling that someone, or some *thing*, is following us, but I haven't spotted anyone."

"Nope. Haven't seen anyone at all tonight except a squad of Bluebands over by the Compound. Haven't heard anything, either, not until you came along. If there is something out there, whatever it is would have to be a lot sneakier than me. And that's not likely, 'cause I'm pretty sneaky." He held a nostril shut with one finger and cleared the other into the dust. Mid took a step back. Sarth wiped his nose with the back of his hand, then wiped his hand on his shirt. "You wanna come to my place and have a bite before you move on? I made some fresh soup."

Mid's eyes went wide. "Uh, no… but… um… thanks?"

"You sure? I'll show you my collection of blue armbands." He grinned right in Mid's face, showing his mouthful of black, decaying teeth. "Sometimes the Bluebands wander a little too close to my hunting grounds, but I don't mind." He cackled. "I eat like a king for a week."

Cheff gently punched Sarth's shoulder. "Thanks anyway, but we need to move along if we're going to be back home before dawn. Maybe another time. Thanks for the directions."

Sarth made no reply—he simply vanished into the dark night. As we continued, Mid asked, "He's joking, right, Cheff? About eating the Bluebands, I mean."

"I don't know. I've never asked, but I always assumed he was kidding. Surely, not even a crazy wild man like Sarth would sink so low as to eat another person." He hesitated. "Right?"

— 9 —

Run!

CHEFF LED US three blocks farther north, then we turned toward the Boulevard through a maze of overgrown rubble. It was strange to think that, long ago, this rubble had been homes and shops, full of people living and working. After another half-mile of sneaking and stumbling through the overgrowth, we came to the outskirts of a rebuilt area.

Cheff stopped us where the ruins ended, and we hid behind a clump of bushes. He shaded his eyes and scanned the darkness behind us. "Did you hear that? It's that same noise again. It's giving me the creeps."

Mid cautiously raised his head and had a look. "I don't see anything. I haven't heard anything, either. Have you, Books?"

"No, nothing. Are you sure you're not imagining it?"

"I don't know. Could be, I suppose. Maybe it's nerves. I've never come this close to the populated areas before. But, to be sure, let's hide here and watch for a few minutes to see if someone passes us."

We crouched in the clump of brush for what seemed like forever, but nothing happened. After a few minutes, Cheff said, "I guess we're clear," and started to stand up, but froze as a heavy, wet snuffle came from somewhere in the darkness behind us. The hair on our arms stood straight up. The snuffling was only a few feet away and rapidly getting closer. A huge, hairy dog burst through the brush at our feet, snarling.

"Nice doggie," Mid quavered, "good boy." He reached out to pet the dog, which snapped his slavering jaws. Mid jerked his arm back just in time, then kicked at the dog, which caused it to bark furiously.

Cheff yelled, quite unnecessarily, *"Dog!"* and then, equally unnecessarily, *"Run!"* He took off like a madman. Mid was right behind him, and I was right behind Mid. I remember thinking how remarkable it was that a fat Troh boy could run so fast on those short little legs. We ran in a blind panic, tripping and stumbling, trying to look behind us the whole time. I fell over a patch of broken pavement, but Cheff turned, scooped me up, and kept on going. We ran until we couldn't run anymore, then stopped in the shadow of a two-story brick building where we struggled to catch our breath.

Cheff looked behind us. There was no sign of the dog. He asked Mid, "Did he hurt you, Old Son?"

Mid examined his arm. "No, he didn't get me, but I thought he was going to bite my arm off."

"He sure made a lot of racket," I said. "I hope he didn't wake anyone."

But all along the street behind us, lights were coming on, and people were calling out, "Who's there? What's going on?" Two blocks to the west, a patrol of Bluebands stopped to talk to a man in a doorway. The man pointed, and the Bluebands looked in our direction. They moved toward us, poking into the bushes and shrubbery with their billy clubs.

Cheff pulled us deeper into the shadows. "This isn't going to do at all. We've got to get off the street. There's too much light. I think we must almost be there, maybe only a few blocks to go. Stick close to me, and be as quiet as you can. We don't want to get any more dogs excited. Try to be invisible."

Run!

Crouching as low as we could, we sneaked into an unlit alley and continued eastward toward the Boulevard, grateful for the darkness. In spots, we couldn't see anything and had to feel our way along. We scurried from bush to trashcan to rubbish heap. Once we left the alley and transversed an entire block through the inside of a burned-out brick building. At the end of every block, where we had to cross a lighted street, we waited until there was no one in sight. Then, hearts pounding, we dashed across to the safety of the next alley.

At last, we could see the well-lit Boulevard two blocks ahead of us. As we crouched in the shadows, we heard sounds of people everywhere—on the streets, in homes nearby, in shops, in restaurants from which strange, mouth-watering aromas wafted into the night. Cheff sniffed the air. "Someone's cooking something."

"Something wonderful." Mid's nose twitched. "I just realized that I'm starving."

"Me, too." I rubbed my empty belly. "Why do you suppose there are so many people moving around in the middle of the night? Don't they have a curfew out here?"

"Probably," Cheff said, "but not for night workers. Here in Old City, people work all night long. All the populated areas are like this. It's why I stay far away from them when I hunt. There's a kid in my class, Trendel—you'll meet him tomorrow, probably—who used to live out here. He said that the restaurants and shops stay open for people coming home from work, and for people who eat their lunches in the middle of the night shift."

We crossed the last street before the Boulevard and crept down the alley until we found ourselves looking across an overgrown yard at the back of a large, two-story wooden building. Cheff read the sign over the back door:

MELTERN'S GUEST HOUSE
PLEASE USE FRONT ENTRANCE

"Not likely," Cheff said. "We'd better stick with the back door."

OPERATION BREAK IRON

— 10 —

MELTERN'S GUEST HOUSE

W E HAD LEFT the shadows of the alley and started for Meltern's back door, when it crashed open. A man staggered down the steps into the weeds. He could barely stand. He fumbled with his trousers, then he relieved himself into the tall grass, singing:

"Oh, great Pallador,

I pee on your floor,

For you're nothing more

Than a stinking old—"

I started to laugh, but Cheff elbowed me in the ribs. "Stay low! Drunk or not, if the Bluebands hear him, he's a dead man."

He bellowed on until he finished, then made a half-hearted attempt to button up before lurching back into the Guest House. We waited for a few more minutes, but no one else came out. Cheff whispered, "Let's go." He led us through the brushy lot, carefully avoiding the wet spot. We stopped alongside the wooden steps and listened to the sounds coming from inside: loud voices talking, off-key singing, and the clanking of dishes and tableware.

Cheff crept up the steps and knocked softly on the back door. No one answered. He knocked again, louder. We heard heavy footsteps coming toward the door. A skinny, unshaven Fessal wearing a filthy apron opened the door, suds dripping from his hands. He pointed at the sign. "Whassamatter? You can't read? Use the front door!"

He started to slam the door, but Cheff growled in the deepest voice he could muster, "Message for Meltern. Urgent!"

The Fessal stared at Cheff, then looked up and down the alley. "Get off the porch, fool." He pointed at the dark spot where Mid and I were hiding. "Wait down there, with your friends." He checked the alley again, then disappeared inside. We heard him shout, "Hey, Mel! Delivery for you, out back!"

Cheff crouched with us in the shadow of the porch, and we waited for what seemed a long time. Finally, the door opened, and a rotund, clean-shaven, apple-cheeked Fruen appeared in the doorway. His reddish-brown hair was parted neatly right down the middle of his characteristic Fruen white stripe. He was drying a large glass mug with a white bar towel. He took several breaths of the cool night air, then he started down the steps. He nonchalantly looked up and down the alley, still polishing the mug. When he got close to our hiding spot, he stopped. Without turning around, he asked quietly, "Who are you, and what do you want?"

Cheff asked from the bushes, "Are you Mr. Meltern?"

The Fruen nodded.

"My uncle told me to contact you. His name is Shoshan Karfendek, but everyone calls him Karf. We live in the Labor Compound. Yesterday he was abducted. The last thing he said was, 'Contact Meltern.' He didn't say why."

"How did you know where to find me?"

"I used to come here with Uncle Karf and my father, Fennel Karfendek."

Meltern finished drying the mug and shook his towel out in the night air. "Sorry, kid. I've never heard of anyone named Karf.

You've got the wrong guy. Now get out of here before I call a patrol." He turned to go back inside.

Cheff stood up. "Wait. I know you're FRM. You've got to help him!"

Meltern dropped the mug, grabbed Cheff, and dragged him back into the shadows. He glanced up and down the alley again, then he shoved his florid face into Cheff's. "What do you know about the FRM? Tell me, quick, if you want to live."

"I think that Uncle Karf is FRM, and I think he sent me to you because *you're* FRM." Cheff looked Meltern straight in the eye. "And when I'm old enough, I'm going to join the FRM, too!"

Meltern's eye showed the briefest hint of a twinkle. "Look, kid, if there was such a thing as the FRM, which there isn't, what makes you think they'd want a brat like you?" He let Cheff go. "Now get out of here before the Bluebands come along and spoil your evening."

Cheff fought back tears of frustration. "But Uncle Karf told me to find you. He must have thought you could do something to help."

Meltern's voice softened. "Look, kid, I told you—there's no such thing as the FRM, and I never heard the name Karfendek before. But if there were an FRM, and if your uncle were part of it, he would have known the risks from the start. By now, he's in the Iron Fortress, and there's no chance of escape from there. Any attempt to help him would be suicide, and I'm sure your uncle wouldn't want that." He patted Cheff on the shoulder. "As far as you're concerned, kid, the FRM is a myth. Go home. Forget about your uncle. Take care of your Aunt Dee. Obey the rules, stay alive, and prepare for your work assignment when you're done with school." He gave Cheff another pat on the shoulder. "Now get home before the sun comes up. I don't know how you got here without getting caught, but if you want to get home alive, you'd better get a move on." He went up the steps and disappeared inside.

Cheff stood, stunned, fists clenched, then he kicked viciously at the ground. "So much for Meltern! I wonder what Uncle Karf would think if he knew his friend told us to forget about him." He savagely wiped angry tears from his eyes. "Fine! Forget Meltern, then! Who needs him, anyhow?" Then he crouched low and led us back into the darkness of the alley.

— 11 —

BLUEBANDS

ALFWAY DOWN THE block, a strange, high-pitched whisper came from the shrubbery along the edge of someone's backyard. "Hide! There's a Blueband patrol right around the corner!"

We flung ourselves into a clump of vegetation and concealed ourselves as best we could. The Bluebands appeared at the end of the alley. It looked like the same patrol that had nearly spotted us earlier. We held our breath until they crossed and started down the side street. We heaved a collective sigh of relief but froze as the patrol stopped. One of them pointed toward us and shouted, "What's that? I thought I heard something over there!"

The other Bluebands returned from the side street and peered in our direction. They conferred, then came down the alley toward us, poking their billy clubs into the bushes and clumps of tall grass. We huddled together, but our cover was pretty thin—it was only a matter of time. They got closer and closer, close enough to identify the squad-leader's pin on the cap of the tallest one. A dog barked in the yard behind us. The squad leader pointed straight at us and shouted, "There! In those weeds!" They all ran toward us. I wondered if being beaten to death with a billy club would hurt much.

When they were a few feet away, a horrific screech came out of the darkness behind them. They stopped dead in their tracks, then spun around to see a small figure in a nightgown jump out of the bushes they'd been poking only moments before. The small figure called, "STARRRRY! STARRRRY, WHERE ARE YOU?"

I asked Cheff, "Isn't 'Starry' your sister's pony's name?"

"Buttons!" Cheff tried to lurch to his feet, but Mid grabbed Cheff's belt and yanked him back to the ground.

"Stay down!" Mid hissed. "You'll get her killed!"

Fortunately, the Bluebands were all watching the little girl and didn't notice Cheff. Buttons ran up to the one with the squad-leader's pin and tugged his pant leg. "Please, mister, she's lost! You have to help me! Pleeease!"

"Stop that! Let me go!" The leader jumped back and shook her off. "What's the matter with you? Who's lost?"

"I told you—*she's* lost!" Buttons began to cry.

The leader shook Buttons by her shoulders. "Stop it! Stop crying right now, do you hear? Now tell me: She, *who*? *Who's* lost?"

Buttons stopped wailing and wiped her quivering lip with her sleeve. "Starry! Starry Stargazer. She's lost, she's gone, and I'll never see her again, ever, in my whole entire life."

The Blueband leader was stumped. "Starry?" he yelled. "Who's Starry?"

"*Who's Starry?*" The girl looked at them as though they were morons. "Starry is *Starry*. Starry Stargazer. *Don't yell at me!*" She started to cry again.

Mid whispered, "Oh, she's good, she's *really* good."

"Buttons!" Cheff whimpered but didn't try to stand up again.

The Blueband leader took a deep breath, got down on one knee, and lowered his voice. "All right, there, there. I've got it now: Starry Stargazer. Who is that, exactly?"

"My *poneee!*" She began to wail again, in earnest.

"Your pony?"

"She ran away! I can't find her anywhere! She's gone, and Moka is all by herself!"

I whispered to Cheff, "Moka is Buttons' other pony, right?"

"Yes, Starry and Moka." Cheff clapped his hand to his forehead and struggled to rise again. "I've got to get her out of there!"

Mid and I held him down until he stopped struggling.

He groaned, "What in the world is Buttons doing out here in the middle of the night?"

"Shhh! Rescuing us from the Bluebands, I'd say," Mid said. "Leave her alone."

The Blueband leader took another deep breath and asked softly, "Who's Moka?"

Buttons gave him another look. "Moka! Starry's sister! Starry's the one with white fluffy feet. Moka's the brown one."

"The brown one—another pony?"

Buttons put her hands on her hips. "Of *course*, another pony. Haven't you been paying attention?" She took Moka from her backpack and held her in the Blueband's face. "See? She's been crying for *hours!*" With her forefinger, she indicated tear tracks on Moka's face.

The Blueband leader sighed. "Of course, right, okay. *Two* ponies. Tell me exactly what happened."

"You see, Starry was sitting on the windowsill getting some fresh air." Buttons pointed at the upstairs window of the house next to where she was standing. "Starry and Moka like to watch the Bluebands patrolling in their uniforms. I do, too. I don't know what happened. I turned my back for a teensy little second, and when I looked around, Starry was *gone*, and Moka was all *alone*. I think Starry got so excited seeing you that she fell out of the window." Her chin quivered again, and a huge tear ran down her cheek. "Now she's out there all by herself, all sad and lonesome." She grasped the Blueband leader's sleeves with both hands. "Please, Mr. Blueband, you've *got* to help me find her. I've looked all over, but I can't find her anywhere. She needs a real hero to rescue her. Like you! Won't you help her, *pleeease?*"

The Blueband leader stood up tall and puffed his chest out a little. "Of course we'll help. I'm sure we'll find Starry safe and sound in no time, right, men? What's your name, little girl?"

Buttons gulped. "Bin… Binnala."

"Okay, Binnala, let's start by looking under the window where she fell out."

Without hesitation, Buttons took the Blueband leader's hand, opened the gate, and pulled him into the front yard of the house. The Bluebands searched under every bush, with Buttons trailing behind, whimpering and calling. "Starrrry! Where are you? Please come out. It's me, Binnala. These nice, strong Bluebands are here to help you. Where are you?"

While they were searching, Mid, Cheff, and I carefully crept back down the alley, and found a much better hiding spot behind some old packing crates. Cheff shook his head. "How could Buttons have gotten all the way out here?"

"I don't know," Mid said. "She must have followed us. Maybe that's what you were hearing on the way here."

"Maybe," Cheff said. "You think?"

Mid shrugged.

The three of us poked our heads up a little bit to see what was happening. Buttons and the Bluebands were still bent over, searching among the shrubbery. Then Buttons screamed, "Here she is! Here she is! You found her! Hurray!" She held up the battered Starry for all to see, then clutched her to her chest. "Oh, thank you, thank you. The Bluebands are our heroes!" She threw her arms around the leader and gave him a big hug. "And you're the most heroic of all!"

With a loud creak, the door of the house swung open. A sleepy-looking man and woman stood in the doorway in their nightclothes. The man said, "What is this? What's going on?"

The Blueband leader started to explain, but Buttons cut him off. "It's me, Binnala, and the Bluebands. They saved her! They saved Starry! She got lost, but these brave Bluebands helped me find her." She put her arms around the woman's waist. "I was so scared, Mommy. I was afraid I'd never see Starry again." She hugged the man. "It's a good thing these gentlemen came along, isn't it, Daddy? I already thanked them, but you should thank them for me, too."

The man stared blankly down at Buttons. Cheff gripped my arm.

Then the man blinked. "Of course, of course, um… Binnala. My sweet little Binnie. Thank you, gentlemen, for your noble and chivalrous service to this damsel in distress. I don't know what might have happened if you hadn't come along." He asked the woman, "I'm sure we have something to thank these gentlemen with, don't we, dear?"

The woman hesitated, then turned and disappeared into the house.

The Blueband leader scowled. "The girl was out after curfew, and she's too young to have a worker's permit. We could have shot her. We're authorized to shoot curfew violators, you know. At the very least, we ought to take her in for questioning."

The woman returned and handed the man a small purse. The man emptied it into his hand, then gave the Blueband leader the fistful of coins.

The Blueband leader eyed the coins with disgust, then barked, "What's this? Bribing a Blueband?"

"Now, now," the man said, "bribing a Blueband is illegal. I'd never do such a thing. It's just that, well, we know you're not allowed to take payment for your services, but after such heroic action, you must allow me to buy you all a nice, hot apple cider. Wouldn't that be okay? Sure it would." He leaned out and peered down the alley. "It looks like Meltern's place is still open. Have a round on us."

The Blueband leader silently consulted his party. "Hmph. Fine. But see that you explain to your daughter why this should never happen again."

"Of course, we'll do that. Thank you again, gentlemen."

The woman rested her hands on Buttons' shoulders, and the man put his arm around the woman's waist. The three of them waved at the departing Bluebands. "Goodbye! Thank you! Goodbye! Stay safe!"

They waited in the doorway while the Bluebands marched right past our hiding place toward Meltern's Guest House. Buttons hugged the man and the woman again. "Thank you, Daddy. Thank you, Mommy." Then she added in a low voice, "And thank you for buying them the drinks. I'll try to pay you back someday."

"Forget about it," the man said. "I hate those stinking Blueband scum! Anyway, it wasn't that much money, and it's worth every last coin to see them made fools of."

The woman hugged Buttons again. "I don't know who you are, honey, and it's probably best you don't tell us. You can stay the night with us if you need to."

"Thank you," Buttons said, "but there are people waiting for me. I have to go."

"Are you sure, dear? You're more than welcome."

"I'm sure, ma'am, but thank you again."

"All right, if you must. Be careful, honey, and get home safely to your real mommy. I know she loves you very much. Now get going, before they come back."

Buttons hugged them one more time, made sure the Bluebands were out of sight, then ran down the steps and out the gate. Without hesitation, she marched right up to our hiding place. We stared at her. Cheff's jaw dropped open. "Buttons! What—? How—?"

"Save it for later, Cheff." Buttons started back up the alley. "You heard the lady—we have to get going before those Bluebands come back."

"Or worse," Mid said, "before Aunt Dee wakes up and finds you missing!"

Mellabee "Buttons" Karfendek

— 12 —

SCHOOL

ISPENT THE NIGHT at Cheff's house, as planned. The next morning, I dashed home to check on Mother and change my clothes. Mother and I had breakfast together, the leftovers of the meal Aunt Dee had brought the night before.

Mother kissed my forehead. "Do your best on your placement test, Birn. I know you'll do fine." And off she went to her new job at the uniform factory. She looked like a new woman. I began to believe in Aunt Dee's restorative powers.

Cheff, Mid, and Buttons came around to walk me to school. The three of them looked bright and chipper. I wondered how they did it. I was groggy, had a headache, and felt exhausted from the previous night's adventure. I had a hundred questions, but when I tried to ask, Cheff said, "Later, Books. Let's get going." As we walked up the street, Cheff asked me, "How is your mother this morning?"

"Much better. Aunt Dee's remedy must have done the trick."

"I told you she'd be okay," Cheff said. "I'm glad to hear that Aunt Dee helped."

Buttons asked, "Why does Cheff call you 'Books?'"

"It's his new nickname," Cheff said. "I'll tell you about it some-time."

"Okay. Can I call you 'Books,' too?"

"Sure," I said.

Cheff asked me, "Are you nervous about your first day at a new school?"

"A little. I did okay in school in Tumberland, so I'm not really worried about the schoolwork. I'm more concerned about…"

"The other kids?" Mid asked.

"Yes."

"It'll depend a lot on which school you get assigned to," Cheff said. "The kids in Regular School can be pretty rough, but it's not so bad in Advanced School."

"What's the difference between Regular and Advanced?" I asked.

"Didn't you have split schools in Tumberland?" Buttons asked.

"No, there was only one school, and all the kids went to it."

"Well," Cheff said, "here in Fellstone City, even in the Labor Compound, we're on what's called the 'Paths of Destiny Academic Program.' It's new—I guess it hasn't made it to Tumberland yet."

"Paths of Destiny?" I asked. "That sounds ominous."

"It's not so bad," Mid said. "Better, in some ways, I think. I'm small even for a Troh. We were still on the old system back then, all the kids in the same school. The big kids picked on me all the time, calling me Big Hands and Squinty. That sort of thing doesn't happen so much under the new system."

"Well," I said, "you do have big hands."

Mid frowned. "Of course I have big hands—all Trohs have big hands."

"Right," I said. "But why 'Squinty?'"

"Because direct sunlight hurts my eyes." He took a pair of sun-glasses from his bag. "When it's bright, I have to wear these."

"Why aren't you wearing them now?" I asked.

"The air is so dirty here that it's not usually a problem," Mid explained. "And the lenses get dirty fast, as I'm sure you've noticed with your own glasses. But away from the Labor Compound, the glasses help. It's not a big deal—most Trohs use eye protection of some kind, some of the time. Didn't you have any Trohs in Tumberland?"

"Some. Come to think of it, the ones I saw were wearing dark glasses. The people in Tumberland are mostly Mountain Loras and a few Lildurs like me. You're the first Troh I've ever known personally."

"I'm honored," Mid said and took a small bow.

"How does the split school system work?" I asked.

Cheff explained, "Instead of one school, we have three, not counting preschool for the little kids. First, there's Basic School. All the kids are together in Basic for our first five grades. When we finish Basic, we get tested and separated into two groups: Advanced if you scored well on your placement test and your teacher didn't hate you too much, Regular for everyone else. Mid and I are in Advanced, and you probably will be, too, but you'll have to get tested first. Buttons will be in Advanced next year—this is her last year in Basic."

Buttons skipped ahead, turned around, and walked backward, facing us. "The Advanced kids are pretty smart, and not nearly as mean as the ones in Regular. You really don't want to be in Regular, so be sure you try extra hard on your test."

"Got it," I said. "What makes the Regular kids so mean?"

"For one thing," Cheff said, "they hate us because they know we're going to get better jobs than they are for the whole rest of their lives."

"What kinds of jobs?"

Mid said, "We'll be the teachers, engineers, managers, researchers, military officers, things like that. They'll be the factory workers, soldiers, clerks, fishermen, and trash haulers. There's nothing wrong with any of those things, of course. Those jobs are important, too, but they don't pay as well."

"It's not only the pay," Cheff said, "or even the job titles and recognition. I think what makes them so angry is that they'll be stuck there for life. Once they're assigned to Regular School, they never get another chance. I'd be angry, too." He considered. "I *am* angry, in fact. Nobody should have their dreams taken away like that." He took a deep breath. "Anyway, try extra hard on your test, okay?"

"Thanks a lot, Cheff. I wasn't all that worried about my entrance tests—until now."

Cheff, Mid, and Buttons laughed.

Mid clapped me on the shoulder. "Don't worry, Books. I'm sure you'll be fine."

"With a brain like yours," Cheff said, "you're not going to have any trouble. Do you have any idea what sort of job you might like? If, I mean *when*, you qualify for Advanced School, you'll have to pick a Track, too."

"You mentioned the Civilian Leadership Track. What other Tracks are there?"

"There are six main Tracks." Buttons made Starry count to six with one hoof.

"They'll make recommendations based on your scores," Cheff said, "but there's a lot of room for personal preference. The first three are the Leadership Tracks." He held up his left hand and counted them off. "First, there's Civilian Leadership, that's the Track I'm on—"

Mid broke in, "Those are the factory managers, teachers, historians—"

"—second, Political Leadership—"

"—the governors, mayors, police chiefs—"

"—third, Military Leadership—"

"—Army and Navy officers, Imperial Intelligence."

"Then come the three Science Tracks." Cheff started counting over again with his first finger. "Pure Science—"

"—they study and research things, and think up new ideas, new medicines, new weapons, stuff like that—"

"—Medicine, Engineering and Technology—"

"—That's me!" Mid said. "We're the ones who figure out how to use what the scientists think up—"

"—and finally, Agricultural Science."

"They try to breed better plants and animals to feed more people," Mid said.

Buttons added, "We call those last three the Thinkers, Tinkers, and Stinkers." She pinched her nose.

We laughed.

I asked, "What about the first three?"

Mid looked around to make sure no snoops were in earshot, then lowered his voice. "We call the civilian leaders the Runners, because they run things, you see, and the military leaders the Gunners, for obvious reasons."

"What about the politicians?"

"Sometimes we refer to them as the No-Funners," Mid continued, "but mostly we call them filthy, rotten, traitorous, no-good—"

"Okay," I said, "I get it."

"—but not when they can hear us."

"Yeah," Cheff agreed. "You never know if one of them will grow up and find you *interesting*."

I shivered. "Right."

Mid said, "The Regulars don't have the free time we have, either. They get out at noon, same as Advanced, but we're supposed to go home and work on projects related to our Track. Because I'm on the Engineering and Technology Track, I get to have a workbench in my bedroom. If you'd like, you can come over after school today, and I'll show you some of my inventions."

"Sure!"

"Instead of free time," Cheff said, "the Regulars have to go to mandatory work assignments, mostly in factories here in the compound. It's usually grunt work: sweeping, mopping, cleaning restrooms, carrying stuff around, whatever needs to be done. Sometimes, if they do well, they can get an assignment where they actually learn something, like operating a machine or helping with construction work."

"There's only one way to get out of the mandatory work assignment," Mid added. "Join the Bluebands."

"The Bluebands! *Me?*"

"Of course not you," Cheff said. "I don't know how you get to join the Bluebands in Tumberland, but around here they're Regular School students who have chosen to become soldiers. So, instead of doing something productive, they run around in packs every afternoon, bullying the rest of the kids and even some grown-ups, looking for evidence of disloyalty and 'unwholesome thinking.'"

Mid added, "You have to be extremely careful what you say and do when they're around. If you give them a reason, any reason at all, even glancing at them, they'll give you a bad time, maybe even hurt you."

"And if you do attract their attention," Cheff said, "don't even think of arguing with them. Look at the ground, answer 'Yes, sir' and 'No, sir.' Give them anything they want and do whatever they tell you."

Mid said, "If you go along with them and don't get upset, they'll get bored with you and go away—usually." He gave me a few small coins. "Here, put these in your pocket. We always carry a few coins to give to them in a pinch. They'll hurt you if you come up dry."

"Thanks." I stuffed the coins into my pocket. "Do the Bluebands bother you a lot?"

"No, not too often," Cheff said. "Mid and I are always pretty careful, and mostly they leave us alone."

Mid looked me up and down. "You're small for your age, like me. They'll notice you sooner or later and give you a trial run to see what you're made of. Remember what we said—look down, answer politely no matter what, and do whatever they tell you. You can't fight them—you just have to endure them."

"Phew!" I said, "That's a lot to take in all at once. I hope I'm up to it."

"Don't worry," Mid said. "You'll be fine. We've all been through it. It's not as bad as it sounds—you get used to it."

"Well, here we are," Cheff said. "Come on, we'll take you to the office."

We had arrived at a large fenced compound. Three dreary buildings stood along two edges of a large square of crumbling asphalt, all surrounded by a high wire fence. I asked, "What's the fence for, to keep us in or someone else out?"

"To keep the Bluebands from biting people." Buttons snapped her teeth viciously a few times, then held Starry up and made her wave goodbye. "I'm going to go on to my class." She pointed across the asphalt yard to the largest building, a one-story brick structure with a sagging wooden roof. "I like to get there a few minutes early and help the teacher. Never hurts to create a little goodwill!"

Operation Break Iron

— 13 —

PLACEMENT TESTING

THE SCHOOL ADMINISTRATION office was a dingy little room in the middle-sized school building. No one was in the office. A tidy desk dominated the center of the room, accompanied by some filing cabinets and well-ordered bookshelves along the walls. Cheff, Mid, and I went right in, stood at the empty desk, and waited. Soon we heard the sounds of a toilet flushing and water running. Shortly afterward, a small, thin man entered the office from the back hallway, smoothing his short, white Sevro beard. Like most Sevros, his white face featured small black eyes and a long, pointy, pink nose. He glanced uneasily at us, then, without a word, took his seat at the desk where he nervously shuffled and organized a stack of papers. He arranged several pens and pencils in a straight line, sorted by type, size, and color. A twitchy smile crossed his face as he studied his newly ordered desktop. Finally, he looked up at us, and demanded, "All right, then. What can I do for you, Karfendek?"

"Good morning, Mr. Walikas," Cheff said. "We've brought you a new student for admissions testing. He arrived yesterday evening."

"How do you do, sir? I'm Birn Tylandine." I extended my hand for him to shake, but he stared at it until I took it back.

He looked me over and sighed. He seemed disappointed, even disapproving.

I involuntarily checked my shoelaces and fly.

He sighed again. "Yes, I have his papers right here on my desk. Very well, then, young man, come with me. I'm sure this won't take long." He waved Cheff and Mid away. "You two run along, now, go on, shoo! I'm a busy man, no time for games."

Cheff said to me, "We'll meet you in the yard at the half-morning break. Look for us at a table under a tin roof. Don't worry, you'll do fine." He and Mid went out the door, and I was alone with Mr. Walikas.

"Well, don't dawdle, boy—let's get moving. I haven't all day." He retrieved a thick sheaf of papers from the pristine file drawer of his desk, then seated me at a small table in the corner. He gave me the papers and two pencils. "Try not to break the points, boy. Pencils don't grow on bushes, you know. If you break both of them, which I'm sure you will, don't bother me. The pencil sharpener is on the wall over there." He glanced at the wall clock. "You only have until the half-morning break, so you'd best get started. And try not to let your pencil scratch on the paper. I have enough trouble of my own without constant distractions." He returned to his desk and pointedly ignored me.

I was dismayed by the size of the test until I looked at the first few pages. The large lettering allowed only a few questions per page. I wasn't going to have any trouble at all—the questions came straight from books I'd already memorized.

I worked my way quickly through the thick test and took it to Mr. Walikas, who was still working at his desk. He consulted the wall clock, then pulled his glasses down his nose and peered at me over the top of them. He checked the wall clock again. Without a word, he began reviewing my test, making a checkmark next to each correct answer. About halfway through, he looked at me over his glasses again, then went back to checking answers and turning pages.

When he finished, he gathered the test papers, tapped them on his desktop to straighten them, then laid them neatly in front of him. He took off his glasses, steepled his fingers, and leaned back in his creaky chair. He contemplated me for a while, tapping his fingers together. After a few minutes, he stopped tapping, rocked forward, and said, "Well, young man, Birn Tylandine, is it? It seems that you've answered the questions correctly. All the questions. *All* of them. Every one. That's remarkable, to say the least. How do you explain this? Were you coached?"

"No, sir. I didn't even know there was going to be a test until this morning."

His eyebrows arched. "Is that so? Interesting." He resumed tapping his fingers together. "Well, then, *Mister* Tylandine, exactly how do you account for a perfect score?"

"I don't know, sir. I learned all the answers in my old school in Tumberland. We had an excellent teacher, sir, and I have an excellent memory."

"Is that so?" he said again. "Hmm... I suppose that *could* account for it. But I, for one, am not that gullible. We don't tolerate nasty little cheaters, here, *Mister* Tylandine. I'm afraid I'm going to have to have you searched." He narrowed his eyes. "Or shall I place you in Regular School this moment?"

"No, sir," I said. "I don't belong in Regular School, and I'm not a cheater."

"Very well." He picked up the telephone on his desk. "This is Walikas. I need two guards for a student search right away." He put the phone back in its cradle, none too gently. "You stay right where you are, Tylandine."

"But, sir—"

"Not one word, Tylandine. Just stand there."

I heard heavy boots in the hallway, then the door crashed open. Two burly Fessals entered, wearing army uniforms and carrying billy clubs. The taller of the two asked, "This the one?"

"That's him," Mr. Walikas said.

The leader put me in a headlock with his club, while the other patted me down and went through my pockets. "Nothing, Mr. Walikas."

"Check his arms," Mr. Walikas said. "Sometimes they write notes on their arms."

He tore my jacket off and examined me. "He's clean."

"Are you sure?"

"Yes, sir, Mr. Walikas. Positive."

"Hmm… all right, then, you may go."

The leader thrust my torn jacket into my arms, gave me a menacing look, then stomped away. He seemed disappointed. I hoped I'd be able to repair the jacket. It was my only one, and there was no way to get another. Maybe Aunt Dee would have some thread and a needle I could borrow.

"Well, Mister Tylandine, it seems I may have been mistaken, but we simply can't afford to take any chances with cheaters. I'm still not convinced. If I ever find so much as a hint of cheating, I will make life hard for you, harder than you can imagine. Do you understand?"

"Yes, sir, I understand. But I'm telling the truth—I do have an excellent memory. And I can prove it."

"Oh? And exactly how do you propose to do that?"

"I'll show you how I got all the test questions right, without cheating. You see, sir, I have an unusual memory when it comes to books."

"Unusual in what way, exactly?"

"I remember them, sir."

"We all remember the books we read. What's so unusual about that?"

"It's not that I remember reading them, sir. I remember *everything* about them. Every word. I can actually see pictures of the book's pages in my mind."

Mr. Walikas narrowed his eyes and studied me, then went to the bookshelf on the wall behind his desk. He took down a raggedy old school textbook and held it up for me to see. "*Salvation from Empire: An Account of Pallador's Glorious Liberation from the Sixth Kingdom.* Did you study this one in... where was it? Tumberland?"

"Yes, sir."

He thumbed through the pages. "Page 12, paragraph 2."

I closed my eyes, brought up a mental image of the page, and recited:

> "'*In the days before the fall of the Sixth Kingdom, Andaran was ruled by the evil Torph kings of the Maghorn Dynasty. For centuries, the Maghorn Torphs dominated the other races, subjugating them and enslaving them. It wasn't until our beloved Emperor Pallador and his faithful companion, Kahph, who would later betray him, formed a plan to liberate all the races. Together, they restored the ancient Cult of Kallor (sometimes spelled Callor or Kullor) and—*'"

"That's enough, young man. That was astounding. I will assume that you are telling the truth—for now." He returned the book to the shelf and sat at his desk. "I've never seen anything like that before. You will forgive me for doubting you."

It wasn't a request. "Of course, sir."

"Very well, then. Obviously, you are to be placed in the Advanced school. Let's decide which Track you're going to be on. Have you given any thought to that?"

"No, sir. We didn't have school Tracks back in Tumberland. I hadn't heard about Tracks until Cheff told me about them. Cheff Karfendek—he's my neighbor, sir. I met him last night."

"Yes, I'm well acquainted with Mr. Karfendek. He's nothing but trouble, I tell you, Advanced student or not. You'd be well advised to steer clear of him, young man."

"Yes, sir."

He opened an official-looking ledger and began turning the pages. "Yes, this will do. Right here under the Civilian Leadership Track: Archiving and Library Management. A most important skill in the Imperium, extremely important, indeed! It consists of, let me see now, yes, it says, 'the collection, organization, preservation, and dissemination of information resources.' In light of your particular talent, I believe that would be a good fit for you. Are we agreed?"

"Yes, sir—whatever you think best."

"Good! It's an important job. It's all about controlling knowledge in the Imperium. And, of course, as Emperor Pallador continues expanding and improving the Imperium, many new books about all of his magnificent accomplishments will need to be written.

"You see, Mister Tylandine, books can be a powerful force for good when they inspire us to perform great deeds. They can encourage faithful, loyal service, but they can also be dangerous. Ancient books from the days of the evil Torph Empire can poison hearts and minds against the Imperium. Library Managers carry the heavy responsibility of ensuring that only the *right* books fall into the hands of the people. Do you understand? Books *must* be controlled."

"Yes, sir, I think so."

"I'm assigning you to Civilian Leadership with a focus on Archiving and Library Management." He wrote something on a small white card and handed it to me. "Keep this with you at all times. Show it to the teacher before class starts." He frowned. "Unfortunately, that puts you in the same class as the Karfendek boy. Remember what I told you about him."

"Yes, sir, I will."

"Go away, now. I have work to do. And remember: I'll be watching you."

"Yes, sir. Thank you, sir." I left the office and went to look for Cheff and Mid.

— 14 —

THE FLASHDARK

I FOUND THEM, ALONG with Buttons, sitting at a wooden table in a grubby, covered break area. The mid-morning sun poured through thousands of holes in the metal roof like water through a colander. "Hi, guys. Hello, Buttons. What are you doing here? Shouldn't you be in class?"

Buttons shook her head, sending her twin shiny black ponytails swinging. "All the schools get mid-morning break at the same time. I always come and sit with Mid and my brother so the Regular kids don't pick on me." She took Starry from her backpack. "We don't like those nasty Regular kids, do we Starry?" Starry shook her head. "Sit next to me and Starry, Books. Starry wants you to sit with me, don't you, Starry?" Starry nodded.

I sat down next to Buttons and Starry.

Mid asked me, "How did your placement test go, Books?"

"Um… pretty okay, I guess."

"'Pretty okay?'" Buttons asked. "How many answers did you get wrong?"

"I, uh, well…"

"Come on!" Cheff said. "Out with it—how many? Five? Ten? Spill it, Books!"

"Well, uh, Mr. Walikas said I got them all right."

Cheff and Mid exchanged a glance.

"All of them?" Buttons said. "Wow!"

"So, you got *all* the answers right?" Mid asked. "That's amazing. I don't think we've ever heard of anyone getting them all right, have we, Cheff?"

"Mr. Walikas said the same thing," I said. "He accused me of cheating. He called the guards, and they searched me to see if I had any cheat notes."

"Did they hurt you?" Cheff asked.

"Only a little," I said. "But they ripped my jacket. I can't afford to get another one."

"Let me see," Buttons said. "Yep. Only a couple of small rips, is all. No big deal. It'll sew right up."

"Do you think Aunt Dee could loan me a needle and some thread?"

"I can do better than that," Buttons said. She found a needle and thread in her special pony-carrying backpack. "I always keep them with me. First-aid for ponies. Look." She held Starry so I could see the row of neat stitches on the inside of the little pony's hind leg.

"I see," I said. "Makes sense. I don't know if I can sew that well."

"How about I do it for you?" Buttons said. "I'd be happy to. You can give me the jacket after school."

"Okay. Thanks, Buttons."

"Don't mention it," she said. She held the ponies up to her ear and listened. "Starry and Moka have some advice for you."

"What's that?"

"From now on, make sure to get a few questions wrong on every test."

"She's right," Cheff said. "It's all about not calling attention to yourself."

"Okay," I said. "I'll do that from now on. I have to say, so far I don't think much of this 'Paths of Destiny' academic system. I thought I was going to get a path straight to the infirmary."

"How did you convince him you didn't cheat?" Cheff asked. "Did you have to show him your book trick?"

"What book trick?" Buttons asked. "Wait, let me guess—you'll tell me later, right?"

"I had to," I said. "It was the only way I could convince him I wasn't cheating. He seemed impressed."

"Did he apologize for having you roughed up?" Cheff asked.

Mid snorted. "Fat chance!"

"No," I said, "but he was a little bit nicer. Sort of."

Cheff said, "I guess you got your choice of Tracks, then?"

"I did, actually. I got Civilian Leadership."

"What focus?" Mid asked.

"Archiving and Library Management."

"Heh," Mid said. "Books the Librarian. I like it."

"Fitting," Cheff said. "Anyway, Civilian Leadership means you'll be in the same class as me. Excellent!"

While we were talking, Mid had been tinkering with a small metal cylinder. "What *is* that?" I asked.

Mid looked around carefully, then said softly, "It's something I've been working on. Top secret."

I laughed. "It looks like an ordinary flashlight to me."

Mid smiled mischievously. "It *is* a flashlight. Watch." He pointed the flashlight upward and clicked it on. A circle of light appeared on the metal roof above us. "See? A flashlight." He looked around again to make sure no one was watching, then whispered, "But this is no *ordinary* flashlight." He aimed it at me, clicked a second button, and a huge dark hole appeared in my chest.

I clutched at my shirt with both hands. My shirt was still there—I could feel it, but I couldn't see it, and now my hands were gone, too. "Turn it off!"

Mid clicked the device off, and the dark hole vanished. My chest and hands reappeared. I held my hands up and wiggled my fingers. They seemed to work okay. I checked my shirt, and it looked okay, too—no blood anywhere. Even the buttons were still buttoned. "Phew! You nearly scared the stuffing out of me. What in the world is that thing? I've never seen anything like it."

The three of them laughed, then Cheff put his finger to his lips. "Shhh… not so loud. Top secret, remember?"

Mid tucked the device into his jacket pocket, out of sight. "I call it a 'flashdark.' It works exactly like a flashlight, except instead of flashing *light*…"

"It flashes dark," Buttons said. "Mid invented it. He invents lots of things."

"What happens if you shine it in someone's eyes?" I asked.

"Why, I thought you'd never ask," Mid said. He aimed the flashdark at my eyes.

"No, wait, I don't—"

He clicked it on. The world went black.

"Ack! I'm blind! Turn it off! I can't see anything!"

I heard another click, and the world came back. "That was not nice, not nice at all!" I blinked a few times. "My eyes seem to be okay, though."

"Of course," Mid said, "I tried it on myself first."

"And on me," Cheff said. "I thought it was great!"

"Me, too," said Buttons. "I was invisible!"

"What makes it work?" I asked. "And what's it good for?"

"Top secret," Mid said again. "Only Cheff and Buttons know about the flashdark, and now you. I'll show you how it works after school. I don't want to take it apart where people can see. You never know when they"—he nodded toward a group of students at another table, all wearing blue armbands—"might get interested."

Cheff said, "They're a bunch of snoops, that's for sure. Careful, don't let them catch you looking at them."

Operation Break Iron

— 15 —

Lhuk

A TORPH BOY ABOUT Buttons' age approached our table. Buttons said to me, "This is my friend Lhuk. Lhuk, meet our new friend, Books. He came to the Labor Compound yesterday. He lives a few doors down from us."

His handshake was cold but gentle, and he didn't look up at me. Unlike the Torphs I'd seen back in Tumberland, who had greenish skin, Lhuk's skin was the most beautiful shade of gold. Tiny golden specks under the topmost skin layer made him seem to glow. He had lovely Torph markings, natural skin patterns that ran up from his hands and arms all the way up his face to his hairline.

"Nice to meet you, Lhuk," I said. "You're the first Torph I've seen in the Labor Compound."

"That's because there aren't many," Buttons said. She patted the bench next to her. "Here, Lhuk, come sit next to me and Starry."

"There's a special camp for Torphs," Cheff said. "It's a long way from here, out west somewhere."

Mid added, "Lhuk's parents were sent to one of the Torph Camps. He's living with a Sevro woman and her three children."

Buttons said, "Lhuk has a pet. Wanna meet him? Show Squeaky to Books, Lhuk. He's Starry's friend, and Moka's, too." She put Starry on the table in front of Lhuk, then took Moka from her backpack and set her down next to Starry. "They really like Squeaky."

Without looking up, Lhuk took a small gray mouse from his jacket pocket and set him gently near Starry and Moka. Buttons made Starry reach over and pet the shivering Squeaky. Squeaky sniffed at the ponies, then stood up on his back legs and looked at the rest of us. Lhuk took a crust of bread from his other pocket and offered it to Squeaky, who took it in his tiny paws and nibbled at it.

Buttons said, "Lhuk taught Squeaky to do tricks, didn't you, Lhuk?"

Lhuk nodded once, but still didn't look up.

Buttons coaxed, "Well, are you going to show us? Pleeease?"

Lhuk held up his forefinger, and the mouse put down the crust, then turned and looked at him. Lhuk tilted his finger to the left, and Squeaky leaned over in the same direction until he was standing on one foot, never taking his eyes off Lhuk's. Lhuk tilted his finger the other way, and Squeaky shifted to his other foot. When Lhuk moved his forefinger in a circle, Squeaky got down on all fours and ran around in a little circle. Lhuk reversed his forefinger's direction, and Squeaky changed direction, too. Finally, Lhuk bent his forefinger in the middle, and Squeaky stood up on his hind feet and made a little bow. We laughed and applauded quietly. The merest hint of a smile played about Lhuk's lips.

"Wow!" I said. "That's amazing!"

"Shhh!" Cheff said, "Keep your voice down."

"Right. Sorry." I wondered if he was using Torph Ability. I'd heard whispered stories about it, of course, but I'd never seen it in action. "How did you make him do that? Training?"

Lhuk looked up at me for the first time. His eyes were golden and huge, and they seemed to look all the way down inside me. I shivered. In a voice so quiet that I could barely hear him, he said, "I didn't *make* him do it. I just made him *want* to do it."

The group of Bluebands at the next table got up and joined a larger group who had arrived in the yard. Cheff jerked his head in their direction. "Be careful not to make him want to do anything unusual where *they* can see."

"That would be a Bad Thing, Lhuk," Mid added. "If anyone even suspected you were starting to get the Ability at your age, you'd be in some serious trouble. You'd be off to a Torph Camp in no time, never to be seen or heard from again."

"Mid's right," Cheff said. "I think it would be best if Squeaky didn't do any more tricks at school."

Lhuk sadly put Squeaky away in his jacket pocket and shuffled off toward the restrooms.

"What's the big deal about Torph Ability?" I asked. "I mean, besides doing some nifty mouse tricks, what else is it good for?"

"Didn't you know any Torphs in Tumberland?" Buttons asked me. "Didn't they teach you anything about it in school?"

"There were some Torphs in Tumberland when I was young, but they moved away. I saw Torphs a few times, but I've never actually talked to one. Before Lhuk, I mean."

"Moved away?" Mid said. "Sent to a Torph Camp, more likely. Torphs mostly come from around Pond Region, but Pallador's been gathering them from all over the continent and testing them for Ability."

"The ones without Ability are given a Certificate of Qualification and released," Cheff explained. "They can apply for employment as long as they show their certificate, but it's hard for them to get work. People who hire Torphs often become 'interesting' to the IID."

"And the ones who do have the Ability?" I asked.

"The official story is that they're transported out west to the Torph Camps, where they live happy and productive lives, serving Emperor Pallador away from the other Peoples."

"Officially," Mid added, "it's for the Torphs' own safety. Many people are afraid of Torphs. Pallador teaches that the misuse of Torph Ability ruined the world, and most people believe it. You have to admit that what Lhuk did with Squeaky was kind of scary, right?"

"Well, I suppose so, a little, maybe," I said.

"Nobody knows why only Torphs have Ability," Cheff said, "but it makes them different enough to frighten the ignorant, and we have plenty of ignorance in the Imperium!"

Mid said, "But Ability isn't the only strange thing about the Torph species, right? For one thing, they don't have much hair, and what little they do have is quite fine. And those spots… you noticed Lhuk's spots?"

"It comes down to this," Cheff said, "Torphs are… well… different. Not as different as the Sephs, of course, but they're not like the other nine Peoples, either." He counted on his fingers: "Ability, spots, superfine hair, flat nose, greenish skin, most of them. A few have golden skin, like Lhuk. It all adds up to: 'Torphs Aren't Like Us.' That's reason enough for many people to simply not like them."

— 16 —

BREX

LHUK RETURNED FROM the restrooms, sat back down next to Buttons, and placed Squeaky on the table, along with a few breadcrumbs. We watched the gang of Bluebands for a while out of the corners of our eyes. A group of ten or twelve older boys and girls stood in the middle of the asphalt yard, shuffling their feet and talking. All of them had a broad, dark-blue band of cloth around their left arms above the elbow. There were also a few younger children with them. They had blue bands, too, but of a lighter shade.

"Why do the younger ones wear a different color?" I asked.

Buttons looked disgusted. "They're *Junior* Bluebands. They go to Basic School with me and Lhuk. They can't wait to join up."

Mid said, "They can't officially be Bluebands until they start Regular School, but they've already decided they want to be soldiers when they grow up, so the Bluebands let them hang around."

Cheff added, "The Bluebands boss the Junior Bluebands around, make them run errands, and get them to spy on the other kids. Or even adults, sometimes. The Juniors love it. They absolutely adore the older ones."

A petite, fine-featured Torph girl carrying four textbooks in her left arm marched up to the group, heels clacking on the asphalt. Her severe shoulder-length blond hair fell in straight obedient lines. I wondered if she used a ruler when she cut it. She wore a full Blueband uniform with a squad-leader pin on the cap. The Bluebands snapped to order, put their feet together, and stood up straight. The Torph girl glared coldly at the Juniors until they, too, stood at attention. She began speaking. We couldn't hear what she was saying, but it was obvious that she was unhappy about something.

"Who's that?" I asked. "The Torph girl. She's the only other Torph I've seen in the Labor Compound."

"Big day for seeing Torphs," Mid mumbled, mostly to himself.

"That's Brex," Buttons said.

"She's a bad one," Mid said, "really bad."

Brex approached a tall, husky girl, growled something we couldn't hear, and stabbed a finger at her messy hair. The tall girl tried to smooth her hair, to no avail. Brex jabbed her finger at several stains on the girl's shirt, which the girl tried to cover with her hands. Finally, Brex put her hands on her hips, stood on her tiptoes, and shouted something into the tall girl's face.

Cheff frowned. "Brex is the worst kind of Blueband: a True Believer."

"True believer?" I asked.

"Yeah." Cheff nodded slowly. "Most of the Bluebands become Bluebands because they're lazy and want to get out of their work assignments."

"Or for the money they can hassle out of the other kids," Buttons said.

"Some of them want a license to be brutal," Mid added. "They enjoy bullying people."

"But Brex is worse than all of those," Cheff said. "She truly *believes*."

"In what?" I wondered.

"In everything: Pallador, the Imperium, the goodness of the Seph Species, the evil of the Torph People. Sorry, Lhuk."

Lhuk raised his eyebrows and shrugged.

Cheff continued, "There's nothing worse, or more dangerous, than a passionate, self-righteous fanatic." He watched Brex out of the corner of his eye. "She's unusually wound up today. She's being pretty hard on those other kids. I feel sorry for them, even if they are there voluntarily."

Lhuk looked up at us, and that hint of a smile played about his lips again. Squeaky, who had been happily munching away, dropped his crust, stood up straight, sniffed the air, then dashed off toward the group of Bluebands. He darted into the middle of the group of kids standing at attention and ran in little circles around their legs, leaping and squeaking. Their discipline fell apart as the Junior Bluebands screamed and ran madly off in all directions. The older Bluebands laughed and pointed at the panicking younger ones. Only Brex remained as she was, standing stock-still, glaring at the little mouse. When Brex was the only one left of what had been the well-ordered Blueband circle, Lhuk smiled again.

Buttons hissed, "No, Lhuk, don't! Don't do it!"

But Lhuk ignored her, crooked his forefinger, and Squeaky headed straight for Brex, who fixed the little creature in a death glare. She waited until Squeaky was within range, then stomped at him viciously. The terrified mouse squealed and fled in our direction.

Cheff said to Lhuk, "If Brex sees him run over here, you and the mouse are both doomed. And likely the rest of us, too."

Lhuk frowned, twitched his finger, and Squeaky made an abrupt left turn into a clump of bushes.

Brex waited by the shrubbery, arms crossed, tapping her foot, but Squeaky didn't reappear.

Lhuk frowned again.

"What's the matter?" Cheff asked him.

"Lost him," Lhuk muttered.

"You *what?*" Cheff wasn't quite shouting.

Lhuk glanced up at Cheff, but didn't reply. He squeezed his eyes closed.

Squeaky bolted out of the bushes and ran straight into Brex's tapping foot. Without hesitation, the little mouse clawed his way up Brex's long stocking and disappeared under her uniform.

Brex let out such a blood-curdling scream that the hair on my neck stood straight up. "He ran up my leg! He ran up my leg!" She was frantically slapping at her clothing and skittering and hopping around, first on one foot, then the other. It seemed that Squeaky was running laps around the inside of Brex's skirt.

The husky Blueband girl Brex had been chewing out earlier giggled, then laughed, quietly at first. Her laugh became a series of loud guffaws, complete with thigh-slapping and belly-holding. The rest of the Bluebands couldn't hold back—they laughed too.

We did our best to refrain, with moderate success, until Mid said, "I think—is she dancing?"

Cheff said, "It's the latest thing—the Squeaky Schoolyard Foxtrot!"

"Mousetrot, more likely," I said, and that cracked us up.

All except Lhuk. Lhuk's eyes were still tightly closed and he wasn't breathing. Finally, he relaxed and took a deep breath. "Got him."

At the same instant, Squeaky dropped out of Brex's skirt and sprinted for our table, completely unnoticed by the Bluebands or by Brex, who was still flailing away at her uniform. Lhuk scooped him up and stuffed him back into his jacket pocket. Buttons handed Lhuk what was left of Squeaky's bread crust, and he tucked it into the pocket with Squeaky.

The five of us avoided looking in Brex's direction, trying our best to be invisible, but it didn't work. When Brex finally settled down, she smoothed her uniform, stood up straight, and looked around. The yard and the break area were empty, except for us.

Brex marched over, trying to rearrange her disheveled uniform. She planted her fists on our table, and one by one she looked into each of our faces. "I can't—" Her voice cracked. She forced herself to calm down. "I can't prove it," she growled through clenched teeth, "but I know you had something to do with this. Maybe one of you, maybe all of you." She leaned into Lhuk's face. "If you weren't so young, I'd pin this on you, you filthy Torph scum!" She glared at him. "If I ever find out you had something to do with this, *any* of you, I'll ruin all of you! Do you understand me? *All* of you!"

Lhuk slowly raised his head and gazed into her eyes, but didn't reply. They were locked together by an invisible thread for a few seconds, then Brex shivered violently, spun around, and strode away.

Buttons held Starry up to her face. "I think that big, bad Blueband was upset about something. Don't you think so, Starry?" Starry thought so. "I don't think she's a very pleasant person, is she, Moka?" Moka shook her head.

"But," I asked, "why did she call Lhuk a 'filthy Torph'? She's a Torph herself."

"I told you before," Cheff said. "She's a capital-T, capital-B, True Believer. Pallador says the Torph species is evil, she believes it. Pallador says the Torph species dominated Andaran to its detriment for centuries, she believes it. Pallador says that all Torphs with Ability should be rounded up and put in camps, she believes that, too. She believes it all, no matter what the cost. She admits to turning in her own mother and father for having Ability."

"More than admits," Mid said. "She brags about it. To her, it's proof that she's Not Like Other Torphs. She even lives with a Fessal family now. She hates all things Torph."

Buttons added, "Including herself."

"Yeah," Cheff echoed, "including herself. The next time you see her, take a look at the Torph spots on her face and neck. She wears her hair down, her sleeves long, and her collar high, so people won't notice them. Or so she thinks."

Miss Averith Brex

I said, "I still don't get how Brex is even *in* the Bluebands, let alone a leader. Since when do they allow Torphs to join the Bluebands? There weren't any Torph Bluebands back in Tumberland."

Cheff said, "Normally, Torphs aren't allowed to become Bluebands. But Brex is a special case. She applied for the Military Officers Track, same as Sable."

"Who's Sable?" I asked.

"A friend of ours from school," Buttons said. "You'll meet her soon, probably."

"But get this," Mid said. "Brex actually qualified."

"She's plenty smart enough," Cheff said, "but Torphs aren't permitted to attend Advanced School. So she got stuck with the Regulars."

Mid added, "She got the gig as Blueband squad leader as a sort of consolation prize."

"That's partly why she's so vicious," Cheff said. "While Sable is living Brex's dream, Brex is stuck as the president of the local thug club."

"She really hates Sable," Buttons said, and the ponies nodded emphatically.

Cheff said, "The authorities want to hold Brex up as an example of how Pallador's educational programs benefit all the other ten Peoples, including Torphs. For her part, Brex goes to great lengths to be the perfect example of loyal submission to the Emperor. I think she imagines that, if she's successful, they'll let her attend the Military Officers Track."

"Will they, do you think?" I asked.

Cheff shook his head. "Probably not."

"So," I said, "she's made herself into the Blueband-of-all-Bluebands."

"Right." Cheff looked sad. "A Perfect Subject of our Most Beloved Emperor. More military than the military. And, of course, she's made the destruction of Lhuk her personal mission in life."

"Of course she has," Buttons said. "He's the only other Torph in the entire Labor Compound school."

Mid said, "I wonder how engineering Lhuk's destruction will work out for her. She'll have to get moving. Next year is her last year in school. You may not know this, Books, but male Torphs don't develop their Ability, if they have one, for several years after Torph females develop theirs. On the average, that is. I'm sure Brex knows it'll likely be years and years before Lhuk develops his."

Lhuk solemnly held up his forefinger and wiggled it. "Years."

"On the other hand," Mid continued, "our most proper Miss Averith Brex is at exactly the right age to get her Ability. Do you suppose she might be a little concerned?"

Cheff laughed. "If she does develop the Ability, her life as she planned it is over forever. Instead of a military career, it'll be off to the Torph Camps for her! C'mon, let's go. You don't want to be late on your first day."

— 17 —

THE ADJUSTED MIND

STARRY AND MOKA waved goodbye. Buttons and Lhuk went back to the Basic School building. Cheff, Mid, and I crossed the yard to the Advanced School. It was as run-down and dismal as the rest of the buildings, but it was a lot smaller.

"The Advanced School only has five classrooms," Cheff explained as we walked, "one for each of the main Tracks except Military Officers Track, which has its own building, as you know. Each Track has its own teacher. We get two sessions each day. In the first session, we study our individual specialties in small groups. I'll be studying Factory Management. You'll be studying Archiving and Library Management. You'll be the only one, though—I've never even heard of Archiving and Library Management before today. In the second session, after the break, the whole Civilian Leadership class comes together, and the teacher usually makes a presentation of some sort on a more general subject, something that affects all the sub-specialties. For the last few days, we've been learning about Mind Control."

"Mind Control?" I asked.

"Yeah. There's a lot to it. You'll see."

"Well, here's my class," Mid said, "Engineering and Tech. You two are in the next room. See you later, Books!"

Our classroom was as shabby inside as it was outside. Long, curling strips of paint dangled in many places, and water stains splotched the ceiling. Countless tape marks and pinholes covered the walls. The room smelled of chalk dust, pencil shavings, old books, and mildew. A teakettle bubbled cheerfully on a little pot-bellied stove in a corner near the front of the room.

Cracked, peeling varnish covered two dozen rusty, battered student desks, arranged in four rows. Besides me and Cheff, there were eight boys and three girls of various species standing around in groups, talking. I was the smallest person in the room, as usual.

Cheff sat at a desk in the front row. "Go check in. When you're done, come and sit next to me."

At the front of the classroom, on a wooden platform raised eight inches above the floor, a tall, slender Fessal gentleman with graying hair sat behind a dilapidated wooden desk. As I approached, he took a sip from his steaming mug, then made a face. "Bitter!" He found a little bottle in his desk drawer, uncorked it, and added a generous amount of sugar to the cup. "Felmoss tea is so bitter, but I love it. Keeps me going all morning."

He peered at me over his wire-rimmed spectacles, accepted the card Mr. Walikas had given me, then pushed his glasses up and examined it. "It says here you're Birn Tylandine, Lildur species, of Tumberland. Just arrive, Mr. Tylandine?"

"Yes, sir. Last night."

He read from the card, "'Civilian Leadership, Archiving and Library Management.' Is that right?"

"Yes, sir."

He handed the card back. "I'm Mr. Rishten." We shook hands. "Tell me, Mr. Tylandine, why did you pick Library Management? We don't get many of those."

"I like books, sir. A lot."

"I see. I'll bet old Walikas was pleased, wasn't he? He has a thing about books."

"Yes, sir, I noticed."

"Here, take this." He handed me a ragged textbook called *Civilian Leadership and Empire*. "That's for the after-break session. Be careful with it. I'll get you your Library Management book tomorrow—*if* I can find one. Now take your seat. It's time for class to begin."

He finished the rest of his felmoss tea, then stood up and came around in front of the desk. "Come to order, class! Take your seats and open your textbooks to Chapter Seven, page sixty-six."

I sat down next to Cheff and found the place in my book. I'd never seen this book before. Chapter Seven was called *Civilian Leadership and the Adjusted Mind*.

Mr. Rishten said, "Before we begin, class, I'd like you all to welcome Mr. Birn Tylandine, recently arrived from Tumberland. He'll be specializing in Library Management."

The class responded with calls of

—"Hey, Birn."

—"Welcome, Birn."

—"Hello, Birn."

—"Good to meet you, Birn."

After the greetings died down, a girl's lone voice said loudly, 'Oooh, he's cute, isn't he?' and everyone laughed.

I blushed, but smiled and waved at her. She blushed, too, and hung her head.

Mr. Rishten continued, "Library Management is an important job. Can you tell the class what Library Management is, Mr. Tylandine?"

"Yes, sir." I stood up and cleared my throat. "Mr. Walikas said it's the gathering and preserving of the knowledge of the Imperium."

"Exactly!" Mr. Rishten agreed. "And I'm sure he also told you that Library Managers are responsible for ensuring that the people read only the *right* books."

"Yes, sir, he did."

"Good! In fact, class, all you future managers will have that same responsibility. It's critical to the Imperium that people read the right books and think the right thoughts. Otherwise, how could they possibly act the right way? And that brings us to today's lesson. Thank you, Mr. Tylandine."

I sat down and glanced over at Cheff. His book was open, but he wasn't looking at it. He didn't return my glance. He wore a sour expression and stared pointedly out the window.

Mr. Rishten continued, "Let's begin. Mr. Tylandine, this week's lesson is about the beneficial effects of Imperial Mental Adjustment. Are you familiar with this subject?"

"Only a little, sir. It wasn't covered in my class back in Tumberland."

"We're in the middle of Chapter Seven. You'll have to read the previous material on your own time. For now, though, let's all help Mr. Tylandine catch up. Who would like to review, briefly, the history of Imperial Mental Adjustment for us?" A Lildur girl in a tattered pink and yellow dress—the one who called me cute—raised her hand. "Yes, Miss Gerina?"

Gerina stood up beside her desk. She glanced in my direction, smiled shyly, and recited,

> *"As we all know, the Seph Species, though highly intelligent, have no arms or legs. Instead, they have the mental Ability to influence members of the other Ten Peoples to act as their Facilitators, their hands and feet."*

While Gerina was speaking, Mr. Rishten poured himself another cup of tea. "Good, Miss Gerina," he said, "you may continue if you wish."

> *"Throughout the centuries, it has been considered a great privilege to serve as Facilitator to a Seph. The Fessal Species, in particular, has proven to be the most suited to the rigors of Facilitating, but members of all the Peoples may qualify to serve."*

She glanced at me again.

"Thank you, Miss Gerina," Mr. Rishten said. "You may be seated. Who will review how the Sephs have used their Ability? Mr. Lannerbin."

A Lora, a couple of years older than me, picked up his book and read in a monotone voice:

> *"The Sephs have nobly and honorably used their Ability to adjust the minds of the other species, bringing peace and harmony, freeing Andaran from war and strife, and creating prosperity throughout the world."*

He sat down.

Cheff muttered, "'Nobly and honorably.' *Right.* And I have a nifty labor compound I'll sell you, cheap." He resumed staring out the window.

"Excellent," Mr. Rishten said, while adding sugar to yet another cup of tea. "Thank you, Mr. Lannerbin. Now, by contrast, who can tell us about the Torph Ability? Mr. Trendel."

An older Fessal boy stood up and recited in a singsong voice:

> *"Of the Ten non-Seph species, only the Torph species has the ability to defy the beneficial influence of Imperial Mental Adjustment, not only for themselves but for members of the other species, too."*

He explained, "It's like an umbrella. They can create a mental barrier, or shield, that counters or even reverses the effects of Adjustment." He began reading in the sing-song tone again:

> *"The Torphs have used their Torph Ability not only to resist Adjustment, but to cruelly and evilly subjugate and enslave the other species, and make war against the enlightened Seph People, thereby bringing poverty and privation to Andaran."*

"Yeah," Cheff murmured, "that Lhuk is a real menace, for sure. All three feet of him."

Mr. Rishten drained his teacup, frowned in Cheff's direction, but continued, "Excellent, Mr. Trendel. Be seated, please. That covers our last two days nicely, I think, Mr. Tylandine. Now let us begin today's lesson. As you can see on page sixty-six, some have raised the question: doesn't Imperial Mental Adjustment take away the personal freedom of the Adjusted? Who can answer that?" A Lora girl volunteered. She looked maybe a year older than I was. "Yes, Miss Desult." Mr. Rishten returned yet again to his teapot for a refill.

She stood up, opened her textbook, and read aloud:

"Does Imperial Mental Adjustment impinge upon our personal freedom? The answer is a resounding 'No!' To the contrary, the blessing of Adjustment is the only way to achieve the purest form of freedom the Ten Peoples have ever known. The Adjusted mind is free from worry about even the slightest thought of disloyalty to our Beloved Emperor and the Imperium. It frees us from the twin burdens of doubt and suspicion. It frees us to support with our whole hearts Pallador's Programs of Progress without reservation. It frees us by making us immune to the traitorous influence of the Fellstone Resistance Movement and others who would oppose the Emperor and his Imperium."

She stopped, overcome with emotion. She put her hand on her heart, took a few deep breaths, and sat down, quivering.

"Thank you, Miss Desult. That was, indeed, moving." Mr. Rishten took off his glasses and polished them with his handkerchief, put them back on, and looked out at us. "Imperial Mental Adjustment is in no way a restriction. Never think so, not even for an instant. To the contrary, Adjustment never keeps us from making our own decisions, nor does it keep us from acting upon them. Quite simply, Adjustment merely ensures that we consistently and reliably make the decisions that *we swear to make before we become Adjusted,* without inner conflict or turmoil, no matter what such decisions should require."

Cheff raised his eyebrows but refrained from commenting.

"Adjustment is a great blessing." Mr. Rishten, face flushed, paced back and forth on the platform, saucer in his left hand, teacup in his right. He stopped to refill it several times, adding liberal doses of sugar each time. His hands trembled, which caused the cup to clatter against the saucer. "Without it, our dear Beloved

Emperor could never have restored Andaran to the glory it had before The Fall. Emperor Pallador could never have so quickly and completely united the Ten Peoples and The One. Why, without Adjustment, the chaos and bloodshed following The Fall might have continued to this day."

His bloodshot eyes burned brightly. "Mental Adjustment is a privilege, not a right. It's for the honored few who demonstrate that they are worthy of it through years of faithful, loyal service. Only the Adjusted may serve in the highest levels of Civilian Leadership. This is equally true of Political Leadership and Military Leadership.

"With Adjustment also come higher position, greater responsibility, greater privilege, and of course, in due time, great wealth. That is why I volunteered for this post, to demonstrate my worthiness. It remains my fondest hope to be Adjusted someday, and claim my share of Pallador's great bounty."

Mr. Rishten stopped pacing and patted the sweat from his forehead with his handkerchief. "That concludes the lecture portion of today's lesson, children. Please use the remaining class time to finish reading Chapter Seven and, if you have time, you may begin Chapter Eight. Thank you." He returned to his desk and fixed himself another cup of tea.

When the bell rang, we remained seated until Mr. Rishten said, "Dismissed. A word with you, Mr. Tylandine, if you please. You may leave, Mr. Karfendek."

Cheff whispered, "I'll wait for you outside."

Mr. Rishten beckoned me to the platform.

"Yes, sir?"

"One more thing, Mr. Tylandine. An annual visit to the Gallery of Pallador's Glorious History at the Silver Palace is required, and we'll be going as a class in a few months. There is also the Imperial Library. It's not required. In fact, you'll need special permission to get in, but I think I can arrange it in time.

"Additionally, once each year, every student in Fellstone City is required to visit Pallador's Museum of History, Security, and

Loyalty. In your case, it is especially desirable, not only because a museum is a type of *archive*, but because you come from out of town. It's important that you experience firsthand the glory of Fellstone City under Pallador's rule. This is *not* a sponsored field trip. Students are expected to arrange the visit themselves. I'd like you to go as soon as possible.

"Of course, you'll need privilege points to leave the Labor Compound, but I have complete confidence that you'll have no trouble earning them. You may ask Mr. Karfendek to assist you. When you have the points, go straight to the administration office any morning. They will notify me of your absence. Run along, now. I'll see you tomorrow."

"Yes, sir. Thank you, sir."

He waved me out the door.

— 18 —

BULLIES

CHEFF AND MID were waiting for me outside. I asked Cheff, "Why were you looking so sour during Mr. Rishten's lecture?"

"I'm worse than sour, Books. I'm furious. It was that bit about making sure we all read the right books and all think the right thoughts. If Pallador's way is so wonderful, why do people need so much convincing? I mean, you heard Rishten going on about what a great thing Adjustment is, right? Keeps us from having disloyal thoughts, and all that?"

"Yes, I did, but—"

"But if Pallador is all that great, then why does he need to mess with our brains to keep us loyal?"

"I don't know, Cheff. I never thought about it before."

"Well, you'd better start thinking about it, because you're part of it now," Cheff growled. "How does it feel?"

"How does what feel? What am I part of? What are you talking about?"

"Being assigned to the book police." He sneered. "Library Management."

"*Book police?* I thought you were happy I got Library Management."

Cheff scowled. "I was, I guess. I mean, I'm glad you're going to have a career doing something you like, working with books and all, but that was before I found out what Library Management is really about: mind control. Making sure that people only read the 'right books?' That's the Book Police. You know, the ones who got your father killed."

"But—"

Cheff imitated Mr. Rishten's rigid posture, then took an imaginary handkerchief from his pocket and wiped his imaginary glasses. "'It's highly important to the Imperium that people read the 'right books' and think the 'right thoughts.'"

He jammed his hands into his pants pockets. "That's what the Imperial Intelligence Division does, Books—they decide which are the 'right' books. And that's gonna be you! In a few years, *you'll* be the one deciding which books are the 'right' books and who gets to read them. How does it feel to be part of the same organization that killed your father and mine? And my mother, and probably Uncle Karf, by now. And would kill *you* if they knew about the forbidden books in your head?"

I stared, speechless.

"Give him a break, Cheff," Mid said. "It's not his fault—he just got here. He had to get assigned to something, didn't he?"

"I'm sorry, Cheff," I said. "I didn't have a lot of choice in the matter. Mr. Walikas picked Library Management for me. He didn't ask me first or say anything about book police. Anyway, if we have to be assigned to a Track, Library Management is as good as any, isn't it? Maybe I'll get to see some extremely old books."

"Who knows?" Mid added. "Maybe Books will discover the Lost Histories of the Sixth Kingdom, or four volumes of Life Before The Fall, or something like that. Anyway, isn't *every* Track about control? What about when you're managing the factory that's making guns for Pallador's goon squads? What about me when I'm designing new military vehicles and advanced weaponry? We all end up working for Pallador. It's the way things are, Cheff."

Cheff scuffed his foot on the asphalt. "Yeah, you're right, Mid. I get so angry." He patted me on the back. "I am happy for you, Books, and I suppose Library Management isn't any worse than anything else. Maybe you'll find ways to do some good. My problem is, who gets to say which books are approved?"

Mid laughed. "Looks to me like it's going to be Books! And maybe that's not such a bad thing. It's good to have friends in high places. Right, Books?"

"I guess. Don't worry, Cheff—I'll be lenient with you if I catch you reading something forbidden."

"I appreciate that," Cheff said wryly. "Thanks, loads. Come on, let's go get Buttons. She'll be waiting for us." Cheff jabbed his thumb back toward the Advanced School. "What did Rishten want with you after class?"

"Not much. He told me about some museums and things in Fellstone City that he wants me to visit as part of my Archiving studies. He was acting kind of funny."

"It's the felmoss tea," Cheff said. "He drinks it constantly, and the more he drinks, the more excited he gets. It acts as a stimulant."

Mid said, "We have to go to both museums once a year. It's not so bad, though. In fact, it's kind of fun. Twice a year we get out of school and out of the Labor Compound for a whole day. It takes a while to get there on the bus, but you get to walk through the market district. Both market districts, in fact. And when you get to the museum, they feed you all you can eat." He patted his ample abdomen.

We met Buttons at Basic School. "Did someone say market district? The ponies like the market—sometimes Cheff buys us treats." Starry nodded.

"It takes some extra coin, though," Cheff said. "We'll have to see about getting Books a job."

"A job?" I asked. "I thought Advanced students didn't have to work."

"It's like we told you before," Mid explained, "Advanced School students aren't supposed to work. We're supposed to spend every afternoon doing our homework and class projects, but as long as we get them done, no one minds if we work a couple of days a week."

"What kind of job?" I asked, but before they could answer, Brex and two husky Fessal Bluebands stepped out of the side street and blocked our way. Cheff whispered, "Easy does it, Books. Remember what we told you."

Brex strutted up and looked me over. Even though she was several years older, she was not much taller than me. She looked like she'd eaten a sourbug. "So, you're the new kid."

"Yes."

"Yes, what?"

I hesitated, so Mid hissed, "Miss."

I hissed back, "Miss? What did I miss?"

Cheff whispered, "Answer 'Yes, *Miss*.'"

I looked at Brex. "Yes, Miss."

She screamed in my face, "What are you looking at?"

I dropped my eyes to the ground. "Sorry, Miss." Her shoes were so shiny I could see my reflection in them.

"That's more like it. I ought to have my boys here teach you a lesson." The two husky Fessal boys stepped forward eagerly, smacking their fists into their palms. "But"—Brex held up a hand, and they stopped behind her, looking disappointed—"since it's your first day, I'm going let you off easy. No beating this time, but you'll still have to pay a fine." She looked at the others. "You three, as well, for not teaching your new friend to show respect to his betters. Well, come on, hand it over."

Cheff, Mid, and Buttons hung their heads and reluctantly dug into their pockets. I followed suit. Still staring at the ground, the four of us offered Brex a few small coins each.

Brex stared at our outstretched hands, then screamed, "That's it? That's all you've got?" She slapped the coins out of our hands onto the cobblestones. The two Fessals got down on all fours and scrambled to pick them up. Brex continued, "It's always the same with you Advancies, isn't it? You never have anything worth beating out of you. Why don't you get a real job instead of fooling around with your stupid projects?"

We kept silent and stared at the ground. Brex paced back and forth in front of us. "Useless, worthless, stupid Advancies. You all think you're so smart, so much better than the rest of us. And you, little girl"—she gave Buttons a shove and Cheff started forward, but Mid held him back—"I'll bet you think you're smart, too, don't you? I'll bet you expect to be an Advancie next year, like your brother, don't you? Well, you won't, you stupid little brat. Yeah, I said 'stupid.' Carrying those ponies around like a three-year-old! And you're not even smart enough to be ashamed of yourself! *Pah!* You disgust me! All of you."

She stood in front of me so close that if she'd had a real nose instead of a flat Torph face, our noses would have been touching. She growled, "I saw you sitting with that filthy Torph brat at lunch, new kid. Take my advice: Stay away from him. Stay away from all Torphs. They're a plague, a blight, a disease. Torphs are the reason Andaran's in the shape it is today."

"Yes, Miss."

"And another thing: stay away from these new friends of yours. They're trouble. How'd you get hooked up with them on your first day, anyway?"

"They're my neighbors, Miss."

"I see. Well, if you know what's good for you, you'll steer clear of them. From now on, my boys and I are going to be watching them. All three of them. I'm going to get them, somehow, and that little Torph brat, too. I know they're up to something, and sooner or later I'm going to find out what it is. And when I do, you won't want to be anywhere near them. Understand?"

"Yes, Miss. I understand. Thank you for the advice."

Her eyes narrowed as she tried to determine if I was sincere. She decided I was. "All right, then, you can go. Go on, get out of here, all of you." She spun on her heel, snapped her fingers at her minions, and left.

We stood silently until she was well down the street, then Buttons held Starry up and made her wave a hoof at Brex's retreating back. "Bye-bye, Miss Brex! She doesn't seem to like us much." She held Starry to her ear. "Starry says that's okay, though—we don't like her either."

I said, "It's a good thing you gave me those coins this morning. I'll pay you back as soon as I can. What kind of job do you think I could find?"

"Don't worry about the coins," Cheff said. "We do that for each other all the time. As for a job…"

"Maybe you can get a job in the munitions factory where Cheff and I work sometimes," Mid said. "It's not every day—we only go when we need some extra money. Cheff helps the manager, and I help the chemists." Mid showed me a red rash on the back of his hands. "I got that rinsing out some chemical bins last Day Five. It stings a little, but it pays better than sweeping. I'll introduce you to the manager next week. He's okay—he's a Lora. He's friendly, and sometimes he lets me take scrap metal or wire for my school projects."

"What kind of projects do you do?" I asked.

"Here's your street," Mid told me. "Go tell your mom you're coming over to my house to study, and I'll show you. We'll meet you there. It's one street over, Building 13, Unit 48."

— 19 —

CLIMBING SPARKS

Mᴀ MOTHER WASN'T home. I figured she was still at work, so I left her a note saying I was going to study at Mid's house, and that I might be home late.

I found Mid's house easily, but before I could knock, Mid called out from the window above the door, "It's open. Come on in."

Mid's apartment was a mirror image of Cheff's. His mom's bedroom was on the main floor behind the kitchen. Upstairs, Mid's room faced the street. Mid sat at his worktable by the window. Cheff reclined on the bed.

"Have a seat," Mid said. "Make yourself comfortable. I'm almost ready."

I asked Cheff, "Where's Buttons?"

"She's home. Said she wanted to do some cooking. Don't worry, Books—she's used to being home by herself while Aunt Dee's at work. All the kids in the Labor Compound are."

Mid was tinkering with a peculiar contraption on the worktable. It had two long, vertical copper wires in a V shape, like a scarlet grasshopper's antennae. Mid pointed at the ceiling, put his finger to his lips, and mouthed the word 'snoops.' He said loudly,

129

"This is a project I've been working on for my engineering class. Want to see how it works?"

Mid switched on an old radio in the back corner of the worktable. "I found this in a scrap heap at Zeek's junkyard last year. My boss helped me find parts to repair it. It takes a minute to warm up." When the radio sputtered, Mid turned a knob until we could make out the scratchy sounds of an old recording of one of Emperor Pallador's speeches.

"Ready." Mid flipped a switch on his contraption. It made a buzzing, snapping sound as a large electrical spark raced upward between the two copper wires. When each spark climbed high, it disappeared and a new spark formed near the base. "There. See what it did to the radio?"

As soon as Mid had switched the device on, the radio broadcast turned into crackling white noise. Mid shut the radio off. "It does exactly the same thing to their microphones. I call it the Climbing Sparks machine. As long as it's running, they can't hear a thing from this room, only static. Clever, don't you think?"

I took a closer look, then wrinkled my nose. "What's that funny smell?"

"My dad called it 'ozone.' Said it has something to do with the effect the spark has on the air. It's made of pure oxygen, but it's not the kind we breathe. Too much of it will kill you, so don't inhale too close to the thing."

I stepped away from the machine.

"Well," Mid asked, "what do you think of my secret laboratory? Are you properly impressed?"

Several jars filled with liquids of exotic colors covered Mid's worktable along with a scattering of small boxes containing bugs, rocks, various shades of sand, and little bits of scrap metal. One of the jars was labeled 'Poison' and had a picture of a skull and crossbones with X's where the eyes should have been.

"Well, um, not so much. Not counting your Climbing Sparks thing, it all looks like a bunch of junk to me. Can you actually *use* any of this stuff for anything?"

Mid turned off the Climbing Sparks device and spoke loudly toward the ceiling. "Oh, this isn't all my stuff. I keep the good stuff in my secret hideout." He pulled back his rug and lifted a floorboard to reveal a secret compartment. Still speaking loudly toward the ceiling, he continued, "I keep all the important scientific stuff in here. You know, the stuff I use for my experiments. See?"

I leaned over and looked into the hole in the floor. "But—"

"Shhh!" Mid turned the spark machine back on again. "Okay, now talk."

"It's the same as the stuff on your table—useless junk. I don't get it."

Mid and Cheff laughed.

Mid said, "Of course it is. I keep it there especially for the soldiers and Bluebands to find. Every so often we have a surprise inspection. They find my little hideout, confiscate my junk—'"

"—over Mid's most sincere protests—"

"—and leave happy. Stupid Fessals!" Mid laughed again. "I wonder what they do with all the rocks?"

"Why don't they take the Climbing Sparks thing away from you?"

"Well, for one thing, it's an official school project. I have a permit for it from my Engineering and Tech teacher. I'm expected to have projects—we all are. So, a certain amount of junk is okay. Generally speaking, neither the soldiers nor the Bluebands are bright enough to tell if something's valuable or not. For another thing, I don't leave my marvelous inventions in plain sight. I keep the good stuff in my *real* secret repository, where the snoops won't find them. I got Climbing Sparks out for our meeting today, right before you got here."

"How many secret repositories do you have, anyway?" I asked.

"I'll never tell! But if you're good, someday I might show you."

"Then tell me this," I asked, "how did you ever learn to make a thing like that? Do they teach electric stuff in Engineering and Technology?"

"They teach a little bit of nearly everything in E&T, including electricity, chemistry, metallurgy, you name it. But I didn't learn to make the Climbing Sparks device in school. When I was young, we lived in Toof-Toof, high in the Tumber Range. Dad was a chemist and an engineer for the Imperial Mines. His official job was to 'research the use of minerals to the betterment of the Imperium,' but he was always fiddling around with some side project. I loved watching him. That's how I learned this little trick. He had a Climbing Sparks device in his lab at work and another one at home. He told the Fessal guards it was for mineral testing." Mid laughed. "Stupid Fessals. When I was old enough, he told me that as long as it's sparking, the monitors can't hear us." He smacked his right fist into the palm of his left hand, then swept his right hand outward. "Rock-smooth, isn't it, Books?"

"'Rock-smooth?'"

"Don't they say that in Tumberland?" Cheff asked.

"No, I never heard it before." I smacked my palm and swept my arm as Mid had. "Rock-smooth… rock-smooth… I like it!"

"Speaking of smooth rocks," Mid said, "do you still want to see how the flashdark works?"

"Sure."

Mid took the flashdark from his jacket pocket and unscrewed the base, then shook out a shiny yellow crystal with a small hole in one end. "It comes from the mines in the Toof-Toof Region."

"What is it?" I asked.

"Amnurite. Watch this." He held the crystal in the ray of sunlight coming through the window. The stone darkened slowly. In less than a minute, it was a deep purple color. Mid closed his hand around the stone, leaving a gap barely big enough to peek through. Cheff and I peered in. The little crystal gave off a faint purple light for a few seconds, then turned back to yellow again. Mid explained, "It sort of soaks up the light, then lets it out again, slowly."

I took the crystal from him and held it up to the light. "It's pretty, but what's it good for?"

"Nothing much, as far as anyone knows. Dad tried all kinds of experiments, but nothing ever came of it. I've been trying a few experiments with it, with electricity and magnets and some other things. That's how I came up with the flashdark. See, I used a regular flashlight: switch, batteries, and light bulb, exactly what you'd expect. However—" he turned the tube so I could see all the way to the bottom "—I added the amnurite crystal, an extra switch, a bit of wiring, and a spring. It's the spring that does the trick. The crystal wants to be slightly compressed first, then you add the current. See?" He reassembled the flashdark and gave the bottom a twist. "That's the pressure. Then you send a trickle of current to the crystal." He flipped the switch, and a beam of dark crossed the room, soaking up the light from the window.

"It only works for a while. Then the crystal gets full or something. When it's full, it glows purple like I showed you. If it's completely full, it'll glow for several hours."

"Pretty nifty," I said. "It'll be fun to see what else you can do with it. Can you make me one?"

"No, sorry. That's the only crystal I have."

"Why does it have a hole in one end?"

Mid lowered his eyes. "It used to be a necklace. It belonged to my sister, Losari."

"You have a sister?"

"Not since we moved here."

"I see," I said, even though I didn't. "How long ago was that?"

— 20 —

LOSARI

"I**T'S BEEN A** while," Mid said. "The trouble started when I was a little boy, and my sister, Losari, was a toddler. We didn't come straight to Fellstone, though. Something bad happened where Dad worked. There was an explosion, and Dad got blamed for it. He lost his job there and was assigned as a contract laborer on a fishing boat in Settport."

"What's a contract laborer?" I asked.

Cheff scoffed. "That's Imperialese for 'slave.'"

"It was a tough time," Mid continued. "Worse in some ways than the Labor Compound."

"What do you mean?" I asked. "What's worse than this?"

"To start with, the army took all our things, except what we could carry. That's the same as here, right? But then they put us into what they called a house, but it was barely even a shack. No electricity, no running water, no glass in the windows. It looked like it was about to fall over. It was made of rough boards nailed to a frame. I could see right through the cracks. At least here we have lights and water and solid walls."

"Wasn't it cold?" I asked.

"Cold? You bet it was cold. The icy wind blew across the Sea of Narabor and right through the cracks in the walls. It was freezing! My mom scrounged up some old newspapers the first day we were there. The next day, Losari and I helped her cover the cracks by sticking the newspaper to the rotten old planks with a paste she made from cooking flour and water. After that, it was a little warmer inside—the wind didn't blow through as much, anyway. But that wasn't the worst part."

"What was the worst part?" I asked dutifully.

"The shack was in the worst part of town, down by the docks. The entire neighborhood reeked of rotting fish all the time."

"Yuck," I said. "Sounds nasty."

"It was," Mid agreed. "And it gets worse: Dad was assigned a job on one of the fishing boats, and he stank of fish all the time, too. The captain of the boat, a Coastal Lora like Cheff, let Dad take a few fish home every day."

"Risky," Cheff said. "If they had caught him, he and your dad would have ended up here, or worse."

"You're right," Mid said, "it *was* risky. So risky, in fact, that my dad smuggled the fish home inside his shirt every night, which made him smell even more. Then I'd give him a hug when he got home, so I smelled like fish, and Losari—"

"I get it—everybody smelled like fish," I said. "Blech!"

"It was pretty bad," Mid said, "especially at first, but we got used to it. After a while, we hardly noticed the smell anymore. But, when we went shopping downtown, people would see us coming and ask, 'which way sets the wind?'"

Cheff and I laughed.

"We didn't starve," Mid said, "in large part due to the kindness of Dad's captain. I don't remember his name—I always called him 'Captain.' Thanks to him, we ate a lot of fish. A lot. Did I mention we ate a lot of fish?"

"How much fish did you eat?" Cheff said, grinning.

"A lot!" Mid said. He and Cheff laughed.

"Mom did her best to make it appealing. She kept finding new ways to cook it. We ate fried fish, boiled fish, baked fish, dried fish. Fish stew, fish chowder, fish soup. Fish and rice, fish and beans, fish and cornbread, when we could get cornmeal. It kept us from starving, and I'm grateful, but, after a while, I got plenty tired of fish. Even now, years later, I don't much care for seafood."

"It's not my favorite, either," I said.

Cheff mumbled, "Oh, you're gonna *love* Labor Compound food. There's this little fishing village to the north of here…"

"So what happened?" I asked. "What about Losari?"

Mid frowned at me. "Hey! Don't get ahead of the story!"

"Sorry," I said.

"I'm kidding," Mid said. "We're coming to that part. First, I have to tell you about how things got better."

"Okay," I said. "Carry on."

"Thank you," Mid said, with mock dignity. "As I was saying, the Captain was nice enough and treated my father kindly. He had a son about my age named Centh. We played together once in a while. One day I went to see him and found him in tears. His uncle, who was also a fisherman, had fallen overboard in a storm and was lost at sea."

"That's terrible," I said. "Did they find him?"

Mid shook his head sadly. "They never found the uncle, but his helper got the boat back to the dock. Centh asked me if I wanted to see his uncle's boat. I did, so he took me down to the dock, and we made sure no one was watching, then we climbed on board. Centh let me sit in the captain's chair. There were all sorts of buttons and dials and levers and things. I pushed or pulled every one of them. I'd never been on a boat before."

"Me neither," I said, "until we took the ship here. But I guess a big ship isn't much like a fishing boat."

"It isn't," Cheff said. "On a big ship, you hardly know you're on the ocean, except during storms. In a little boat, you get bounced around by the ocean except on extra-calm days."

"Of which there aren't many on the Sea of Narabor," Mid said, "which I found out a short time later."

"Oh? How?" I asked.

"It was like this: I wanted to start up the steam engine, but Centh said it got broken during the storm. So I told him I'd fix it."

I laughed. "You what? I thought you'd never been on a boat before?"

"I hadn't been. I didn't know a thing about steam engines or boats. I have no idea why I said that. It popped right out of my mouth. Anyway, Centh wouldn't let me see the engine. He was afraid we'd get in trouble. So we messed around a while, then went home."

"A couple of days later, right after supper—I remember we had fish sticks—there was a knock on the door. It was the captain. He told Dad that Centh and I had been on the boat without permission. Dad started to say that he would punish me, but his boss interrupted. He said he wasn't worried about that, boys will explore, it's their nature. Then he looked at me and said that, from now on, I could never go on the boat without asking permission first. I gulped and nodded."

"That could have been worse," I said. "What happened?"

"The captain told my dad that Centh said I could fix the engine. He asked Dad if that was true. Dad looked at me for a while, stroking his chin. Finally, he said it might be true, that although I didn't have any experience with steam engines, he wouldn't put it past me. They both laughed. Dad said that I just might be able to if he were to help me."

"Did you fix it?" I asked.

"We did," Mid said. "The next day, Dad and I and the captain went to the uncle's boat and got the engine working. It took all day. At lunchtime, the captain's wife, a beautiful Mountain Lora with smiling eyes, brought us some sandwiches and beer. I was worried, at first, but they weren't fish sandwiches. It was the first time I'd had meat in over a year, and it was delicious! I was allowed to sit in the captain's seat. I even got a small glass of beer. The captain said that I was doing a man's job and deserved a man's chair and a man's drink. Dad agreed." Mid's eyes glistened. "That may have been the proudest moment of my life. Up to that point, anyway, because in the next few minutes, I was even prouder."

"Is this the part about Losari?" I asked.

Mid ignored me. "The captain said that if we could keep it running, Dad could be the captain of it and earn a share of what the boat made. Maybe we could get out of the shack and get a proper house. Then he looked right at me. 'If,' he said, 'your Dad can find a suitable mate to help him run the boat.' He smiled, and I still remember the twinkle in his eye."

"Sweet!" I said. "So you got a real job."

"Not just a job—a *man's* job. I was the engineer. It was my job to make sure there was always plenty of coal on board and to keep the firebox full when we were underway. I'm not sure why, but that cranky old steam engine and I got along fine. Maybe because I was nice to her and kept her all clean and shiny."

"What about school?" I asked.

"I was excused from school to work on the boat."

Cheff said, "Turns out that our Beloved Emperor approves of child labor."

"Things got better for us after that. As soon as we made some decent money, we moved out of the shack into a regular house in town. We had better food and more of it. We still ate a lot of fish, but sometimes we had real beef, too. My mom made the best stew I ever tasted. Still does, except well, not so much with the beef."

Cheff grimaced. "Fence chicken."

"Fence chicken?" I asked.

"That's what we called rat meat when Buttons was little. It's the only way we could get her to eat it."

We heard Mid's front door open, then close again.

"It must be getting late," Mid said. "That was Mom coming home from work. I don't want her to overhear us talking about what happened back then. She gets upset."

Cheff reached over and closed the bedroom door.

Mid continued in a low voice, "Anyway, the better times lasted for a little more than a year. Then *they* came in the middle of the night. The army. They kicked down the door and dragged my father away. We never saw him again. They said he was suspected of FRM affiliation like they always do. My mom and I and little Losari were put on a boat and brought here. Like you, Books, except for one thing—as we got to the main gate of the Labor Compound, a big black steam car drove up to the guardhouse. An enormously fat Fessal woman in expensive clothes extracted herself from the car and spoke to the guard. The guard pointed at Losari.

"The fat woman came over, bent down, and smiled all sickysweet. 'Hello, darling. My, you sure are a pretty little thing.' She took Losari by the hand and pulled her away from Mother. Mother tried to go to Losari, but the guards held her back. The fat woman asked Losari, 'How would you like to come live with me and be my girl?'

"Losari pulled loose, ran screaming to Mother, hid behind her skirt, and started to cry. While the woman wedged her bulk back into the car, two men in black uniforms got out, picked Losari up, and stuffed her into the back seat, kicking and begging Mother to save her. Then they drove away. We haven't seen her since."

"Do you know what happened to her?" I asked.

"A long time later, we heard from a guard that the fat Fessal woman is the wife of some high-up official who works in the Silver Palace. She couldn't have children of her own, so she bought my sister. Anyway, that's what the guard told us. He told us she lived in a big, fancy house in New City, that her life there was much better than it could ever be here in the Labor Compound, and that we ought to be grateful. I tried to believe it for a long time, but now I'm not so sure. If she wanted a child to raise as her own, why pick a Troh? Why not a Fessal, like herself?"

Mid got up and stared out the window, pretending to wipe some soot from his eye. "Sometimes I dream about Losari. I dream that she's that fat woman's slave, cleaning, scrubbing, waiting on her hand and foot."

Cheff growled, "We know which guard it was: Manyard. He's the meanest of all the guards. Someday we'll take care of him. I don't know how, but we will."

Mid recovered and sat down at his worktable again. "Anyway, that's all we know. Which isn't much. I hope she's having a good life. I miss her. Stupid Fessals…"

"They can't all be bad, can they?" I asked. "The entire Fessal species, I mean."

"I don't know. I suppose not, but sometimes it seems like it. You know, Dad told me that the explosion in his factory was caused by the incompetence of a Fessal foreman. He was dangerously stupid, and Dad had warned his bosses about him many times. His *Fessal* bosses. One day, the foreman's stupidity caught up with him, and something blew up. No one died, but several people were badly hurt. They blamed Dad for it and fired him. Dad had never much cared for the Fessal People, but after that, he hated all Fessals. He became bitter and blamed Fessals for everything wrong with Andaran." Mid thought it over. "I don't know any decent Fessals myself, but I suppose there might be some. It doesn't help that the Seph prefer Fessals as their Facilitators and employees. I'll maybe start thinking about forgiving them when they bring my sister back.

"The amnurite crystal was hers. Dad made it into a necklace for her. She wore it all the time, but when we got on the transport ship that brought us here, she asked me to keep it in my pocket until we got to our new home. She was afraid it would fall off into the Sea of Narabor and be lost forever. She was so little when they took her. I don't know if she'd even remember me anymore."

He wiped his eyes again with his sleeve.

"She'd be a couple of years older than Buttons. I like to think they'd be friends."

— 21 —

FIELD TRIP

THE DOOR SWUNG open and Mid's mom stepped in, carrying a pitcher of milk and a tray of glasses. Her expression was vague, her eyes unfocused. A livid scar ran from her forehead, across her left eye, and down her cheek. She said in a peculiar, lilting tone, "Hello, boys. Look who came for a visit." Buttons was right behind her, holding a plate piled high with cookies. "Buttons has been baking. Look what she brought for you." She put her tray down on Mid's worktable, then filled the glasses. "Mid told me about your uncle, Cheff. I'm so sorry. How's your Aunt Dee doing?"

"Not so well, Mama Kee," Cheff said. "She's trying to put on a good face and hold things together, but she's pretty well undone."

"Of course she is, dear. If she needs anything, anything at all, you'll come get me, won't you, Cheff?"

"Yes, thank you, I will."

Buttons passed the plate of cookies around. "They're not fancy, Books. We don't get fancy ingredients here in the Labor Compound. Mostly flour and sugar with a little egg. But they're still cookies, and Starry said you'd like them anyway. They're fresh, see? Still warm."

I took a cookie and tasted it. "Tastes like a real cookie to me. Starry was right: I like it. Thanks, Buttons."

Buttons shook congratulatory hooves with Starry.

Mid's mom turned to me and extended her hand. "You must be Mid's new friend. It's so nice to meet you."

"It's nice to meet you, too, ma'am."

"'Ma'am?' Oh, my! I think it would be best if you call me Mama Kee. Everyone else does. How would that be?"

"That'd be fine, Mama Kee."

She smiled absently and retrieved the empty pitcher. "I'll leave the cookies here. Help yourselves. You, too, Starry and Moka." She winked at me. "The ponies love cookies, you know. By the way, I'm Mama Kee. It's nice to meet you." She extended her hand for me to shake again.

I shook it, puzzled. "Er… nice to meet you, too, Mama Kee."

Mama Kee said, "Have fun with your homework. I'm going downstairs now. Bye-bye, ponies."

Buttons made the ponies wave goodbye.

Mama Kee pinched Mid's chubby cheek. "Don't eat too many cookies, Mid, okay?" She kissed him noisily on the forehead.

Mid tried, unsuccessfully, to duck. "Okay, Mom. I won't." He was blushing.

"Is your mom okay?" I asked Mid when she had gone. "She seems… um…"

"Not so much, no," Mid said. "She's been like that since we lost Losari."

"She's functional enough," Cheff said. "She goes to work every day and takes care of Mid and the house."

"But she's not altogether there anymore," Mid said. "She treats me like a little kid. I've gotten used to it. I forget how strange it can seem."

"The ponies wish there was something we could do for her," Buttons said, "but they haven't been able to think of anything."

"It is what it is," Mid said. "It could be a lot worse."

"I suppose," I said, dubiously.

"We all find some way to cope," Cheff said. "There's simply too much hurt. So she moved her mind to where the hurt can't reach."

I let this sink in. "It's hard to imagine. So far, I've only lost my father."

Buttons climbed up on the bed and sat next to me. "And your home, and your previous life, and your mother's not doing too well."

"It stacks up," Cheff said, "and just keeps on stacking." He checked to make sure the climbing sparks machine was still working, then lowered his voice anyway. "Which is why I want to do something about Uncle Karf. I can't stand it anymore. Little by little, Pallador and his Labor Compound and his Bluebands and his goon squads are going to take everything. *Everything.*"

"Easy, Old Man," Mid said. "I feel the same way, but what can we do about it?"

"That is the question, Old Son," Cheff said. "What *can* we do about it?"

"The ponies think we should make a plan!" Buttons said.

"The ponies need to go bake some more cookies," Cheff said. "It wouldn't be safe for them to be part of this conversation. We must keep the ponies safe." He opened the door and gestured for Buttons to go.

She said in a flat voice, "You're joking."

"I'm not joking," Cheff said. "I'm trying to keep my little sister safe."

He tried to push her off the bed, but she scrambled out of his reach. "Hold it, Cheff, I'm safe enough right here. And aren't you a fine one for talking about being safe after last night?"

"You had no business following us last night. That's what I'm talking about—I can't let you get involved with that kind of stuff."

"Really, Cheff? *You* can't *let* me?" She shrugged and slid off the bed. "Okay, fine. But it'll be a shame when Aunt Dee hears about how a certain little pony went for a midnight ride, won't it? I'm sure Aunt Dee wouldn't approve of your dragging me with you to Old City. Why, I could have been hurt! *Anything* might have happened. Yes, she'll be furious. It really wasn't responsible of you to take me along like that." She batted her eyelashes at him, smiled sweetly, and reached for the doorknob.

Cheff grabbed her arm and growled, "You wouldn't *dare* tell Aunt Dee about last night."

"*I* wouldn't," Buttons said, "but the ponies might. You're hurting my arm."

"You know, Cheff," Mid pointed out, "she *was* pretty clever. After all, she *did* save our skins. Those Bluebands were within inches of finding us. I think she's earned the privilege of being included. It's as much her secret as it is ours now. Don't you think so, Books?"

"Umm…"

"You stay out of this," Cheff snarled at me.

"If you say so, Cheff," I said. "But I was there, too—we all were. Uncle Karf is her uncle, same as yours, and I don't blame her for wanting to help him."

"He was my uncle, too," Mid said, "even if not by blood. He watched out for all of us."

"I'm sorry I didn't get to know him," I said. "He sounds like a good man. And I could use an uncle right about now."

"I get that you want to keep Buttons safe," Mid said, "but are any of us truly safe in this place? I mean, you could shut her in—"

"—he could *try*—"

"—but that's no way to live. What if the Bluebands came for her while you were out? That could happen anytime. Safety and security aren't real—they're merely illusions."

Cheff frowned and set his mouth, but nodded reluctantly. "You make some good points, Old Son." He put his arm around Buttons and gave her a squeeze. "I just don't want anything bad to happen to her."

Buttons hugged him back. "Thanks, Cheff. I love you, too. And to show you how much, I'll be quiet while we make our secret plans." Buttons took a huge bite of cookie. "I promise," she said, spraying cookie crumbs all over the bed. She swallowed and wiped the crumbs from her lips with the back of her hand. "I'll be so quiet that you won't even know I'm here. 'Quiet' is my middle name. Yep, Mellabee Quiet Karfendek, that's me. I'm the quietest little girl in the entire Fellstone Labor Compound. I'm the quietest girl in all of Fellstone City. I'm the quietest girl you'll ever meet in your life. I'm the quietest girl in the whole, wide wor—"

"All right, enough!" Cheff covered her mouth with his hand, then jerked it back with a yelp. "Hey! If you have to bite, bite your cookie." He shook his head. "With her here, we don't need your Climbing Sparks, Mid. We could point Buttons at the ceiling and let her talk." He patted her on the back. "Mid's right, you know. Your performance last night *was* brilliant. Even while I was worried that you'd get caught, I still thought you were spectacular. I'm proud of you."

"Why, Cheff!" Tears welled up in Buttons' eyes. "I guess hanging around Books is good for you. You've never been that nice to me before in my whole entire life." She wiped her nose on Cheff's sleeve.

"And I never will be again, most likely. You're too funny-looking."

"*I'm* funny-looking? You guys should have seen yourselves running from that dog. Now, *that* was funny-looking!"

"Andarans' bones," Cheff said. "That was one *big* dog! You could have been eaten!"

"What, Mister Snuggles eat me? He'd never do such a thing!"

"Snuggles?"

"*Mister* Snuggles. That's what I call him, anyway. It's probably not his real name. He's a nice wittle snuggle-uggle-uggums. And, besides," she added, "he likes Starry."

Cheff smacked his forehead. "Nice little snuggle—? He must weigh two hundred pounds (90 kg)!"

"Silly boys, you don't even know how to get along with a cute little puppy dog. He just needs hugs."

Cheff shook his head. "All right, then, let's get down to business."

He and Buttons and I arranged ourselves on the bed. Mid pulled his chair up close, and the four of us leaned our heads together. For the next few minutes, Buttons and I kept quiet as Cheff and Mid talked over the situation. Next, Cheff briefly related to Buttons what had happened at Meltern's Guest House.

Buttons frowned. "I can't believe the FRM wouldn't help us."

Mid threw his hands up. "Help us? He wouldn't even admit that he's FRM!"

Cheff said, "Uncle Karf must have thought he could help, or he wouldn't have asked me to contact him."

"I suppose that's true," Mid said. "Maybe Meltern *can't* do anything. He said that once someone gets put in the Iron Fortress, there's nothing anyone can do."

Cheff shrugged. "If he were FRM, he'd know, I suppose. Aunt Dee is devastated. She's talking as if Uncle Karf were already dead."

"He might be, for all we know," Mid said. "Think about it—a lot of people get put into the Fortress, but no one ever comes out. No one we've ever heard of."

"So?"

"So," Mid said, "either the Iron Fortress has thousands of prisoners in it, or they're going somewhere else."

"Or being killed," Buttons added.

Mid shook his head. "They can't be killing that many people. Surely that many bodies would be noticed."

"Not if they burned them," Cheff said, "or ground them up and fed them to the fish. Or took them out to the desert to bury them."

"What if," Mid said, "instead of killing them, they're secretly shipping them somewhere? Maybe to some other kind of labor compound or camp. If they are, we might be able to kidnap him from the transport truck, or before they put him on a ship or something."

Cheff thought about this possibility. "Maybe, but I've never heard of anything like a transport truck or a transport ship leaving the Fortress. It would be pretty hard to hide an entire ship from everyone."

"Then what do we do?" Buttons asked.

Cheff sagged, defeated. "I don't know."

Mid got up and stared out the window at the gathering darkness.

Cheff slumped against the wall and pounded his fist into his palm. "I guess Meltern was right. It's hopeless. There's nothing anyone *can* do. Maybe it would be best to forget about him and move on like Aunt Dee is trying to do." He sank his face into his hands. "Besides, even if we could get him out, what would we do with him? We can't bring him home. He'd just be arrested again."

Mid turned from the window. "Speaking of Aunt Dee, I thought of something."

"What's that?" Cheff asked.

"Meltern said you should forget about your uncle and take care of your Aunt Dee. He actually said her name: *Aunt Dee*. We never said it."

Cheff uncovered his face. "You're right! He lied! If he lied about not knowing Uncle Karf, he probably lied about not being FRM, too." Cheff got off the bed and began pacing. "You know what we're going to do? We're going to get Uncle Karf out of the Iron Fortress and drop him right on Meltern's doorstep. *Then* we'll see who's FRM or not!"

"That's a great plan, Cheff," Mid said, "except for the part where no one's ever allowed into that place."

Buttons said, "That's not exactly true."

"What isn't?" Cheff asked.

"It's not true that no one's ever allowed into the Iron Fortress."

"What are you talking about, Buttons? It's sealed up like a can of beans and guarded around the clock!"

"But we *are* allowed in. Not only *allowed* in—we're *required* to go in. Every year."

"You know, Cheff," Mid said, "she's right."

"What are you talking about?" I asked. "I don't get it."

Cheff brightened. "I get it, Books, and so do you. Remember what Mr. Rishten told you this morning? You're required to visit Pallador's Museum of History, Security, and Loyalty."

"I still don't get it."

"It just so happens that the museum is located inside the Iron Fortress."

Mid said, "The Fortress also houses the IID."

I scratched my head. "Still, they must keep the IID and the prison part locked away from the museum, right?"

Cheff waggled his hand, palm down. "Yes and no—sort of. There's only one entrance, the main gate."

Mid said, "Visitors, IID operatives, and prisoners all have to go through the main gate on the causeway, up the steps, and through the front door. There's got to be some way to get from the museum to the prison. And if we can find it—"

"—We might be able to rescue Uncle Karf," Cheff said.

"Do you think so?" Buttons asked. "The ponies really hope so!"

Cheff put his arm around her shoulders. "I don't know, Buttons. I don't know if I can get him out of there, but I have to try. I can't sit around here and do nothing, pretending that he's already dead." He stood tall. "I guess it's time we had a look around that place—a *good* look."

"I'm ready." Buttons slid off the bed and stood next to her big brother. "How're we going to do that, Cheff?"

"Exactly the way you said, Mel. It's time for a field trip." Cheff grinned at her, then asked me, "Didn't you say that Mr. Rishten recommended a trip to the museum? Well, you're going to go a little sooner than he expected."

"But how—?"

"No worries," Cheff said. "Mid, Buttons, and I are about due for our annual visit anyway, and we have plenty of privilege points saved up." He put his hand on my shoulder. "Books, old buddy, it looks like we're going to have to get you some travel papers."

$$— 22 —$$

Captain Utaliak

The next morning, Cheff, Buttons, and Mid came by to walk me to school again. Buttons carried a parcel wrapped in brown paper. Along the way, several crews swept up the residue left by the sooty rain into little mounds of wet, black mud.

I turned into the schoolyard, but Cheff caught me by the elbow. "No school for us today, Books. Today's field-trip day, remember? We're going to see the captain in charge of the Labor Compound."

We approached the main gate where I'd come in only two days ago. To the right of the gate was the Labor Compound Administrative Office, a one-story building obviously built by the same couldn't-care-less builders who constructed the residences. In big clay pots on each side of the door were the dried skeletons of a pair of long-dead, scrawny little bushes, black with grime.

Cheff cleaned a spot on the door glass with his shirt sleeve and peeked in, then frowned. "Oh, no."

"What's the matter, Cheff?" Buttons asked.

"Captain Utaliak's on duty today."

Mid whispered, "What are we going to do? Should we forget about it and go back to school? We'd only be a few minutes late."

"No, Uncle Karf can't wait. We'll have to take our chances. Buttons, give Books that package. Hide it under your coat, Books."

"What am I going to do with it?"

"You'll know when the time comes," Cheff said. "I'll give you a nod." He took a long, deep breath, then pushed the door open, and we followed him in.

A huge, unshaven Fessal in an Army uniform sat behind the desk, painstakingly filling out a form with a broken pencil. The Captain squinted up at Cheff, then jumped to his feet, sending his chair tumbling across the floor behind him. "YOU!" He pointed at Cheff. "WHAT ARE YA DOING HERE? YA SHOULD BE IN SCHOOL!" He pulled out his pistol and aimed it straight at Cheff's forehead. "I TOLD YA THE NEXT TIME WOULD BE YER LAST!" The gun made a loud metallic *ker-click!* as the captain pulled the hammer back.

Cheff ducked instinctively and covered his face.

Without thinking, I jumped in front of Cheff and put my hands up. "Don't shoot. Please! We're here on official business. I'm a new kid. Mr. Rishten sent us. He said Cheff should help me."

The captain aimed carefully at my forehead. I squinched my eyes shut and tried to keep my bladder from cutting loose. He barked, "Are ya ready to go, New Kid? Huh? Well, are ya?"

I wanted to say that no, I wasn't ready to go, not even a little bit, but my voice didn't work. My mouth was opening and closing, but no sound came out.

The captain put the pistol back into its holster and laughed. "Haw, haw, fooled ya! Ah, the look on yer face!"

The world went dark around the edges, and I nearly collapsed. The captain hauled me back to my feet, then slapped me on the back so hard that my glasses shot off and skidded across the floor. "Did I scare ya, New Kid? C'mon, admit it! Ya really thought I was gonna shoot ya, dintcha, New Kid? I wasn't, y'know. Dis is a little game I like to play wit' da kids sometimes. But ya sure fooled me—I din't expect ya to jump in front of Cheff. You mus' be pretty brave."

Still guffawing, he retrieved his chair from behind his desk and fell into it, holding his sides and wiping the tears from his eyes. "Ya shoulda seen yer face, New Kid! Oh, man, ya shore looked scared."

Mid handed me my glasses and murmured, "Sorry, Books. I guess we should have warned you. Utaliak pulls something like this from time to time. Never with a gun before, though. That *was* pretty brave, jumping in front of Cheff like that."

Buttons came over and took my hand. "*So* brave."

"Well," I said, checking to see if I'd actually wet my pants (I hadn't), "I didn't feel brave. I nearly had a heart attack."

Cheff whispered to us, "We need his help. Follow my lead." He led me up to the desk. "Books, meet Captain Utaliak. He's always kidding around, aren't you Captain?"

I stepped forward, wiped my palm on my pant leg, and shook his hand.

The captain boomed, "Haw, haw, I got ya good, din't I? Don't lie, I can tell—your hand's all sweaty." He turned to Cheff. "I got him good. Haw, haw, haw." He leaned back in his chair and crossed his filthy boots on the desktop, still shaking with laughter and wiping his eyes. "You kids sure brightened up my morning! I'll be laughing all day. Who's dat you got witcha there? Is dat little Mellabee? Hi, Mellabee, where's da ponies?"

Buttons held Starry up for inspection. "Starry doesn't like it when people call me 'Mellabee.' She prefers 'Mel,' and so do I."

The captain somberly gave Starry a pat. "Thanks for da intel, Starry. I'll keep 'at in mind from now on. Now, what can I do for you kids today, Cheff?"

"Captain Utaliak, we want to get traveling papers to visit the Museum at the Iron Fortress. It's time for our annual visit."

"Shouldn't be a problem." He opened a large metal box stuffed with hundreds of folders. "Let's see... Karfendek, Cheff... check. Karfendek, Mellabee, I mean, Mel... check. Persil, Mid... check."

"Well..." The captain shook his head. "I'd like ta help yas, I sure would, but rules is rules. I'm afraid not." He started to put my folder back in the box.

Cheff glanced at me and said, "We wouldn't want to spoil his strag—er, *strategy*, would we? That could discourage such an enthusiastic subject of our Beloved Emperor."

I got the hint. I stepped forward and quoted:

> *"'It is good when young ones want to learn of their Emperor's ways. And even as I have once so wisely said, 'The youth who treasures his master's mind and life will himself find his own mind and life!'*

"That's from the Illustrious Emperor Pallador's green book, *Loyalty and Livelihood: Prosperity through Pallador*, page 45, paragraph 3."

The captain applauded. "Say, dat's a neat trick. Can ya do it again?"

"Yes, sir." I cleared my throat and said:

> *"'Anyone who holds back a young person from loving me, from knowing about me, will himself be swallowed down by my wrath, never to return. Therefore, all must encourage and aid young ones to come unto me.'*

"The same green book, page 47, paragraph 9."

"'Encourage and aid young ones,' eh?" The captain wrinkled his brow. "Say... yer not maybe tryin' ta tell me sumpin, are ya?" He laughed. "Of course you are. Ya really *are* ent'usiastic, ain't ya? Still, I dunno. I could get into a lotta trouble..."

Cheff gave me a tiny nod. I slipped the package from under my coat and set it on the desk.

Captain Utaliak looked at me, then at Cheff. "Something ya found sleepwalking, perhaps? Dat might be worth a few privilege points for the new kid."

Cheff winked.

A bell tinkled and the office door opened. The package disappeared into a desk drawer.

Captain Utaliak called to the newcomer, "I'll be witcha shortly, Tocette. I hafta fill out travel papers for dese lovely children first."

"Oh. Okay, Captain," she brayed. I thought of a donkey I knew back in Tumberland. The tall, big-boned Fessal girl's Blueband uniform was wrinkled and had several dark stains. Her blue armband had been tied carelessly and was drooping. She slouched over to the window and picked her teeth with a grimy fingernail. I was pretty sure she was the same disheveled Blueband that Brex had chewed out in the schoolyard the day before.

The captain finished filling out our papers, noisily stamped each one, then handed them to us. "Dere you go, kids. Have a good time, okay? Jus' make sure yer back before curfew. Oh, hang on, I almos' forgot. Yer gonna need a chaperone, ain't yas?"

He called the tall girl over to his desk. "It's a good thing yer here, Tocette. Dese four is goin' on a tour of the Iron Fortress today, and dey need someone to escort 'em. Ya came just in time."

Cheff's eyes went wide. He murmured, "Oh, no, please, not her, please…"

Tocette glanced sharply at Cheff, then smiled, showing her crooked teeth covered with yellow crud. "Sure, Cap, I'd love a trip to New City today. I'm, uh, all ahead in my, uh, classwork, Cap."

"Of course ya are." He picked up the phone, listened briefly, then shouted into the receiver, "Hey! Get off dis line. Dis is Utaliak. I got a emergency."

He waited for the line to clear, then jiggled the receiver hook several times. I heard, faintly, a female voice say, "Operator."

"Yeah, uh, dis is Utaliak over at the Labor Compound. I got some kids comin' for deir annual field trip… Utaliak. *Captain* Utaliak… The Fellstone Labor Compound… I tol' ya alreddy." He thumped the desk with his fist. "I'm sendin' some kids to see ya… Five—three boys, two girls. One's a Blueband chaperone." He slowly spelled out our names, then said, "Dey're leaving here right now. Should be dere in maybe t'ree hours. Right."

He looked up at me and stared hard. "What's your name, New Kid?"

"Birn Tylandine, sir."

He thumbed through the files. "Here ya are. Hmm…" He frowned. "Seems we got a problem here. Ya can't go to the Fortress anytime ya like, Tylandine. We got rules, see? A trip to da Fortress requires a minimum of fifty privilege points, and accordin' to dis, you don't got any."

Cheff explained, "It's because he only got here a couple of days ago, from up Tumberland way. He lives a few doors down from me. He's a good guy, Captain. I'm sure he'll make up the points in no time."

Mid added, "Cheff and I were telling him about the Fortress and the museum and all, and, well, he got pretty excited and wanted to go right away. We explained about the privilege points, but he begged us to ask you, anyway. Isn't that right, Books?"

I gulped. "Yes, sir, it's true. My teacher, Mr. Rishten, strongly advised me to go. He said I could go anytime, and it would be okay. He said that you'd notify him when I left the compound."

"I get it," the big captain said. "Yesterday was yer first day at school, and ya want to make a good impression on yer new teacher. Is that it?"

I nodded.

Captain Utaliak stroked the stubble on his chin. "Commendable. I approve of kissin' up to da authorities. It's a good stragedy for youngsters. And adults—I certainly do my share. More dan my share, ya' see, and it's paid off, too! Look where it's gotten me!" He leaned back and gestured grandly at the dismal administrative office. "A comfy, cushy, indoor job! Still…"

Buttons went around the desk and gave the captain a big hug. "He really wants to go, Captain Utaliak. Couldn't you make an exception this time? I promise he'll make up the privilege points. I'll help him." She batted her eyes. "Pleeease?"

He filled out another travel pass, stamped it, and handed it to Tocette. "Here ya go, honey. Take good care of 'em."

"Oh. Sure thing, Cap." Tocette put her arm around me. She blared, "And who's this little fellow?" spraying me with drops of reeking spittle and bits of ancient decaying food particles.

Cheff said, "New kid from Tumberland."

I slipped out of her surprisingly strong grip, then wiped my face with my sleeve.

She laughed, like fingernails on a chalkboard. "Awww, he's cu-uute! I'm gonna enjoy this trip, Cap! C'mon kiddies, let's go catch a bus."

"I told you the next time would be your last!"

— 23 —

Bus Stop

WE APPROACHED THE main gate of the Labor Compound, located to the right of the administration office. In the daylight, the gates looked quite different from when Mother and I had entered. Razor-sharp wire topped the rusting iron plates, which were held together by hundreds of giant rivets. The gates could roll sideways on rusting iron wheels in an iron track set into the pavement. The massive twelve-foot-high gates looked small compared to the outer wall of the Compound, which towered another six feet above them.

Mid called my attention to a large gray metal box to the left of the gates at the end of the iron track. "There's a big electric motor inside that box. The gates are too heavy to open by hand, even with the wheels. The guards hate it when the power goes off and they have to use the hand crank, especially when it's raining. We'll go out through the little gate." He indicated a smaller door set into one of the massive doors. "That one's for people. They only open the big doors for cars and trucks and such."

Mid kicked at the ground and muttered so that Tocette wouldn't hear, "Yeah, trucks full of kidnappers."

Buttons slipped her hand into his.

As we approached the guard shack, Tocette stopped us. "Uh-oh—Manyard's on duty today. You kids better wait here and let me handle this. I'll be right back." She took our papers and approached the dingy guard shack.

Mid took me by the arm, turned me around, and whispered, "Keep your eyes down. Don't look at Manyard."

Cheff added, "It's best not to look any of the guards in the eye. They're mean. It's part of the job description."

"That captain back at the office," I asked, "Captain Utaliak? He seemed okay, sort of."

Cheff snorted. "Don't you believe it. He likes the meat I bring him, that's all. He can be as nasty as the rest of them when he wants to be. He was in a good mood today, though. I think it's because he likes 'Little Mellabee,' here."

Buttons frowned. She took Starry out of her backpack and brushed off the pony's head. "I hate it when certain people touch her. Especially Fessals."

"Cheff's right." Mid's face darkened. "We've seen Utaliak when he was in a bad mood. It isn't pretty, but Manyard's far worse. He'll hurt you if he gets a chance, just for fun. Stinking, rotten, twisted Fessal monster." Mid clenched his fists so hard that his knuckles turned white. He turned and walked a few paces away. Buttons trailed after him.

I whispered to Cheff, "Isn't Manyard the one who—?"

"Sold Losari? Yeah, that's him. Mid hates him. So do I."

A few minutes later, Tocette came back. The small door buzzed open, and as we filed through, I couldn't help glancing at Manyard. His eyes were glowing black coals of pure hatred. I forced my eyes back to the ground and kept moving, but I felt Manyard's eyes burning a hole in the back of my head all the way across the street to the bus stop.

Several people were already waiting, including Brex, looking every bit as pinched and severe as she had the day before. Tocette said, "Look! It's Miss Brex! I'll bet she's going on the same bus as us." She gave us a stern look. "You all wait for me here. I'm going to talk to her."

The four of us huddled together a short distance away from the others. Mid glanced back at the guard house out of the corner of his eye. "Be careful. He's still watching." I shivered and looked toward the gate in time to see a tall girl come out dressed all in black. She looked older than me, about the same age as Cheff and Mid.

I'd never seen anyone like her in my life. She was tall, lean, and extraordinarily dark. Her skin was the most beautiful silky black, so black that it was hard to tell where her skin stopped and her black military uniform began. I thought of how the water looked on one moonless, starless night during my recent trip across the Sea of Narabor. Her face was hidden behind her long straight hair, which was even blacker than her skin, if that was possible. She reached up and brushed the hair away from her face. Her eyes were the most fascinating brilliant green. My breath caught in my throat.

Cheff noticed me looking at her. "Quite a sight, isn't she?"

"I've never seen anyone quite as… as…"

"Stunning? Striking? Breathtaking?"

I sighed. "Yeah, those."

Mid and Cheff laughed. Buttons said, "She's a Kreff."

Cheff said, "You can tell by her lithe build."

"And her fangs," Mid added. "Kreffs have fangs." He shivered. "I'd sure hate to be on the wrong end of those. Her green eyes are unusual, though. Most Kreffs have brown or black eyes."

"I thought she might be a Kreff," I said. "There weren't many Kreffs in Tumberland, only a few, but I can't recall any like…"

Cheff said, "You didn't have any Kreffs like Sable, that's for sure!"

"Why, what's so special about her—besides being so beautiful, I mean?"

"You'll see." Cheff waved. "Hey, Sable, come on over."

She flowed gracefully to us. "Field trip?" Her voice was deep, quiet, and mellifluous with an exotic accent I didn't recognize.

"Iron Fortress." Cheff said. "We got special permission to show our new schoolmate from Tumberland."

She held out her long, elegant hand. "Sable."

I tried to shake her hand, but my arm wouldn't budge. "I… I, uh… I'm…"

Mid said, "He's Books."

"Books." Sable looked deep into my soul. "Pleased."

While I gazed into her green eyes, Buttons picked up my hand, put it in Sable's, then shook them together. "He's glad to meet you, too, Sable."

Sable laughed, the sound of crystal waters trickling down a green hillside in the spring.

I jerked my hand back and turned away, blushing.

Cheff and Mid laughed again. Cheff said, "Don't worry, Books. She has that effect on everyone."

"Not *every*one," Mid said, nodding toward the little group of Bluebands, where Brex was glaring in our direction.

"Andaran's bones!" Cheff said. "I hope she's not going to the Iron Fortress today, too. That would be a nasty coincidence."

Brex stalked over and examined us. "Hmph. Who let you losers out today?"

"Mr. Walikas, Mr. Rishten, and Captain Utaliak," Cheff said.

Buttons said, "It's our annual field trip to the Fortress Museum."

"Shut it, brat!" Brex said. "No one asked you."

"You just did," Buttons said. "I heard you. You asked, right out loud. You did." She held Starry up to her ear. "Starry heard you, too."

Brex's golden skin turned a dark bronze. She drew back her arm to backhand Buttons.

Sable stepped between Brex and Buttons. "Brex. Uniform. Nice."

"Oh, shut up, *spiderlegs!* At least I have a proper one." She spun around and stomped back to her troop of Bluebands.

Cheff grinned. "I don't think Miss Brex likes you, Sable. Or you, either, Sis."

Sable raised her eyebrows.

Buttons giggled.

"You'd better behave," Cheff said. "If Brex is on the same bus, we'll have to be extra careful. Got it?"

"Okay, Cheff, I got it."

Mid asked Sable, "Where are you going today?"

She brushed her hair from her face again. "Fortress. Museum. Research. Special project."

"Good," Cheff said, smiling. "You can come along with us."

Sable nodded and went to sit on the bench.

I whispered to Cheff, "What did Brex mean when she said, 'at least I have a proper one'? Sable has a uniform, doesn't she? Although I don't recognize the colors. What outfit wears black with red trim?"

"None," Cheff said. "That's what Brex was referring to. Sable's on the Naval Officers Track. She should be wearing blue and silver."

"How does she get away with having her own personal uniform colors?" I asked.

"It's a mystery. They issued her a regular uniform on our first day at Advanced School. I remember because she showed it to me. The next day, she was wearing this one, black with red trim, and she's worn it ever since." He shrugged. "No one seems to object, or even notice. Sable's going to be a naval officer, like her father was. Her mom says it's the best way to restore the family honor. More to the point, Sable figures it's her best chance at getting far away from Fellstone City."

"The Naval Officers Track—that's interesting," I said. "What do they learn there?"

A great rattling and rumbling came from down the street. Mid said, "We'll have to explain it later—here comes the bus."

— 24 —

OLD CITY

WE HAD STEAM buses in Tumberland, but nothing like this. This one was huge! The biggest of our buses in Tumberland, with their cheerful little steam engines, could hold twenty people, at most. This monster had seats for fifty-two, and standing room for another twenty-five. Its gleaming black boiler stood proudly at the front, belching clouds of foul-smelling black coal smoke into the air. It hissed loudly as it came to a stop, then released a blast of steam around its black rubber tires. The door opened, and a middle-aged Fessal in a sooty conductor's uniform stuck his head out. "All aboard for Old City, the Docks, the Market District, and the Old Bridge" —he hung his head and sighed—"er, that is, The Bridge of Pallador's Glorious Unification."

We showed our papers to the conductor, then climbed up the narrow steps and looked for empty seats. The bus was nearly full. The passengers were of almost all the Ten Peoples, mostly Fessals and Loras, of course, but I spotted a few Kreff, Frae, Fruen, and Sevro among them. As far as I could see, I was the only Lildur, Mid was the only Troh, and Brex was the only Torph. I didn't see any Altaars. In fact, I hadn't seen any Altaars since I arrived

167

in Fellstone City. I wondered if Altaars were scarce here. Some passengers were elderly, some were coughing, and some merely stared blankly out the soot-stained windows. Others wore uniforms, probably on their way to work, and carried meager lunches in brown paper bags that smelled like the ghosts of food. Most were middle-aged, haggard, and tired.

Our group and Brex's Bluebands were the only young people on the bus—most people our age were in school. Cheff, Mid, Buttons, and I found some empty seats near the back. Tocette sat near the front, still chattering loudly at Brex, who seemed to be completely ignoring her. Sable came over and sat down next to me, nudging me aside with her hip. I turned and looked out the window so she couldn't see me blushing again. Sable and I sat quietly, watching the scenery go by and listening to the others chat.

The bus lumbered down the hill and soon passed the dock where Mother and I had arrived. It looked less foreboding, more cheerful, than it had in the rain. Long, wooden piers reached out into the bay. Brightly colored seabirds circled, squabbling and diving for fish in the water. I opened the bus window a crack to smell the creosote-scented salt air, a welcome change from the smoky stench of the Labor Compound.

Men shuffled about, loading and unloading a half-dozen ships, carrying goods to and from the long warehouses, either over their shoulders or on hand trucks. Most of the ships were steamers, probably carrying ore, lumber, and other raw materials from the Northeast. A few boasted sails in addition to their steam engines to help conserve coal. Even a few old wooden sailing ships were taking on freight despite their varying states of disrepair.

Near the end of every pier, a few sad, dilapidated street carts sold bowls of soup and hot drinks to the workers who clustered around square metal grills with iron legs, warming their hands over the charcoal fires. From time to time, someone would buy a potato or a small fish and cook it on one of the grills.

On the inland side of the road, scores of factories sent columns of dark smoke into the air, each surrounded by rows of shabby houses, small shops, and dingy eateries.

As we continued southward, the industrial district and the docks ended abruptly, giving way to blocks and blocks of old ruins. Pilings that had once supported docks stood alone except for the seabirds that built their nests on them. A few rotting wooden hulks lay on their sides in the mud flats, the once-proud ships now mere sun-bleached skeletons painted white with droppings from generations of seabirds. Sea lions and harbor seals slept and barked on the rocks, at times vying for position, like fat slugs sunbathing all in a row.

Among the remains of old buildings on the inland side of the road, thousands of newcomers seeking work in Fellstone City had built a shantytown of canvas tents and scrap lumber. Women cooked over open fires while nearly naked children played in the dirt. A few of the tents had wooden floors, but the rest were simply pitched in the mud. Ragged clothing hung on makeshift clotheslines, darkening with soot before they could dry.

Not all the newcomers lived in tents. Out in the bay, opposite the tent city, there was a thriving floating city. Hundreds of boats, large and small, were anchored or tied to the old pilings. Cheff explained, "Whole families live on those boats—parents, children, grandparents, even dogs and cats. I've heard that some of them live their whole lives without ever setting foot on solid ground. I don't know if it's true, but it could be."

"How do they live?" I asked.

"Some work in Old City, others fish. Pickled eels are a local specialty. I had them when we lived in the Toddary District. They're pretty good. But since I found out where they're caught, I've lost my appetite for them—there's no sewer system in the floating city. Still, pickled eels sell for a good price in the New City Market. Or so I've heard, anyway."

The bus stopped several times to pick up more passengers. Cheff and Mid got up to give a pair of middle-aged women their seats. A couple of stops later, Sable and I did the same.

As we lurched along, we clung desperately to the overhead rails to avoid being flung loose every time the bus hit one of the million or so potholes that dotted the ill-maintained roadway.

Some were worse than others—one was so deep I thought we'd have to finish the trip underground.

Buttons said, "See all those empty bags the women are carrying? We're almost at the market district now. When you see those bags again, they'll all be full to bursting. Just try to get a seat, then!"

When I thought my arms were about to come out of their sockets, the bus pulled into a paved yard and rolled to a stop near several other buses unloading passengers. Our conductor called, "Old City Market District. End of the line. Everybody out!"

"We have to go through the Old City Market on foot," Cheff said, "and cross the Old Bridge."

Sable scowled at him.

"Sorry, Sable, I mean 'The Bridge of Pallador's Glorious Unification.' Anyway, after that, we'll walk a few blocks through the New City Market and catch another bus. Care to walk with us, Sable?"

When we stepped off the bus, we were assaulted by a harsh, discordant mixture of sounds, sights, and smells. Dozens of hawkers with bags of peanuts, pistachios, and sweet treats crowded around the doors of the buses, clamoring for attention. Mid blinked against the bright sunlight, then put on his dark glasses. We followed closely behind Cheff as he pushed through the crowd, with Sable bringing up the rear. All five of us kept up with Cheff for a while, but somewhere along the way, Tocette got sidetracked. When I realized she was gone, I tugged on Cheff's sleeve. "Tocette fell behind. Should we wait for her?"

"No," Cheff said, "don't worry, she knows where we're going. We'll meet up with her in short order, I'm sure." He laughed. "I'll bet she finds us before we leave the Old Market."

"Why's that?"

Mid answered, "On field trips, it's customary for students to buy their escort a little snack treat, or a drink, or whatever. Does Tocette look to you like she misses many treats?"

Buttons said, "*I* don't miss many treats." She held Starry up. "I'll bet you don't miss many treats, either, do you, Starry?" Starry didn't.

The Old City Market District was a big, open area of packed dirt with hundreds of individual booths, tents, and street carts lined up in jagged rows, their awnings and tarps flapping in the morning breeze. Horse-drawn wagons and flatbed steam trucks filled with market goods rumbled up and down between the stalls. This market was far bigger than the one back home in Tumberland and was jammed full of early-morning shoppers haggling for the best deals. The bloody smell of raw meat was overwhelming as we passed several butchers' stalls piled high with freshly carved beef, pork, mutton, and carcasses of plucked birds hanging above the counters. The rows of pig's heads seemed to stare at us, their dead eyes following us as we went by.

When Sable stopped at a shoemaker's booth to examine some boots, I asked Cheff, "Why did Sable scowl at you? About the Old Bridge, I mean."

"She's rather strict about complying with the Emperor's wishes in everything, including using all the new names for places and things. It's partly her military training—showing proper respect for authority and all that—but it's also part of who she is, her family's military tradition. She's a good sort, but you have to be careful what you say around her."

"Why?" I asked. "Would she report you?"

"Never," Cheff said. "She'd never do that. But she has strong feelings about anything that even resembles disloyalty to the Imperium or Emperor Pallador."

Sable caught up with us, and we crowded through a section filled with bins and tables piled high with fruits and vegetables. Another section was devoted entirely to baked goods. Cheff led us to the counter of one stall and pointed to a peculiar-looking cream-filled pastry. "We'll take five of those, please. No, wait—better make that six." He pulled a handful of coins from his pocket and grinned. "Proceeds of the sleepwalking business. Comes in handy sometimes."

Sable pretended not to hear.

Cheff counted out the coins and handed them to the woman behind the counter.

I asked Cheff, "Shouldn't we have gotten the meat-filled ones, so they'd last through lunch?"

"Nope, although ordinarily, that would be a sound plan. But today is no ordinary day—today we dine on Pallador's Bounty."

"Pallador's Bounty? What's that?"

"You'll see when we get there. Meanwhile, enjoy your treat."

While we were eating the oddly delicious concoction, a swirl of lemony cream inside a flaky, buttery crust, we joined a crowd watching a troop of jugglers, fire eaters, musicians, and tumblers. Each new feat brought forth a round of applause, shouting, stomping, and whistling.

A small red flyer monkey dressed in a tiny blue suit collected money from the onlookers. Whenever someone gave him a coin, he carefully put it into a basket set out for that purpose. If it was a large coin, the monkey kissed the onlooker's hand, but if the monkey deemed the contribution too small, his red face glowed redder. Then, instead of putting the coin into the basket, he handed it back with exaggerated disdain, making the crowd laugh. While we were watching, Tocette caught up with us, looking frazzled, a stray strand of greasy hair dangling in her face. Cheff gave her the sixth pastry. "Here you go, Tocette. We saved the best one for you. We sure do appreciate your taking the time to escort us today. Especially our new friend Books here. Isn't that right, Books?"

I nodded.

Tocette smiled a little, then devoured the pastry in three huge bites. "Fanks, Feff," she yelled over the noise of the crowd, spraying flakes of crust over a dozen people. "It's delifious."

"I'm glad you like it," Cheff said, brushing the sticky flakes off his vest. "It'll hold you over until we get to Pallador's Bounty."

"Pallador's Bounty!" Tocette shouted. "Yay! I can hardly wait!"

"What's Pallador's Bounty?" I asked again, but Cheff didn't answer.

We finished our snacks and continued past a row of booths with all kinds of savory soups and stews in enormous cauldrons and grills with sizzling bits of spiced fish and meat. "Someday," Cheff said, "when we're all rich, we'll come back here and have one of everything. You can come, too, Tocette."

She looked at Cheff and smiled again, this time more confidently.

The last section of the market before we got to the bridge was a collection of clothing and shoe shops. I drank in the smell of new leather, then glanced at my own worn shoes. I was growing fast, and I wondered how I'd pay for a new pair. Sweeping floors? 'Sleepwalking,' maybe? I'd have to think of something pretty soon.

— **25** —

THE OLD BRIDGE

O NCE THROUGH THE market, we found ourselves at the east end of the Bridge of Pallador's Glorious Unification. The magnificent stone-arch construction, with seven full arches, spanned the Fel River near its mouth.

At the end of the bridge, a large sign displayed several colorful pictures. Cheff said, "Let's go have a look." We crowded around the sign, except for Tocette, who had wandered a little way down the riverbank, still licking the remnants of her pastry treat from her dirty fingers.

The sign explained that Emperor Pallador built this bridge shortly after the Liberation of Fellstone City, the last battle after The Fall. In a huge ceremony, Pallador personally dedicated the bridge to the Glorious Unification of Old Fellstone City and New Fellstone City, which was already under construction.

When Sable went to round up Tocette, I whispered, "Cheff, this sign isn't right. I read about this bridge in one of my old books, an ancient one. It even had a picture of this exact same bridge."

Cheff whispered back, "Are you sure it was the same bridge, Books? Was it a photograph?"

"No, it was a drawing, but it was exactly the same. *Exactly.*"

"I don't doubt your memory, Books, but…"

"I'm *positive*, Cheff. My book says that some old Torph king called Maghorn built this bridge nearly three hundred years *before* The Fall. That's over four hundred years ago. Look." I pointed to a faint square patch on the stonework that was a few shades lighter than the surrounding stone. "You can barely make out where they filled the holes in each corner of the square. In the picture, there was a plaque there with Maghorn's name on it."

Mid said, "Come to think to of it, there are a lot of signs like this around Fellstone City. Do you suppose they all replace older plaques?"

"They might," I said, then I quoted:

"'Knowledge of the past is a burden and a snare. True Enlightenment looks toward the future.'

"Pallador's blue book, page fifty-seven, verse four."

Cheff grunted. "Maybe this is Pallador's way of 'looking toward the future.' I can't say I'm surprised."

Mid said, "Surely the people who witnessed Pallador's 'dedication' knew the truth?"

"Almost certainly," Cheff said, "but I'll bet they were forbidden to talk about it, and now, more than a hundred years later, who's to know?"

Mid said, "I guess that's one advantage of outliving your enemies—you get to rewrite history to your own specifications."

Sable came back with Tocette. I wondered how much she might have overheard. I waited to see if she was going to give Cheff and Mid another severe look for 'disloyal speech.' She was frowning, and she looked thoughtful.

"Let's get moving," Cheff said, "and be careful what you say. There are snoops everywhere." He glanced pointedly behind us at Tocette, who had stopped to look wistfully at a ruffled pink-and-white dress hanging from a bar at the last of the clothing stalls. "Never forget that she can't be trusted, not even for a moment. '*Never trust a Blueband.*' Cheff's green book, page one, verse one."

Sable went back to have another look at the sign. The rest of us walked over to the edge of the water. Both banks of the river had been finished with brick and stone a long time ago to keep them from eroding. On the bay side of the bridge, a huge dredging machine on a barge lifted enormous buckets of mud from the mouth of the river. Mid explained, "I learned in my engineering studies that an awful lot of sand and silt wash down the river every year. The entire harbor has to be dredged constantly to keep boats from getting stuck like the wrecks we passed earlier. It's an interesting engineering problem. In fact, the problem isn't solved yet. Pallador's dredging crews are falling behind—there's less usable harbor every year. The story around the Labor Compound is that Pallador is most unhappy about the whole situation. I wonder if I could figure out a way to…" He stared out at the dredger, deep in thought.

Meanwhile, Tocette had pulled herself away from her daydreams of fine clothes and caught up with us. She said to Buttons, "Did you see that pretty dress back there? I wish I could have one like it."

"How much is it?" Buttons asked her.

"More than I'll ever be able to make as long as I'm in the Labor Compound. I wish I lived in Old City where I could have a real job. Or even New City." She sighed. "Someday, maybe."

Sable put her hand on Tocette's shoulder. "Bluebands. Uniform. Loyal. Proud." Then she added, "Navy."

Tocette looked puzzled. Cheff explained, "Sable means don't worry. That's why you joined the Bluebands, to show the Emperor that you're loyal. Wear your uniform proudly. Someday you'll get out of that place. That's why she's joining the Navy."

"Oh." Tocette looked at Cheff curiously, then at Sable, who nodded. "I hope so." She scratched her head and asked Cheff, "How did you know what she said?"

Cheff said innocently, "I'm sure I don't know what you mean."

"I mean…" She looked at Sable once more, who was gazing serenely back through her long, black hair. "Why doesn't she say it herself? Can't she talk?"

"She talks quite well," Cheff assured her. "She just doesn't like to."

"Oh." Tocette shook off her bewilderment. "All right, kiddies, it's time to cross the bridge. Line up, and remember, this is serious—no goofing around. Got it? Good." She marched off toward the guardhouse at the far end of the bridge with the rest of us following like ducklings, all in a row.

The guardhouse at the entrance to the bridge was freshly painted and clean, unlike the shabby guard shack at the Labor Compound's main gate. The outdoor area around the guardhouse appeared to be recently constructed: clean, modern, and decorated with an impressive array of electric street lamps. As we waited, we watched the stern Fessal guards in their severely starched uniforms carefully inspecting and stamping the travel papers of those ahead of us. Most of the bridge-crossers wore shabby work clothes.

Mid explained, "They're cooks, janitors, street sweepers, gardeners. It takes a lot of work to keep New City all clean and shiny. Of course, the delicate denizens of Pallador's Paradise don't want them as neighbors, so they have to live in Old City and commute every day."

Cheff added, "You won't see any of the rich, high-and-mighty New City residents waiting in this line, either. They don't travel to Old City often, and when they do, they come in their fancy steam cars." He turned up his nose, closed his eyes, and mocked, "Simply wouldn't do to rub elbows with the riffraff."

Immediately ahead of us in line, a Sevro man in his early thirties began arguing loudly with the guard. "But I come here every day! Don't tell me you don't recognize me! I know you know me! I can't miss another day or I'll lose my job!"

The guard shook his head. "Travel papers are out of date. Go away."

The man cried, "Please! My children will starve!" The guard shoved him away, but he staggered back and clutched at the guard's sleeve. "Please, sir, have mercy!"

The guard casually cracked the man's head with his billy club, and he fell to the cobblestones at our feet, bleeding profusely. Two officers came out of the guardhouse and dragged the wounded man off the bridge back toward the Old Market. The guard returned his billy club to his belt, went back inside the guardhouse, and shouted, "Next!" He looked Tocette up and down and leered. "What can I do for you, Miss?"

Tocette stepped forward and presented our travel papers. She pointed at the blood spot on the cobblestones. "Do you think he'll be okay?"

"Probably not," the guard said proudly. "I thumped him pretty good."

"Oh," Tocette said. "Do you have to do a lot of thumping?"

The guard stood straight and tall. "All in a day's work, miss, all in a day's work." He stamped our papers, looked us over, and waved us through the gray and green crossing gate. "Enjoy your visit, kids!"

As we started across the bridge, Cheff mumbled, "Yeah, right, enjoy our visit. Another great day in Pallador Town."

My palms dripped with sweat, and a heavy, sinking feeling grew in my stomach. We hugged the side of the bridge as steam cars, steam trucks, and horse-drawn wagons rumbled past us. Halfway across, the deep, echoing blast of a steam whistle nearly made us jump out of our skins.

Buttons pointed at a huge battle cruiser approaching New City docks to the northwest. "That's the biggest ship I've ever seen!"

Sable's eyes gleamed as she watched the tugboats nudge the magnificent vessel to her berth. "*Pallador's Pride*," she said softly. "Captain."

Tocette looked at Cheff for clarification.

Cheff explained, "That great big ship over there is the *Pallador's Pride*, the largest ship in Pallador's fleet. She's the first and only of the new Dauntless class of steamships. Sable plans to be her captain one day, or captain of one like her."

"Oh." Tocette laughed out loud. She asked Sable, "You really think you'll be the captain of *that* someday? You're a dreamer!"

Sable turned and studied Tocette until Tocette squirmed, then spoke quietly, "Yes. Dreamer." She turned again and continued across the bridge.

"She scares me," Tocette said, and shivered. "I don't like it when she looks at me like that!"

"Like what?" Mid asked innocently.

"Like she just did. Hungry." Tocette shivered again, then followed Sable across the bridge.

As we walked, I asked Cheff, "Do you think she'll be a ship's captain someday?"

"I'd bet on it. Her father was captain of the first steamship of the Conveyor class, the class before this one. She told me once that he sailed all around Andaran: Tumberland, Cozzbole, Sawtooth when the ice melted, Lone Island, even Faelport once, in the far west. It's her idea of how to get as far away as possible from Fellstone City while still serving the Emperor. Of course, she'll have to start as a junior officer and work her way up to captain, but she's a talented student and a good recommendation from her Naval Studies teacher will go a long way."

— 26 —

THE TERMINAL

At the western end of the bridge, we passed through another marketplace, the New City Market. It had all the features of the Old City Market—meat, vegetables, fruit, clothes, shoes, baked goods—but what a difference! Unlike the Old City Market, this one was inside a huge iron-framed building with a spotless concrete floor. The clean and tidy stalls were arranged in straight, even rows. The vendors weren't shouting. Rather, they waited serenely for their elegantly dressed clientèle—or their servants—to approach.

In the center of the market, a low, decorative iron fence enclosed a food court filled with tables and chairs. Servers in white jackets carried trays of food to groups of patrons, mostly middle-aged women, seated at the tables, sipping beverages, nibbling dainty pastries, and gossiping. A quartet of musicians tediously played highbrow music in the background. The women's gloves muffled their applause after each piece. A few froze in mid-bite and stared down their noses as we passed. Buttons held Starry up and made her wave at them. They declined to return the salutation.

One restaurant specialized in seafood: grilled fish, steamed shellfish, shrimp, crab in enormous cauldrons, and rows of fresh fish on beds of ice, waiting to be cooked to order. Buttons inhaled deeply. "That smells scrumptious!"

"Enjoy it." Cheff stabbed his finger at the menu board. "At those prices, the smell is all you're ever likely to get in this lifetime."

Mid looked a bit green at the sight and smell of the seafood, but quickly rallied. "I think I might just barely make it until we get to the Bounty." Mid dramatically tightened his belt a notch. "Good thing we ate that pastry on the other side."

On the far side of the market, Tocette held open the door of a gleaming steel-and-glass bus terminal. "You kiddies find some chairs. I'm gonna go get our tickets. The bus will be here in a few minutes."

Sable escorted Buttons to some seats overlooking the bay, where they could watch the boats. Cheff and Mid took me with them to the boarding area where we stood and watched the buses arriving and departing. I was intrigued by their destinations, announced by lighted signs above their windshields, exotic names such as 'The Bight,' 'New Moon Beach,' 'Silver Palace,' 'Imperial Docks.' So many places, all new to me. I hoped I'd get to visit them all someday.

Cheff studied each bus carefully. "Keep your eyes on the destinations. Our bus will say 'Fortress Express.' A lot of people from Old City work there, so it has its own route."

Unlike the old, smelly, steam-powered buses in Old City, these buses were new, and there wasn't a single steam pipe or smokestack. Instead of rumbling and rattling, these sleek machines glided up to the loading area on soft rubber tires with only a few gentle creaking noises and a whispering swish of air when they stopped. I asked Mid, "If they don't have steam engines, what makes them go?"

"Electricity. The buses in New City are all electric. If you listen, you can hear the hum of the electric motor. Do you see those long poles on the roof of the bus, the ones with the little wheels on the end? They're called trolley poles. Come on, I'll show you." We walked over to the window to look at the overhead wires in the street. "Outside the terminal, out in the streets, the trolley poles rise and connect with those wires to get power, but inside terminals, the buses use batteries. The batteries get charged up again when the bus re-connects to the wires."

Cheff took a deep breath. "Smell that nice, clean air? Our beloved Emperor doesn't like New City's air dirtied up by steam buses." We filled our lungs with the delicious sea breeze, then Cheff said, "I'm going to go check the bus schedule. I'll be right back."

Mid and I found seats next to Buttons and Sable.

Sable asked me, "Tumberland?"

I tried not to blush this time, but I did anyway. "That's right. My dad was a mechanic for the railroad until… you know. I was wondering about your accent. Do all Kreffs talk like you? I've never heard an accent like yours before. I like it. It's rather pleasant." I knew I was babbling, but I couldn't make myself stop. Sable didn't seem to mind. "We don't have many Kreffs in Tumberland. I'm not sure why. Mostly we have Loras and Troh, and a few Lildurs like me. And Fessals, of course. Always Fessals. But I never heard anyone talk like you, and I'm curious." I felt my face flush again. "If you don't mind me asking, I mean."

Sable smiled kindly. "Farpoint."

"Farpoint? Where's that?"

"South."

"Um, okay. What did your father do, so that you ended up in the Labor Compound?"

She bolted to her feet and loomed over me, a black thundercloud, green eyes blazing into mine. *"Traitor."* She turned and stalked past Cheff who was coming to join us.

Cheff watched her all the way to the other side of the terminal, where she crossed her arms and glared out the window at the street. He plopped down beside me in Sable's seat. "Wow, she's angry! What did you say to her? You didn't mention her father, did you?"

I stared at him, then buried my face in my hands.

"Oh, that's bad." Cheff patted me on the back. "But don't worry, she'll get over it. I guess I should have warned you—asking about fathers isn't something we do much in the Labor Compound. Not everyone feels the same way about their families as you and Mid and I feel about ours."

He glanced over at Sable. She was still glaring out the window at the street. Cheff whispered, "Her father was a naval officer who turned traitor. He betrayed the Emperor and ruined her family's good name. That's why she wants to be a naval officer. She says that she's going to prove to Emperor Pallador that not all her family are traitors."

"I see. That's a heavy load for her to carry." I reflected, then asked, "She *said* that? Sable *said* all that? To you?"

Cheff squirmed in his chair. "Well, yeah, she did, sort of." He hesitated, then added, "She and I went through Basic School together. I've known her as long as I've known Mid, since my first day in the Labor Compound. We don't always see eye-to-eye, as I'm sure you've noticed. She's staunchly loyal to Emperor Pallador and the Imperium, which might seem odd to you considering what happened to her family, but I agree with her reasons. And I respect her as a person, too. She's not like me. I try to be a good person, and I do the best I can. But Sable, she's good all the way to the bone."

"What happened to her family?"

"They're from Farpoint, a tiny little town all the way south along the east coast of Andaran. There's a small naval base there, a lighthouse, and not much else. Sable's family has, or had, a huge estate there. They lived there for generations. When her father was accused of treason, the Emperor confiscated her family's estate and everything in it. Sable and her mother went to the Labor Compound, but the rest of Sable's relatives were put into the street. Sable hopes that, in time, she can earn her family's estate back."

"Are you saying she's a True Believer like Brex?"

"Yes and no. She is a True Believer, but she's the complete opposite of Brex. Brex is motivated by hatred, for herself and all her species. Sable, on the other hand, is all about love. She loves the Emperor and the Imperium because she believes that they're our best hope for a better future. Take her father, for example. She hates what he did, but she loves *him*. That's a tremendous difference." He glanced around. "Like I said before, be careful what you say in front of her. Try not to say anything in front of her that could put her in an awkward position. Understand?"

"Like our little outing last night?"

"Exactly. Your forbidden books, too. Mid and I keep things like that to ourselves. Again, I don't think she'd turn us in, but—"

"—But there's no point in taking chances," I said. "Don't worry, my lips are sealed."

"Okay, kiddies," Tocette called from the ticket counter, "it's time. That's our bus pulling in right now."

Sable Theshta

— 27 —
THE ELECTRIC BUS

OUR BUS HISSED as it rolled to a stop in the boarding area. We piled on board and sank into the clean, plush seats, all together in the back. A dignified, elderly, barrel-chested Frae gentleman wearing a spotless conductor's uniform came down the aisle checking everyone's travel documents. He chatted amiably with the passengers as he moved along. After Tocette handed him our papers, he tipped back his conductor's cap and peered at me over the top of his silver-framed glasses. "First time to the Fortress, sonny?"

"Yes, sir."

"Well, let me tell you, you're in for a real treat! Plenty to see at the Fortress Museum. And you're early enough for Pallador's Bounty!" He handed our papers back to Tocette. "You'll enjoy the Bounty, that's for sure! Hope you're hungry!"

Cheff and Mid sat together on the left side. I sat across the aisle in a seat by myself. Sable and Buttons were right behind me. I was about to ask Cheff again what Pallador's Bounty was, but before I could speak, Tocette flopped down next to me, pinning me against the window. She put her arm around me and brayed, "You're a cute little fellow for a Lildur, aren't you?"

I closed my eyes and endured the shower of foul spittle and food bits. "Um, I don't know, I never thought about it."

"Oh. Well, I just *know* we're gonna be buddies. I always wanted a baby brother." She gave me another squeeze.

"That's, uh, nice, I guess."

Out of the corner of my eye, I caught Cheff grinning at me behind her back. He mouthed silently, "Awww, she likes you! That's so sweeet!"

I scowled fiercely at him, but he laughed. He tapped Tocette on the shoulder. "Hey, Tocette, what do you think they'll have for lunch at Pallador's Bounty today?"

While she chatted with Cheff, I watched the other passengers boarding and getting settled. A few elegantly attired mothers organized their equally elegantly attired children. Two women in teachers' uniforms herded a group of younger children, mostly Fessals and a few Lora onto the bus and into their seats. One lone Altaar boy, easily identified by his sloping forehead and long arms, sat in a seat by himself.

Buttons pointed and said, "Look, Books, it's a class tour. Kids from New City have to go every year the same as us. I like those uniforms! That's what New City kids get to wear to school."

I looked at my own clothes and made a futile attempt to smooth out some of the wrinkles. "Must be nice." I scraped at a stain to no avail, then crossed my arms to hide my patches and hid my shoe with the floppy sole under the seat.

Buttons noticed me trying to tidy up. "Don't worry, they're used to the way Old City kids dress. Did you notice the Altaar boy? You don't see Altaars often, not around here, anyway. He looks lonesome." When the Altaar boy glanced over, she caught his eye, then held Starry up and made her wave a hoof. He hesitated, then tentatively waved back. Buttons smiled, and the boy smiled back, then hung his head and stared at his lap. Buttons cuddled Starry to her cheek and made her wave again, but the boy didn't look up.

"He might be from out of town," Mid said. "I've heard there are quite a few Altaars up north, around Graymoore."

"He seems so sad," Buttons said. "It can't be fun being the only Altaar in his class."

"Graymoore's a long way from here," I said. "How do they afford the trip?"

"It's all part of Pallador's 'Path of Enlightenment' program," Mid explained. "The government awards trips to the capital as prizes for academic achievement."

"Which means kissing up to the right teachers and officials," added Cheff. That earned him a glare from Sable. Cheff said, "Well, it's true. Same as we do."

"Anyway," Mid continued, "each group gets the whole tour—Silver Palace, Iron Fortress, naval yards, the lighthouse—all the best things in Fellstone City."

Cheff said, "They get special patches to sew on their jackets to show off back home. They're supposed to tell everyone how wonderful Emperor Pallador is, and how beautiful he's making the world."

The bus rocked as six tall Bluebands boarded, four boys and two girls, all Fessals. Like everything else in New City, they appeared to be perfect. Their uniforms were crisp and clean, pleats pressed in, black boots and belt buckles recently shined. They wore identical Blueband berets. The tallest of the boys sported a squad-leader's pin in his.

They paused at the top of the step while they scanned the passengers and the empty seats. We kept our heads down, but it didn't work. The leader strode down the aisle and, ignoring Tocette completely, snarled at Cheff, "Move, Labor Compound scum, and take your scuzzy friends with you."

When none of us moved, or even looked up, a female Blueband swatted Buttons with her billy club. "MOVE, BRAT!" She grabbed Buttons by the shoulder to pull her out of the seat.

Cheff clenched his fists.

Tocette, eyes wide, reached over and held my hand.

The leader grabbed Cheff by the front of his vest and jerked him to his feet. "Whaddya gonna do? Hit me?"

Cheff raised his fist and said quietly, "Let her go."

The leader smacked his billy club against his palm and grinned. "Go ahead, hit me. You know you want to." He pointed at his own pimply, peach-fuzz-covered chin. "Right here. Come on, what are you waiting for?"

Mid was tugging on Cheff's belt from behind. "Sit down, Cheff. Please."

Buttons wriggled and yelled, "Ow! Leggo! You're hurting me!"

Cheff drew his fist back.

Mid yanked Cheff down to the seat.

At the same instant, Sable stepped right in front of the Blueband Leader. She said in her command voice, "Stand down."

The Blueband leader was stumped. He couldn't get his brain wrapped around the idea that this tall, slender, beautiful girl was blocking him from carrying out his lawful duties. He frowned as he looked Sable up and down, trying to recognize her uniform, without success.

Sable repeated, "Stand down. *Now.* Unless you prefer a month in the stockade?"

"No…"

"What?" Sable asked.

"No… Miss."

Sable gestured toward the rest of us. "They're with me. Understood?"

"Yes, Miss."

"Dismissed."

He stared at her stupidly, then led his group to the front of the bus.

Cheff went to Buttons, who was rubbing her arm. "Let me see that, Sis." He looked it over. "Nothing broken, but it's going to be bruised. Does it hurt?"

Buttons said to Starry, "Brother Cheff wants to know if it hurts. Shall we let him work that one out for himself?" Starry nodded.

Cheff laughed and gave her a little hug. "Sounds like you're perfectly okay to me." He sat back down heavily. "This is shaping up to be a really fine day. Really fine."

"Well," Mid offered, "one good thing: Brex didn't get on this—"

And there was Brex, standing next to the driver's seat. She had apparently witnessed the entire incident, or most of it, anyway.

Cheff shook his head. "A *really* fine day. Did I mention that it's shaping up to be a *really fine day*? Here's a riddle for you: what do you get when you put Brex and six humiliated Bluebands on a bus to the Iron Fortress?"

Mid said, "Um… a really fine day?"

Cheff and Mid shook hands with great dignity.

"Couldn't have said it better myself, Old Son," Cheff said. "Thanks for saving my bacon."

"Don't mention it, Old Man," Mid said. "Anyway, thank Sable, not me."

"Yes, indeed, Old Son," Cheff said. "Thank you, Sable. Once again, you have saved the day. That's twice so far, and it isn't even lunchtime yet. Not bad, not bad at all."

Sable smiled, showing her Kreff fangs. "Go for three?"

"Yes, well," Cheff said, "let's try not to make it three."

Buttons said, "The ponies say that two is plenty, and they thank you very much."

As soon as Tocette saw Brex, she jumped up eagerly and went to stand in the aisle between Brex on one side, and two of the New City Bluebands on the other side. The New City Bluebands took one look at Tocette's patched and ragged makeshift uniform, then turned and looked out the window.

Brex glared at Tocette, briefly surveyed the other passengers, then nodded curtly to Tocette and moved over to the window seat so Tocette could sit down.

I scooted over to the recently vacated aisle side of my seat, still damp from Tocette's perspiration, and whispered to Cheff, "Tocette sure seems to like Brex, but I don't think the feeling is mutual."

"Brex is Tocette's ideal, the perfect Blueband. She's everything Tocette isn't and never will be. Tocette, on the other hand, represents everything Brex hates about the lower classes of the Imperium: poverty, filth, and ignorance. I guess it's partly why Brex puts up with her—if she can change Tocette into a 'proper' Blueband, that would make a big hit with her superiors."

"Whew!" I said. "That's a tall order. Think she can do it?"

"I hope not," Cheff said. "It would be a shame."

$$-\;28\;-$$

NEW CITY

WHEN EVERYONE WAS seated, the door closed with a hiss, and the bus rolled out of the terminal. I heard the trolley poles on the roof rising to meet the overhead wires. The wires made a strange hollow ringing sound as the bus picked up speed. The rubber tires whispered gently on the smooth pavement. Potholes didn't seem to be a problem in New City.

We soon left the spotless New City Market District behind and passed rows and rows of beautiful homes, but as I watched out the window, I realized who kept it that way. Everywhere I looked, shabbily dressed workers from Old City were sweeping, cleaning, painting, polishing, and gardening. Their sad eyes never left their work as we passed.

We turned north onto West Bay Drive and drove along the western edge of Fellstone Bay. We passed a little marina on our right filled with brightly colored pleasure boats and surrounded by dry docks, marine-supply shops, and other boat-related businesses. Next came the Imperial Docks. Unlike the dark and dingy Old City docks, these were bright and lively, filled with energetic people bustling about.

On our left, across from the marina, large, white mansions with beautiful flower gardens and manicured lawns dotted the side of Mount Kellona, the heart of New City.

Cheff said, "Pallador requires all the houses in New City to be made of white stone or else be painted white, but the people get to pick the trim colors around the windows and doors. I guess it gives them a feeling of individuality."

We passed the Imperial Naval Base, with its modest gray houses, on the harbor side of the road. Cheff said softly, "Military housing is gray instead of white. This whole neighborhood is housing for Naval Officers and their families."

Sable pointed to a small gray house with blue trim. "My house."

Cheff explained, "That house on the corner is where Sable lived when her father was still an officer."

Sable looked back out the window and indicated another house. "Work."

"You work there?" I asked. "How'd you get a job in New City?"

Cheff answered for her, "The officer who lives there was an associate of her father and a fellow Kreff. I guess his wife was nice to Sable when she was little. After Sable's father was arrested, the wife specifically requested Sable from the Labor Compound, supposedly to clean and help her with household chores, go shopping with her, and things like that. She's been kind to Sable."

Sable nodded.

"All those houses back there," I asked, "the ones on Mount Kellona? Who lives in them? Why do *they* get to live in New City? What's so special about them?"

Cheff sneered. "Pallador rewards some people with permits to live there. It keeps people hopeful. You know—if we work hard and do our best, we, too, might be allowed to live there someday. It's what keeps people like Brex and Mr. Rishten striving."

"According to the official version," Mid said, "it's based on a completely unbiased merit system."

Cheff scoffed. In a low voice, he said, "Sure, right, of course it is."

"Don't you believe that?" I asked quietly.

"Nope. For one thing, lots of folks in Old City work twice as hard as these people, and they don't ever get chosen. Think about this: the people who live here are mostly government employees."

"So?" I asked.

"So, you couldn't afford to live here on a regular government salary."

"Meaning?" I asked.

Cheff glanced around to make sure no one was listening. "Meaning that the people who live here are Pallador's cronies and sycophants. People who have earned Imperial favor by one corrupt deed or another."

Sable glared at Cheff, burning right through him with her bright green eyes.

"I apologize, Sable," Cheff said. "I don't mean to sound disloyal. But everyone knows someone who has had to pay one of these people a special 'tip' or 'gift.'"

"You mean a bribe?" I said.

Sable scowled, but before she could speak, Mid pointed out the window to our left. "Here it comes… wait for it… wait for it… there! Capital Parkway! Quick, look up the street!"

As we passed the end of Capital Parkway, we had a perfect view of its tree-lined splendor all the way up to the summit of Mount Kellona, topped by the gleaming Silver Palace. I'd heard of it, but I wasn't prepared for what I saw. It was truly magnificent in the late-morning sun, so bright that it hurt my eyes to look at it. "What's it made of? Surely not real silver?"

"No," Mid said. "It's made from a new alloy of steel that doesn't rust, like the conductor's glasses and the grab rails in the bus. Didn't you notice them? It's mostly made of iron with a few other metals mixed in. It doesn't rust like regular iron. My father had some in his laboratory back in Toof-Toof. He brought a piece home, and we did an experiment. We left it outside for weeks, but it never rusted or even got dull."

Buttons said, "It's so pretty, isn't it, Starry?" Starry thought so.

"It *is* pretty," Cheff said. "It's supposed to symbolize something, I forget what."

I quoted:

> *"'My palace shall reflect the enduring quality of my untarnished empire.'*

"Pallador's green book, page one hundred two, a caption under a photograph of some buildings."

Sable smiled.

A huge steam-powered bus-like vehicle passed us going the opposite direction. It was ornately decorated and had dark tinted windows we couldn't see into. The workers along the road knelt, took off their caps, and kept their heads bowed until the vehicle had passed, as did the passengers on our bus. We watched out the back window and saw that the vehicle turned up Capital Parkway.

"That's a Seph," Mid said, "heading up to the Silver Palace, no doubt."

"Why is the Seph vehicle so big?" I asked. "I mean, I know that Sephs are big, but I didn't think they were *that* big."

"You're right," Mid said, "they're not that big. The thing is, they never travel alone."

"Why not?" I asked.

Cheff answered, "They always travel with Facilitators to do things for them. Lots of Facilitators, and food for the Facilitators, and so on."

"I see," I said. "Where do you suppose the Seph might have been? I have no idea where Sephs go."

"Hard to say," Cheff said. "It might have been coming from the Iron Fortress. Or, I've heard they have a resort of some kind over the mountains on the edge of the Great Desert. But that's in the other direction, to the south."

Mid added, "Sometimes they go hunting out in The Fel."

"The Fel?"

"To the southeast of Old City," Cheff said, "there's a vast marshland, full of yummy critters that the Sephs like to eat, such as marsh pigs and Fel bears. 'Fel' is the old Lora word for 'marsh.' It's how Fellstone got its name, partly."

Buttons said, "The 'stone' part comes from the Great Stone of Fel. You'll be able to see it from the Fortress. There's a lighthouse on it."

We turned off West Bay Drive onto the narrow causeway that led to the Iron Fortress. The overhead wires sang as the trolley poles switched to the power lines that ran along the causeway. The causeway itself was narrow, barely wide enough for the road and the power poles.

A dozen yards (11m) along the causeway, a large yellow sign with red letters hung above the roadway in an elaborate wrought-iron frame. It read:

CAUDON FORTRESS 4 MILES (6.4km)
SECURITY CHECKPOINT AHEAD
NO WEAPONS OR FOOD ALLOWED
ENTRY BY APPOINTMENT ONLY

The elderly conductor came and stood next to us, leaning on the back of my seat. "We're almost there, only a few minutes more." He patted me on the head before I could duck. "Look! You can see it from here." Far ahead, the dark Fortress loomed ominously above a dry, rocky hill. "I'll bet you're pretty excited."

"Yes, sir, I am." I cleared my throat and hoped he didn't see me shiver. "I was wondering, sir, about the causeway. Is it a natural formation, or is it man-made?"

"Good question, sonny. You have a good eye, and a good brain, too, I'm guessing. This causeway is man-made. They don't mention it in the official tour anymore, but I remember from when I was young. It's no secret—the Iron Fortress used to be on an island, but after Emperor Pallador moved to the Silver Palace, they built the causeway and this road out to the Fortress."

"How did they get to the Fortress before there was a road?"

"Boats, of course. The Sephs rarely left the Fortress back in those days, or so I've been told, but when they did, it was by boat. It's usually a big hassle for a Seph to get on a boat—ramps, nets, cranes, you know. Sephs don't like water much to start with. To make it easier, on the bay side of the Fortress, there's a loading dock as high as a ship's deck. Inside the Fortress, there's a slitherway leading right to it."

"Excuse me, sir. I don't know that word."

"Slitherway? It's what we call ramps or passages specifically designed for Sephs. We walk, Sephs slither." He made a slithering motion in the air. "See? It's what you do when you've got no legs."

"Yes, I see. Thank you, sir."

"Anyway, the Sephs could slither on and off the boats with no special equipment. Of course, it's all closed up now. They welded the doors shut after they built the causeway." He turned and pointed behind us. "See that old warehouse on the mainland, right on the waterfront? The one with the big sea doors? That's where they kept the Sephs' road vehicles back then. They'd float their transport boat right inside the warehouse, so the Sephs could slither to their transports. They could make the whole trip, start to finish, without having to be outside for more than a minute or two." He noticed my puzzled look and added, "It's the cold, you see. The Sephs get cold fast. They don't like being outside much except in the summer. Nowadays, of course, they keep their vehicles in a giant garage right inside the rock under the near side of the Fortress. When you get there, you'll see the big garage doors right at the end of that little side road. There are doors exactly like them in the Silver Palace, too."

Several blasts from the air brakes signaled the approach to the front gate. The conductor called out, "Iron Fortress, end of the line! Everybody out!"

— 29 —

THE IRON FORTRESS

THE ORIGINAL ISLAND upon which the Fortress stood was mostly barren rock with only a few scant wisps of vegetation sticking up here and there. The Fortress' front entrance gates were a full fifty feet (15m) wide and stood twenty yards (18m) in front of the Fortress itself. It was actually two gates. Above the gate on the left, a sign read:

IMPERIAL INTELLIGENCE DIVISION
AUTHORIZED PERSONNEL ONLY

It was heavily guarded by armed Fessal soldiers bristling with weapons. A few of the soldiers had huge, fierce-looking dogs on leashes.

The sign over the gate on the right read:

WELCOME TO PALLADOR'S
MUSEUM OF HISTORY, SECURITY, AND LOYALTY
CHECK-IN REQUIRED

As we waited in line for the group of New City school children to sort out their papers, Buttons tried again to catch the little Alta-ar boy's eye, but he never even glanced her way.

Brex pushed past us without a word and presented her papers at the Imperial Intelligence Division's gate. The guard barely looked at her documents, then waved her through, but instead of going in, she came back to where we were standing. She marched up to Cheff and demanded, "Show me your papers!"

Tocette started toward Brex, but Sable put a hand on her arm. "Wait."

Cheff smiled. "Why, thank you, Miss Brex. It's kind of you to make sure our papers are in order. We appreciate it. Still, we wouldn't dream of detaining you unnecessarily. I'm sure you have important business at the IID today."

"That's none of your concern," Brex snapped. "Show me your papers, now!"

"Of course, of course," Cheff soothed. He patted his shirt pockets one at a time, then checked inside them. Next, he did the same with his pants. "Hang on, I'll find them. I'm sure they're in here somewhere." He started with his vest, which had six pockets. "But I assure you, Miss Brex, everything is in order."

"We'll see about that! I find it hard to believe that your new friend here—"

"Birn Tylandine," I volunteered.

"Shut up, filth! I find it hard to believe that Mr. Tylandine has been in the Labor Compound anywhere near long enough to earn sufficient privilege points for a field trip. Now, *where are those papers?*"

Cheff put on his best innocent face and tried to look like he was deep in thought. "I had them a while ago. I'm sure I did. Gimme a minute, lemme think. We showed them at the bridge, then we got on the bus and showed them to the conductor... right. Then we... let's see now..." He began checking his pockets again, starting over with his shirt.

Brex tapped her foot. Her normally pale face grew darker and darker. When I thought she was about to explode, Cheff snapped his fingers. "I've got it! I know where they are. We gave our travel documents to our escort, the Beautiful and Intrepid Tocette! Isn't that right, Tocette?"

At the word 'beautiful,' Tocette stood up a little straighter, smiled, and tried to brush the hair out of her face, but she caught Brex's glare and snapped to attention.

Brex strode up and pushed her flat face into Tocette's. *"Well?"*

"Yes, Miss Brex, it's true. They all gave me their papers, and I checked them through the Old Bridge. Er, I mean, The Bridge of Pallador's Glorious Unification, Miss."

Brex held out her hand for the papers and waited.

Tocette shifted uneasily from one foot to the other and finally asked, "What is it, Miss?"

"The papers, you moron!" Brex screamed, "What's wrong with you? Can't you follow a simple conversation? Give. Me. The. Travel. Papers. *Now!*"

"Yes, Miss. Of course, Miss. Here they are, right here." She scrounged around in her pockets for a long time, then withdrew a wad of wrinkled papers and brushed the lint off of them. Before she could hand them to Brex, Sable walked up behind Tocette, snatched the papers from her hand, moved a few steps away, and looked them over.

I could see the vein in Brex's forehead throbbing as she yelled at Tocette, "Get those papers back, right now!"

Tocette tentatively approached Sable. Sable shook her head slightly, and Tocette subsided.

"Useless girl!" Brex snapped. "Forget it! I'll get them myself!"

Brex whipped around to face Sable. "What do you think you're doing?" she screamed. "Give me those papers!" She lunged to snatch them, but Sable casually raised her hand high above her head.

Brex jumped for the papers a few times, but they were safely out of her reach. When she realized how undignified she must look, she forced herself to stand still. She glared daggers at Sable, grabbed the front of Sable's cadet uniform, and growled through clenched teeth, "Hand over those papers this instant, you long-legged goon, or I'll make your life a living nightmare from now on."

Sable calmly stared at Brex's hands clenching her dress-uniform jacket, and murmured, "Uniform."

"WHAT?" Brex's voice was shrill now. "What are you talking about? What's *wrong* with you?"

"Excuse me, Miss Brex," I offered, "but I think you're wrinkling Sable's uniform."

"Shut up, fool!" Brex yelled, but she let go of Sable.

Slowly and deliberately, never taking her eyes off Brex, Sable lowered the handful of papers down to her eye level and looked them over. Brex started to jump for them again, but Sable transfixed her with a piercing glance. "In order."

Brex's mouth worked, but no sound came out. She seemed incapable of comprehending that Sable wasn't going to hand over the papers. Sable gazed serenely at Brex then suggested quietly, "Dismissed."

Brex aimed her index finger at Sable's head. "You… you… I'll have your shiny black Kreff hide for a rug. Just you wait and see!"

"Excuse me, Miss Brex," Cheff asked, "but doesn't 'dismissed' mean it's time for you to run along? You wouldn't want to be late for your IID appointment."

Brex's jaw dropped. She stared at Cheff.

Mid laughed outright, but Cheff merely said sweetly, "No offense, Miss Brex, but I'd like to remind you that our friend, Sable, here, is on the Naval Officers Track, as you well know. That means that someday, someday soon, she'll be your superior officer. As much fun as it would be to have a nice new rug, you might want to rethink your strategy." He held up his finger knowingly and quipped *"'It's a Good Thing to be in the good graces of your superiors.'* Cheff's red book, page 12, paragraph 2."

"That may be, Karfendek," Brex snarled, "but *you're* not going to be my superior anything, and neither are your other little friends. I know where you live. *All* of you!" She spun on her heel, strode through the IID gate without looking back, and disappeared into the Fortress.

Cheff, Mid, and I breathed a huge sigh of relief. Buttons brought Starry to Sable and made Starry pet Sable's silky skin. "Starry thinks you'd make a beautiful rug."

Sable petted Starry on her muzzle.

"What did you do that for?" Tocette asked Sable. "Why didn't you let her see the papers?"

"Why," Cheff said, "for you, of course, dear Tocette."

"Oh. For me? What do you mean?"

"You know when Brex said that Books hasn't been in the Labor Compound long enough to earn enough privilege points for a field trip?"

Tocette nodded.

"Well, it just so happens that it's true. Captain Utaliak made a little, uh, 'adjustment' on the form so that Books could go with us today."

"Oh. He didn't say anything about it to me," Tocette said.

"Well, of course not. It's for your own protection. If you don't know, you can't be blamed. Besides, no one ever checks travel papers that carefully."

"Oh. Except Brex?"

"Exactly, except Brex. So that's why Sable couldn't let Brex see the papers. If she had seen them, you would have been in a lot of trouble."

"Oh. Even though I didn't know about it?"

"Do you think that Brex would care whether you knew or not?"

"No." Tocette shivered. "You better watch out, Cheff. She didn't like you before. Now she's really going to be watching you." She looked at Cheff with a new light dawning in her eyes. She smiled hesitantly, "That was sweet of you."

"Tocette's right," Mid said. "We didn't exactly make a new friend today."

"That's okay." Cheff shook his head sadly. "I can't even envision a world in which the likes of Brex would ever approve of the likes of me." Then he grinned. "For which I will be eternally thankful!"

We laughed. Even Tocette ventured a hesitant chuckle. Then Mid said, "Still, Cheff, that wasn't exactly rock-smooth. We're going to have to be extra careful around her from now on. I think we may have become her brand-new hobby."

Sable said from behind her hair, "Dangerous."

"Dangerous," Tocette echoed and shivered again.

"We'll have to keep an eye on her, for sure," Cheff said. "C'mon, let's get ourselves inside before Pallador's Bounty is over."

The guard stamped our travel papers without so much as glancing at them or us. He handed Tocette six day-passes, then waved us through the gate. We found ourselves in a little courtyard between the security gate and the Fortress' main doors. A high wall separated our courtyard from the Intelligence Division's side.

Tocette handed us the day-passes, and we pinned them to our jackets. The yellow-tagboard passes had the date, the words 'Good for Day of Issue Only,' and a stylized drawing of Pallador's head in his full ceremonial headdress. Across the bottom, in huge letters, were the words 'Labor Compound.' I asked Cheff, "Why are our passes yellow, and everyone else's are red?"

"Yellow means we're from the Labor Compound." He looked disgusted and pointed at the huge words. "For people who can't read, I suppose."

"Or can't tell from the way we dress, or the soot on our clothes," Mid added. "There's nothing for it—we are what we are."

I savored my first close-up view of the mighty Iron Fortress. It towered much larger than it had appeared from the causeway. Octagonal in shape, six of the eight walls faced the land. The other two walls stood right on the edge of the cliff facing Fellstone

Bay and plummeted straight down to the waterline. I looked, but I couldn't see the sea doors the conductor had mentioned.

Each of the eight walls stretched a hundred feet (30m) wide and sixty feet (18m) tall, or maybe more. Rivets the size of my hand secured their thick, ancient iron plates. Time and weather had worn the black paint away in many places, allowing cancerous rust spots to form and grow.

A large, roofed turret topped each of the eight corners, with another turret at the top of the old keep in the center. Each turret housed one large cannon plus a curious dish-shaped device on its roof. I asked Mid about them, but he only said, "Mind control. You'll find out all about it inside."

Before we climbed the weathered concrete steps to the door, Tocette stopped us. I winced and tried to get out of the spray zone. "Okay, kids, you all know the drill." She put her arm around me and held me close. "That is, except my little buddy Booksie, here." I struggled to get loose, but her grip was like steel.

Cheff laughed behind his hand and said, "'Little Buddy Booksie?' Awww that's so cuuute!"

I scowled and struggled again, but I was stuck.

Tocette continued, "As you know, regulations dictate that I inform you of The Five Rules of Decorum." She fumbled in her hip pocket and found a battered square of cardboard. She blew some bits of leftover sandwich off the card, then held it up to her eyes. "So here they are. *Ehem.*

"The Five Rules of Decorum

"One: Remain with your tour guide at all times.

"Two: Disturbances of any kind will not be tolerated.

"Three: No running.

"Four: No, uh—" she flicked some fresh flecks of spittle off the card, "—loud voices. Yeah. No loud voices.

"Five: Respect areas designated Off Limits. Which you'd better do, 'cause if they catch you, they'll kill you. Or worse!"

She looked at us fiercely. "You kiddies get all that?"

We nodded dutifully.

"All right, then, in we go!"

OPERATION BREAK IRON

— 30 —

PALLADOR'S BOUNTY

INSIDE THE DOOR, a tall Fessal boy in a Blueband uniform handed each of us a bright red ticket that read: "Admit One—Pallador's Bounty Cafeteria." He announced, "Our Beloved Emperor insists that everyone enjoy a delicious meal before entering the museum." Then he smiled and said, "Hi, kids! You're early today—it's still well before noon. You know what that means? No waiting! Go on, hurry in and get in the serving line." He waved us toward a set of double doors, above which a large sign read:

PALLADOR'S BOUNTY CAFETERIA

Enormous murals of Emperor Pallador engaged in various activities festooned the dining hall and its high, vaulted ceiling. The clatter of tableware and the sounds of cheerful talk filled the room. Tantalizing aromas made my mouth water—I hadn't realized how hungry I was. The serving line overflowed with huge, steaming mounds of all sorts of food.

"Well? What do you think?" Cheff asked me. "Did you ever see anything like it?"

"No. Never." I realized I was gaping at the buffet and closed my mouth.

"Enjoy it as much as you can," Cheff said. "We only get two meals like this a year. This one, and the one at the Silver Palace Gallery. It's even fancier than this one."

I recognized two dozen types of fruit, plus a few that were new to me, eight kinds of meat, a variety of cooked vegetables, several kinds of salad, and a wide array of pastries. I chose a rather large pastry that caught my eye, glistening with a sticky frosting and leaking thick, purple juice around its edges.

We left the serving line with our trays piled high. Buttons' tray was piled half again as high as everyone else's. I asked her, "Can you eat all that? Why did you take so much?"

"Because Starry and Moka are growing ponies."

Tocette found a table that could seat all of us. Before I sat down, I whispered, "Tocette, I have to *go*. Which way is the—"

She pointed to an arched doorway on the far side of the room. "Over there. Hurry up—you want to eat this before it gets cold."

I wasn't gone but a few minutes, but by the time I got back, the others had already made a serious dent in their lavish meal. I took a bite of some kind of meat, and it was warm and yummy all the way down.

After a few more bites, I stopped eating to watch the others. Cheff's eyes were much too bright. Mid sported a grin from ear to ear. Buttons had taken Starry from her pack and was dancing her all around the table so that Starry could eat a bite from everyone's tray. Sable hummed softly as she ate.

I wondered what had come over them, then realized that I had a subtle metallic aftertaste in my mouth. I whispered to Mid, "I think there's something in the food."

Mid grinned even wider. "You're right, there is! It's called flavor! Isn't it delicious?" He shoveled another huge spoonful of potatoes and gravy into the grin.

"No, Mid, listen. This is important." I took hold of his elbow to keep him from taking another bite. He struggled, but I held on.

"Mid, you have to stop eating. There's something in the food, I'm sure of it. If you stop eating, you can taste it."

He stopped struggling and smacked his lips a few times. "I think you may be right."

"I know I'm right. You have to stop eating, right now, and you have to get the others to stop too."

Mid sighed and reluctantly set his spoon and fork down on the tray. He tapped Cheff on the shoulder. "I have to talk to you right now. It's urgent."

Cheff's eyes narrowed as he stabbed at another bite of meat. "How urgent, exactly?"

"'Code Red' urgent, that's how."

Cheff dropped his fork. "Meet me in the restroom *now*." He sprang from his seat and strode rapidly across the hall.

Mid stood up and said casually to Tocette, "I gotta go, too. Back in a minute." He followed Cheff toward the restrooms.

Tocette waited until Cheff and Mid were out of sight. "They shoulda thought of that before they left home," she said as she stole a few chunks of meat from Cheff's tray and a particularly juicy piece of fruit from Mid's. "I don't mind—all the more for me. Right, Booksie? Booksie my buddy?" She speared another sizeable chunk of meat from Cheff's tray. "Finders losers, weepers keepers, right Budsie Booksie?" She frowned, then mumbled, "Buddy Booksie, Booksie Buddy, Budsie Books… hmm…" She resumed selecting juicy tidbits from the others' trays.

Cheff waved at me from behind the restroom door across the hall, mouthed, "Sable, Buttons," and made beckoning motions.

I said, "Sable, you need to take Buttons to the restroom right now."

Buttons protested, "But I don't have to—"

I held my finger to my lips and glanced over at Tocette, but she was much too busy stuffing her mouth to notice anything. "Yes, you do," I insisted, and nodded in Cheff's direction.

Buttons put down her fork and spoon and stood up. "That's right, Sable. I have to *go*. Won't you take me? I don't want to go by myself. *Please?*"

Sable looked at Buttons, then at me again, then stood up. In her normal tone of voice, she said, "Restroom." She took Buttons by the hand and crossed the room.

Tocette smacked me on the shoulder so hard I thought I might lose a tooth. "I guess it's just you and me, Budsie Booksie. We'll be lunch budsies," she blared, splattering most of the table with bits of half-chewed food. She reached over and helped herself to half of Sable's salad and all of my glistening pastry.

Cheff and Mid returned, followed by Sable and Buttons. They all took their seats. Buttons held her stomach and groaned. "I don't feel too well. I threw up in the restroom."

Mid said, "Maybe it was those pastries we bought at the market."

Cheff said, "I guess that bakery stall wasn't as clean as I thought it was."

Tocette said around a mouthful of rice pudding, "They didn't bother me none! I feel fine! I thought it was *deee*-licious! Well, if you all are sick, I guess you're not gonna be wanting the rest of your Pallador's Bounty, now, are you?" One by one, she picked up each of our trays and scraped our food onto her tray. "There, now. No need for you to worry. The Facilitators will think you ate your food all up!" She dug into the stack of food like a steam shovel filling a dump truck.

In mere moments, her tray was as clean as the rest of ours. She let out a ripping belch, then pounded her chest with her fist. She blinked rapidly in a futile attempt to focus her eyes. "All done! Let's see us some museum-um-um!" As she stood up, she nearly lost her balance and clutched at me to steady herself. "Whoa! I'm a little dit bizzy, I mean, a little bit dizzy. I guess I ate too fast." She thumped her chest and belched again. "Well, it'll settle. C'mon, what're you waiting for? We got a museum to see to see-um. We're gonna see-um the big museum!" She giggled. "Leave your trays. Someone'll be around to collect 'em." She steadied herself one last time with one hand on the table then wove her way to the cafeteria exit and into the Main Hall of the museum, still singing "I'm gonna see-um the big museum" over and over.

Tocette Crindel

— 31 —

TOCETTE VS. THE BOUNTY

CHEFF AND SABLE dashed after her, and the rest of us followed. Tocette stood in the center of the main hall of the museum, arms raised, a look of ecstasy on her upturned face. "It's so beautiful, so magnificent!" she moaned. She clasped her hands to her breast. "Oh, my beloved Emperor Pallador, you truly are magnificent, and your deeds are truly great!" She wiped tears from her bleary eyes with her food-stained sleeve, then skipped across the floor to a bust of Pallador which had been carved so that Pallador's immense head was low enough for children to touch his reptilian face. Tocette draped herself around the massive head and tenderly stroked the cold marble. "Isn't he the dreeeamiest? Our dear, beloved Emperor." She pulled away and began spinning with her arms outstretched.

We watched, helpless, as she crashed into a glass display case containing a figurine depicting Pallador's loving mother coiled tenderly around her infant son. Tocette swayed as she peered at the glass case with one eye. "No cracks," she announced and resumed spinning.

Cheff and Sable each took one of her arms and forced them back down to her sides. Cheff hissed, "Easy, Tocette! Those two

213

guards by the door are looking this way. You'll land us all in the other side of this place."

Tocette whispered loudly, "Oh. Riiight. We don' wanna land us all there, do we? The IID isn't very nice to their guests." She giggled.

Cheff admonished, "Try to keep your voice down. There you are, easy does it. Shall we show our new friend Books around the museum?"

"Books? You mean Booksie? Is my little Booksie Budsie here?" She craned her head around. I waved. "There's my little Booksie! How ya doin', li'l buddy?" She staggered but recovered. "Sure, I'll show my li'l buddy around." She flopped her arm onto my shoulder. "C'mon, my dear li'l friend."

Cheff grinned at me behind her back, then patted Tocette on the shoulder. "That's the girl! But remember, we must be very, very quiet."

"Oh. Riiight!" She put her finger to her lips. "We're gonna be very, very quiet. Are you ready, li'l buddy? Let's go see Pallador's date greeds." She stopped, frowned, and scratched her head. "Date greeds, drate geeds, weeds, seeds, deeds. Yeah, that's it, great deeds." She bent down and whispered loudly right into my face, "Me and you are gonna see Pallador's date greeds. Let's go!"

With Cheff and Sable supporting Tocette we formed a semblance of a group of students quietly enjoying the exhibits: Emperor Pallador at the fall of the Sixth Kingdom, leading his troops into the burning ruins of Worldheart. Pallador leading his troops into Old Fellstone City. Pallador landing on Fortress Island. Pallador at the dedication of the Silver Palace. Pallador posing by a model of the Bridge of Pallador's Glorious Unification, along with a photograph of the opening ceremony of the Bridge.

I tugged at Cheff's sleeve. "That's what I was trying to tell you. Look—in the picture, you can see that bridge looks exactly like it does now: old. Pallador couldn't have built—"

"Not now, Books. I've got my hands full with our fearless leader." Tocette sagged and leaned on him. "Oof! She's a big girl. Come on, Tocette, let's move on, shall we?"

But Tocette pulled free and began to spin across the floor again, singing loudly, "Our dear Pallador… leads the Cult of Callor… that's what he's for… forever more…"

"Shhh, Tocette. We're being quiet, remember?"

"Oh." She whispered loudly, "Sorry, Cheff, I forgot." She held her hand over her mouth and mumbled through her fingers, "Very, *very* quiet!"

Tocette leaned on the glass display case with both hands, squinting. "I can't see 'em, Cheff," she lamented. "I think there's something wrong with my eyes." She wailed, "Oh, no, I'm going bliiind!"

Cheff laughed and held his hand in front of her face. "Can you see this?"

"Of course I can see that. It's your hand, Cheff."

Buttons giggled.

"Then you're not blind, are you?"

"Oh. Well, I guess not, but—"

"Good! Because you don't want to miss this next part."

"Oh. I don't?"

"No," I said. "It's a film."

"Oh. I like films."

Mid guided her to a dark little kiosk with several rows of wooden chairs facing a large viewing screen. We sat for a while and watched an old, scratchy, black-and-white film showing parades in honor of the Beloved Emperor. Tocette became more agitated by the minute. Cheff and Sable had a pretty hard time keeping her calm. Buttons tried to get Tocette to pet the ponies, to no avail. Finally, we had to go back into the main hall. From there we steered Tocette into a small side room out of sight of the guards.

We coaxed Tocette into sitting on a small wooden bench, but it didn't last. Tocette promptly leaped to her feet, almost fell over Buttons, then ran back to the main hall where she stood stock still in front of the huge bust of Pallador and raised her arms slowly along her sides until her hands were slightly above her shoulders.

Her face was flushed, and her eyes were glazed over. She began spinning slowly counterclockwise and chanting, quietly at first, but louder with each revolution, "Beloved Pallador, great and powerful, all good things come from you. Beloved Pallador, great and powerful, all good things come from you. Beloved Pallador, great and—"

Cheff grabbed her shoulder. "Tocette, stop it!" She shook him off and chanted even louder, "BELOVED PALLADOR, GREAT AND POWERFUL, ALL GOOD—"

Cheff lunged to grab her again, but she twisted away. "Sable! Help me! I'll take her right side, you take her left! Buttons, don't try to help—she's too big. Come on, Sable, we've got to get her out of here before the guards get interested!"

But it was too late—the pair of guards by the cafeteria door who had been watching us earlier were coming our way. One of them signaled to another pair of guards near the gift shop. I pointed them out to Cheff. Cheff and Sable crept up behind Tocette and each grabbed an upraised elbow, but the maneuver backfired. Tocette screamed, "LET ME GO!" and waved her arms wildly. Cheff told me later that it was like trying to hold on to a windmill.

Sable and Cheff lost their hold. Sable dropped to her knees, but Cheff went careening into one of the display cabinets, sending glass shards in all directions. In seconds, the four uniformed guards surrounded Cheff and Sable. Four more guards appeared, took hold of Tocette, and stood her upright. The sergeant of the guards helped Cheff to his feet, brushing shattered glass from his clothing. "Can you tell me what's going on here?"

"Yes, sir. Our friend isn't feeling too well. I think she ate a little too much Bounty."

The sergeant scowled. "Surely you're not implying that there's something wrong with Pallador's Bounty?"

"No, sir, of course not. It's just that—"

"Uh-oh," Tocette said, then her eyes glazed. "I don't feel so good." She doubled over and deposited the contents of her stomach at the guards' feet. She fell to her hands and knees, retching and drooling.

The guards covered their faces with their sleeves, gagged, and turned away. The sergeant coolly regarded the steaming mass on the floor and cocked an eyebrow. "I understand what you meant now," he said to Cheff. "I wouldn't have believed one person's stomach could hold that much Bounty if I hadn't seen it myself." He turned to one of his subordinates. "Go get the nurse and a stretcher." He ordered another, "You go get that Fessal mop-boy. Have him bring a bucket and a mop. As for you kids, you need to leave immediately."

Cheff stepped forward. "Please, sir, is there any way we might be able to stay? It's our friend Books' first time. He came from Tumberland recently and this is his first field trip, on his teacher's recommendation. The rest of us are feeling fine."

Mid added, "It took us three hours to get here, sir, on the bus. We'd hate to have come all this way, only to go home early."

"Sorry, kids, but I can't turn you loose without your escort. That's absolutely not permitted. Get your gear together. We'll see that the big girl gets home."

Sable stepped forward and snapped a smart military salute. "I'll take full responsibility for the group, sir."

"You know these kids?"

"Yes, sir. Same school. Labor Compound."

"I see." The guard examined her uniform. "Naval Officers Track?"

"Yes, sir."

"Unusual uniform colors."

"Yes, sir."

"Special program?"

"Yes, sir."

The sergeant looked thoughtful, but didn't ask any further questions.

"All right, then. I'm putting you in charge of the rest of these kids, from now until closing time. But if there's any further incident..."

"Yes, sir. Thank you, sir."

The nurse arrived with the stretcher and the guards loaded Tocette onto it. The nurse examined Tocette, then announced, "She'll be fine. She's suffering from a case of Bounty overload. Sergeant, could you please have your men carry her to the infirmary? She'll have to sleep it off, but I'm sure she'll be all right by closing time."

"Thank you, nurse. Okay, men, two of you get this girl to the infirmary. *Phew!* She's going to need some cleaning up." He turned to Sable. "Carry on, cadet. But remember what I told you: no more trouble." He led the remaining guards out of the room.

— 32 —

SOMETHING IN THE FOOD

CHEFF GATHERED US together and led us away from the smelly pool of vomit. "It seems that Books was right—there *was* something in the food."

"I don't get it, Cheff," Buttons said. "Why would Pallador *want* people to act crazy?"

"Maybe he doesn't," Mid said. "Maybe it's supposed to do exactly what it did for Tocette—make people happy. Not *that* happy, only happy enough to get a warm feeling about Pallador and his mighty accomplishments as they view the exhibits."

Sable said, "No need."

Cheff asked her, "You think his accomplishments are great enough to generate loyalty in people without drugs? You might be right, but what if Pallador—"

"—or someone who *works* for Pallador—" Mid interjected.

"—doesn't want to take any chances. After all, people can be unpredictable, right? Maybe someone decided to put enough of something in the food so that visitors to the museum are guaranteed a boost in loyalty and affection for our Beloved Emperor, to make sure they think the right thoughts and feel the right feelings."

I said softly, "Like making sure they read only the right books."

Cheff looked thoughtful. "Yeah, like that. It's not right. People should be free to make up their own minds."

"Nothing in the food," Sable insisted. "People would notice."

"I don't think we're supposed to notice," Mid said. "I think it doesn't affect a person too much if they only eat one meal."

"Books noticed," Cheff said.

"Books just got here. Maybe he's not used to it." Mid looked pensive. "You know, Cheff, it does make a certain kind of sense. What if there is something in the food here, and we don't notice it because we're used to it?"

"But Tocette was all wound up," Cheff said. "I've never seen anyone else act like that!"

"She reminded me of someone," I said, "but I can't think who. Anyway, Tocette had a lot more than one meal. She ate, let's see"—I counted on my fingers—"all of mine, most of Buttons', and half of Cheff's, Mid's, and Sable's. That's almost five entire portions, maybe closer to six."

"No wonder she went goofy," Mid said.

"Of course!" Cheff said. "Even as large as she is, six times the regular dose is bound to have more than the usual effect, right?"

"Six times more, I'd expect," Mid said, and laughed. "She was more than a little bit content. She was overwhelmed with feelings of love and admiration for Emperor Pallador. That's not normal for Tocette."

Sable said, "First time."

"You're right," Mid said. "I think that's the first time I ever saw Tocette enthusiastic about anything."

"How about the rest of us?" Cheff asked. "We didn't have a chance to eat much. Do we feel any different?"

"Different from what?" asked Buttons.

"From how we felt on the bus," Mid said, "or even different from how we felt when we came here last year."

Cheff said, "I think maybe I do. I've been here once a year for the last six years. All the other times, I was completely absorbed in the exhibits, and I felt proud of Pallador's great accomplishments."

Sable furrowed her brow. "Not today. Sick."

"Sick?" Cheff asked. "Sick how?"

She pointed at a gruesome panorama depicting one of Pallador's many 'Liberation Campaigns'—life-size paintings of unarmed people, mostly Torphs, being slaughtered by hordes of Fessal soldiers.

"Me, too." Buttons gulped. "All that blood is making my tummy feel funny. All those poor Torphs…" She turned away.

Sable took her by the hand and the two girls went to look at a cheerful display depicting large, hairy-footed Grand Graymoore horses pulling old-growth fir trees out of the snowy woods. Buttons held Starry and Moka up so they had a good view of the display.

"Here's something else I feel quite different about," Mid said. "You know that I've always been interested in, even excited about, Pallador's technological advances. But today I'm wondering if he's trying to catch up to something."

I broke in, "That's what I've been trying to tell you, Cheff! All the 'glorious achievements' in these displays—I've read about them before. *All* of them and a good many more."

"Wait," Cheff said. He signaled the girls. "Sable and Buttons should hear this." When they joined us, he said, "I don't want you to think we're being disloyal, Sable, but Books has some information from Tumberland that conflicts with some of the information in the museum exhibits. Go ahead, Books."

"Right." I lowered my voice. "It's just that, in certain books I read, all the inventions that this museum says Pallador invented had already been invented *before* The Fall. Listen: this is from an old history book called *History of the Sixth Kingdom — The Reign of Queen Brindshale.* I squeezed my eyes shut and recited:

"'One of her advisors persuaded the Queen to fund the development of steam power. A blacksmith from Stoopone, one Smid Fenspeen of the Lildur People, produced the first working steam engine, thus making possible steam-powered cars, trains, ships, and factories, for the benefit of us all.'

"—Page 88. See? Steam cars, trains, ships, all of it, from way before The Fall."

"How?" Sable asked.

"I remember books," I said. "I see them once, and a picture of them stays in my mind, so I can read them again anytime."

"Forbidden books," Sable said.

I squirmed inside, but I summoned my courage. "Yes. My dad's. I—I've read quite a few. And I remember them in perfect detail."

Sable regarded me with a new interest, then frowned.

"I'm sorry, Sable," Cheff said gently, "I know how strong your feelings of loyalty are, and how important restoring your family's honor is to you, but if what Books says is true, if all that stuff existed before The Fall…" He made a sweeping gesture around the exhibit hall. "This is all lies."

"If," Sable said. "Proof."

"Yes," Mid echoed. "We need more proof than Books' memory. We need something concrete, tangible. No offense, Books."

"None taken," I said. "I agree completely."

"Let me ask you this, Sable," Cheff said. "What if we can *prove* that what Books says is true? Would you still be loyal to Pallador and the Imperium?"

Sable was silent for a long while, then whispered, "True loyalty must be based on truth."

Cheff said gently, "Thank you for that. I can only guess how hard this must be for you. I know my skeptical cynicism clashes with your loyalty, sometimes, but…"

Sable put her hand on Cheff's shoulder. "Truth first, then loyalty."

Mid nodded thoughtfully. "Well said, Sable. I agree."

"Me, too," I said.

"Agreed." Cheff took a deep breath. "Buttons?"

"Of course. Who wants to be loyal to a lie? Starry doesn't, do you Starry?" Starry didn't. "Neither does Moka."

Cheff smiled. "Fair enough. That makes two things we have to investigate: historical inaccuracies and what's in the food. I think we owe it to ourselves to discover the truth."

A grating, grinding, squealing sound filled the room. Buttons pointed. "Look! The wall!"

Pallador in Full Ceremonial Dress

— 33 —

LERY

A CRACK OF LIGHT appeared right in the middle of an enormous mural in which Emperor Pallador blessed the fields of some poor farmer. Pallador's scaly belly eerily split down the middle and opened wide until it grew into a doorway. A tall, thin, young Fessal in a green army janitor's uniform pushed a mop and a wheeled bucket into the museum hall. An oversized pipe wrench hung in a holster on his belt and he held a wastebasket under one arm. Without even glancing at us, he rolled the bucket toward the giant pool of vomit. His right foot twisted inward at an odd angle, making him limp. The handle of the pipe wrench bounced against his leg.

Cheff beckoned, and we followed a little way behind him. We pretended to be interested in a display case entitled *How Pallador Invented Steam Power*.

The tall Fessal swept up the broken glass, then took a dustpan and began scooping the malodorous mess into the empty wastebasket.

Cheff grimaced. "I don't envy him that job."

Sable said, "His place."

"I know we all have our place in Pallador's Imperium," Cheff said. "But I'm sure glad I don't have *his* place. I don't mean any disrespect, but it doesn't seem like a pleasant job."

Mid asked, "You don't want to be the Duke of Puke?"

I cracked up. "Or the Earl of Hurl?"

Sable murmured, "Comet."

Cheff laughed. "A comet of vomit!"

Buttons giggled. "You'd have to clean up all kinds of stuff, like Stew Spew and Mush Gush."

Mid added, "You'd have to follow everyone who might excrete meat or exude food."

I laughed so hard that I could barely see straight until I caught a glimpse of the cleanup guy. He glanced over at the sound of our laughter, then resumed his unpleasant task. I said, "Shhh, guys, quiet down. I think he thinks we're laughing at *him*."

Sable said, "We are."

"Well, yes, we are," Cheff said, "sort of, but not in a mean way. I hope we didn't hurt his feelings. Do you suppose whatever was in that food is making us act silly?"

"Maybe." Buttons pinched her nose shut against the freshly agitated vomit smell. "He's being pretty quick about it, like he's had a lot of practice. Do you think people throw up here a lot?"

"That's a good question," Mid said. "If there is something in the food, I'll bet that guy has a lot of cleaning up to do."

Buttons said, "If you want to know if people vomit a lot, why don't you go over and ask him?"

Sable said, "Smart."

"Good plan, Buttons!" Cheff said. "Books, you and Buttons and Sable wait here, okay? We don't want to scare him off. Come on, Mid, let's go start our investigation."

Cheff and Mid approached the cleanup man, but he didn't raise his eyes, only kept mopping, head down. Cheff cleared his throat and said, "Excuse me, but I was wondering what that big pipe wrench is for?"

The man didn't answer. He turned his back toward Cheff and continued mopping.

Mid whispered to Cheff, "I think maybe he's nervous. Let me try. I'm a lot less intimidating than you."

Cheff raised his eyebrows but gestured Mid forward.

Mid circled around in front of the young man and said, "Say, you're pretty good at that, aren't you?"

The Fessal didn't reply, but he smiled a little.

"I couldn't help admiring your system," Mid continued. "First, scoop up most of the mess into the wastebasket. Then, when you've gotten nearly all of it, mop up the rest. Smart! Keeps the mop water from getting too nasty."

The cleanup man glanced up at Mid tentatively. "No… nobody ever called me smart… before."

Mid stuck out his hand. "I'm Mid."

The man flinched. He stared at Mid's outstretched hand.

Mid prompted, "And you are…?"

"I'm… I'm… Lery."

Mid reached out, took Lery's hand, and shook it. "Pleased to meet you, Lery. He's Cheff."

Cheff waved. "Hi, Lery."

Lery frowned, took his hand back, removed his cap, wiped the sweat off his forehead with his sleeve, then leaned on his mop handle. "I… I didn't do it that way… at first. They just… just… gave me this mop… and this bucket… and told me to… to mop it up. It… it didn't work too well. It smeared it… all around and… and then everybody got mad at… at me."

He reflected. "Nope… didn't work so well… at all. So I got to… to thinking… and then it… came to me. That's not… not what a mop is… for. Picking up stuff… I mean. Mops are for *wiping* up stuff… not *picking* up stuff. Shovels and… and things like… like that are for… for picking up stuff.

"So I asked them for… for a shovel… but they… they wouldn't give me one. Then I looked… around for a while… and I asked myself… what do I have that's… that's like a shovel? After… after a while I got it. I had been… been looking at it the… the whole time… right there next… next to the broom… my dustpan. It works like a… a little shovel. And that's how I… figured it out. They didn't say anything… though. They just… just looked at me… shook their heads and… and went away."

He wiped the sweat off his face with his handkerchief, then took a deep breath. "Sorry… I'm not… not used to talking so… so much at one… time."

"You're doing fine!" Cheff clapped Lery on the shoulder, which made Lery flinch again and duck his head.

"Well, that sounds pretty smart to me," Mid said. "The right tools for the right job. You gotta use the right tools for the right job. Isn't that right, Cheff?"

"Absolutely right, Old Man."

Lery grinned and put his cap back on. "The… the right tools for… for the right job." His grin spread slowly until it reached from ear to ear. "Yeah… Smart."

"Yup," Cheff said, "I guess you gotta be pretty smart with people puking up here all the time."

"You… you got that right." Lery rinsed his mop, squeezed it in the wringer, and resumed mopping. "People sure do puke a… a lot around here."

"Why do you suppose that is?" Mid asked.

Lery stopped mopping and made sure no one else was close enough to hear, then bent down and whispered, "It's the… the jexan."

"Jexan?" Mid asked. "What's jexan?"

"It's what they… they put in… the food."

Cheff and Mid exchanged a look.

"They put jexan in the food?" Mid asked. "What for?"

"To… to make people… happy."

"Happy?"

"Like your big… big girlfriend… happy. But if… if they eat too much… they puke."

"She sure did, didn't she?" Mid said.

"And I clean it… up." Lery smiled. "With… with the right tools… for the right… job." He frowned. "I shouldn't have… said anything about the… the jexan. They don't know that… that I know. I… I'm not… supposed to know. *Nobody's* supposed to… know." He looked anxiously at Cheff, then at Mid. "You won't… won't say anything… will you? They… they'd get mad if… if they found out I… I told someone."

"Of course we won't say anything," Cheff said. "Friends don't tell on friends, not ever. Your secret is safe with us!"

"Friends?" Lery smiled again, slowly. "I… I never had any… any friends before."

"Well, you do now," Mid said. "The two of us, for a start, and three more over there who are waiting to meet you."

Lery glanced shyly in our direction.

We smiled and waved.

Mid continued, "Say, Lery, if you're not supposed to know about the jexan, how *did* you find out about it?"

Lery said, "They… they make me carry… cases of it… up from the boats."

"The boats?" Mid asked.

"Boats. Jexan only… only comes on boats. Never by truck… only boats. And only… at night. They make me carry it… upstairs from the… the sea doors. They… they think I'm too… too stupid to understand what it is… so they talk in front of me… sometimes. I… I don't ever say anything so they… they keep on thinking I'm… I'm stupid. It's… it's better that way… they mostly leave the… the 'dumb guy' alone."

"Good plan," Cheff said warmly. "Always keep 'em guessing. Say, Lery, do you suppose we could get a look at those sea doors where they bring in the jexan? The conductor on the bus we came in said those doors have been sealed for decades. If they're sealed, how do you get the jexan inside?"

"The big… the big sea doors… I've never seen them open. But the jexan… comes in through the… the little sea doors."

"That bus conductor didn't say anything about little doors," Cheff said. "You see, Lery, I'm studying architecture as part of my Civilian Leadership class. It would help me with my schoolwork to get a look at those doors. Is there any chance you could arrange that?"

"Excuse us a minute, Lery," Mid said, taking Cheff aside. "What are you doing? That guy's a *Fessal*. Getting information is one thing, but are you going to put our *lives* into the hands of a Fessal?"

"I don't think we have much choice. Right now, he's all we've got." He grinned. "Think of it as your big chance to find out if all Fessals are rotten."

"I don't know, Cheff," Mid began, but Cheff was already talking to Lery again.

Lery hung his head sadly and stabbed his thumb toward the wall he came out of. "I… I don't know… no one's allowed to… to go in there. I'd like to help my… my new friends… but I… I don't want to… to get into trouble. Sometimes… sometimes they… they hurt me." He pointed at his twisted foot. "Sometimes… they hurt me bad."

"I don't think there'll be any trouble," Cheff said. "That sergeant, the one who helped our friend, he said it was okay for us to look around."

"He didn't say you could… could look around in… in *there*." He finished mopping and stuck the mop into the bucket.

"That's true," Cheff said, "but he didn't say we couldn't, either. And it sure would help me with my schoolwork."

"Cheff," Mid said, "maybe this isn't such a great idea."

"We wouldn't have to stay long," Cheff said, "just a quick look. No one will ever know."

"Friends don't… tell on friends." Lery thought it over. "Okay… New Friends. But we… we gotta go quick. Getting caught… would be… bad."

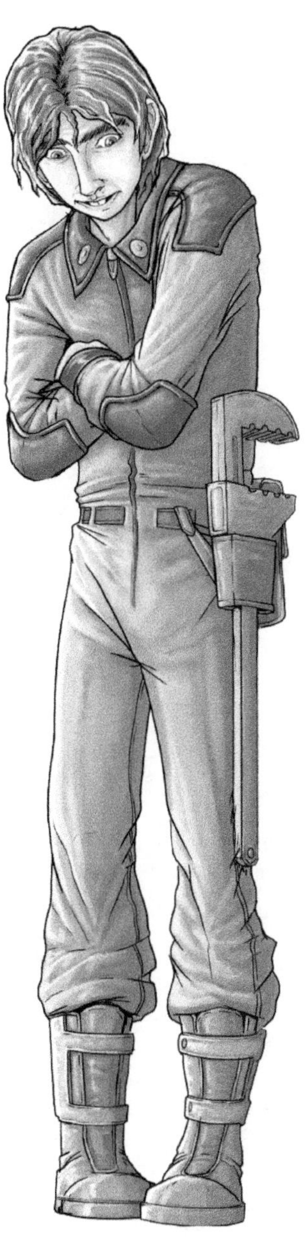

Lery

Operation Break Iron

SPECIAL DELIVERY

SABLE HAD BEEN watching Cheff and Mid carefully. When they started to follow Lery through the hidden door, she hurried over and grabbed Cheff by the sleeve of his jacket. Buttons and I followed her. Sable hissed, "What?"

"We're gonna have a quick look around," Cheff said.

Sable stared at him.

"It's like this"—Cheff's voice was barely audible—"our new friend, Lery, here, just confirmed that they do, indeed, put something in the food, something called jexan. We're going to see what else we can learn. Truth first, then loyalty, right?"

Buttons tugged on Sable's sleeve. "Whatever we're doing, we'd better do it quick. That sergeant came back into the museum hall and he's looking all around, probably for us."

Sable glanced over Buttons' shoulder. The guard hadn't spotted us yet. Sable grabbed Buttons and me by the arms and shoved all of us through the hidden door.

Lery softly closed the door behind us.

As our eyes adjusted to the dim light, we found ourselves in a long, dark corridor with walls made from rusty iron plates. The corridor faded into darkness in both directions. I sniffed, then wrinkled my nose at a peculiar smell, one that I didn't recognize.

"Sephs," Lery said. "Sephs… smell bad. It's… worse… downstairs."

Mid grumbled, "Great, just great. 'A quick look,' he says, and now we're criminals. What next? If that sergeant sees us coming back out of this door, we're all dead. Or worse."

Lery pushed the mop bucket down the dark hallway. "The… the sergeant won't… see you. There's… another door… farther on. Nobody ever… comes this way… except… except me… mostly."

"Mostly!" Mid whispered. "What do you mean, mostly?"

"Quiet," Cheff said. "We're in it now. Go easy."

Mid subsided, but he didn't look happy.

We followed Lery, doing our best to be silent and invisible. I heard footsteps nearby, coming closer.

"The… guard…" Lery said. "Faster."

We went faster.

Lery stopped abruptly in front of a large gray metal door. He unclipped an enormous bunch of keys from his belt, found the right one, and opened the door. "All come… inside. Close… close the door. All safe… inside."

I was the last to enter the dark room. I pulled the door closed. We waited in the dark, motionless, as the footsteps grew louder, passed our door, and continued down the corridor.

We gave a collective sigh of relief. Lery switched on the lone, bare bulb hanging from the ceiling, revealing that we were in a combination janitor's closet and storeroom. In the dim light, I made out a floor sink, various mops and brooms hanging from the walls, and several shelves filled with cleaning products. A rumpled bed stood in one of the rear corners. Next to the bed was a single chair, and a table with a tin box on it. A nearby shelf held a few items of clothing, folded neatly.

"Lery," Cheff asked, "do you, um, *live* in this room?"

Lery was emptying the reeking wastebasket into the drain of the large, square floor sink. "Yes. This... this is my room. I... live here." He washed the bucket out and set it aside.

Cheff asked, "Where did you live before?"

"I... I don't like to... to think about... about before." Lery shuddered. "Before wasn't... wasn't..."

"It's okay," Cheff said. "You don't have to talk about before."

Lery concentrated on filling the mop bucket with fresh water, then rinsed out the mop. "Gotta clean... clean it out and... fill it up... all ready for... for next time." When he was done, he asked Cheff, "Who... who are these other people? Are they your... your friends... too?"

"Yup. This is Sable. She goes to school with me and Mid. This is Books. He's our new friend, got here a couple of days ago." He put his arm around Buttons' shoulders. "And this is my little sister, Mellabee, who likes to be called Mel."

"Hello... Mellabee-who-likes-to-be-called-Mel. That's a... a nice horse."

"She's a pony, not a horse. Her name is Starry Stargazer, but you can call her Starry." She handed Starry to Lery, who petted her gently. She took Moka from her backpack. "And this is Moka, Starry's sister and faithful sidekick. They're best friends."

Lery petted Moka, too. "Hello... Starry. Hello... Moka." He gave Starry and Moka back to Buttons, then shook my hand. "Hello... New-Friend Books. Why... why are you called... Books? Do you... read a lot?"

"I do."

"I... I only know how to read a... a little bit. I'd like to... to learn to read well... someday." Lery turned and stared at Sable, then shook her hand. "Hello... Friend Sable. You... you sure are pretty." He scratched his head. "Your eyes are... are green."

Sable smiled. "Yes."

"Very... green."

"Yes."

Lery cocked his head and studied her eyes. "I saw green eyes… *your* eyes… before… one time… a long time ago."

"Not mine."

"No… not you… a man. A Kreff… like you… but… tall… taller than me." He held his hand a few inches above his head. "This tall."

Sable stood motionless and asked in a whisper, "Black, like me?"

"Yes… black. Pretty… like you. His hair was… was black like yours."

Sable said quietly, "My father."

"Could be," Cheff said. "Is he the only other black Kreff you know of with green eyes?"

Sable nodded.

Cheff explained to Lery, "Black Kreffs usually have dark brown or black eyes. But Sable's father was special. His eyes were green, and Sable inherited them, along with the deep black skin color. Sable's mother was dark, too, but not as dark as Sable and her father, and her mother's eyes were brown. Lery, what was the Kreff's name? Do you know?"

"No… I don't know… his name. They… they don't let me talk to… to the ones who… who… who…" He glanced at Sable, then hung his head, turned his face toward the wall, and began wringing his hands.

Sable gently took one of his hands and held it between both of hers, then looked up into his face. "The ones who *what*, Lery?"

Lery snatched his hand away and darted toward the door. "Anyway… he's… he's gone… a long time ago. Better go… go see the… the jexan door now." He opened the door and looked both ways down the hall. "No one there… all safe."

Sable started to speak again, but Lery was already gone.

Lery led us through a maze of corridors until we came to a long slitherway that descended to a large, open room. The walls were all made of the same thick iron plates, covered with rivets. Crates and barrels of all shapes and sizes were stacked haphazardly along the walls. Our shoes made faint ringing sounds on the iron deck plates.

Lery pointed. "The jexan doors are… are over there."

There were two sets of iron doors, an enormous pair on the right, and a much smaller pair on the left. Mid ran his hand along the crack between the two large doors. "Sealed, like the conductor said. Welded shut, looks like a long time ago. It would take a miracle to get these doors open again. However," he said, as he inspected the smaller doors, "these are another matter entirely. Lery, can you open these for me?"

Lery selected a key and opened one of the small doors. A delightful flood of fresh sea air billowed in, bringing much-needed relief from the overpowering stench of Seph musk. We stepped outside, squinting against the bright daylight, and found ourselves on an iron platform about thirty feet (9m) above the water. The magnificent view stretched all the way across Fellstone Bay to the eastern shore. I closed my eyes and soaked up the sound of the birds, the feel of the wind, and the aroma of the salt air.

"Enjoy it while you can," Cheff said. "Tonight we'll be back *there*."

He pointed to the huge, gray Labor Compound looming at the top of its hill, plumes of black smoke darkening the sky.

Sable examined the platform. When she came to a long double gate in the railing, she observed, "Freighter dock."

"Sounds right," Mid agreed. "This platform is the right height for the deck of an old-time freighter. Those old freighters loaded and unloaded from the rear. They'd back up to this platform, open those gates in the railing, and unload the cargo through the big doors. Does the jexan come on a big ship, Lery?"

"No… the jexan comes on… on a small boat. They tie… tie up down there." In the shadows below, a small wooden dock floated at the waterline. "We pull… pull the cases of jexan up with… with ropes. And I carry them… upstairs."

"How many cases are there, usually?" Cheff asked.

"Sometimes twenty… sometimes more. A lot more." Lery ran his hand over the large cargo doors. "Big ships don't… don't dock here anymore."

"The big doors are for the Sephs," Buttons said. "That's what the conductor told us. The little doors aren't big enough for a Seph to get through. The Sephs don't come in through here, do they, Lery?"

Lery stiffened. "No Sephs. A… a long time ago… maybe… when this was still… still an island. Not… anymore." He shivered. "Sephs only come in… from the road… now. When… when Sephs come… I stay in my room… unless they call me." He shivered again.

We watched the heavy waves crash against the rusty iron plates at the base of the Fortress until Lery said, "I should… should close the… the door now. It… it would be bad if… if someone saw us… out here." He asked Cheff, "Did you see enough of… of the sea doors to help with… with school?"

"Yes, thank you, Lery. It was quite helpful."

"You're welcome… Friend Cheff. We… you… let's… um…"

"Maybe we could go back to your room for a while, Lery?" Cheff suggested.

"Okay." He herded us back into the Fortress, locked the doors behind us, and practically sprinted up the slitherway. It was all we could do to keep up.

— 35 —

PIECE OF CAKE

WHEN WE GOT back to his room, Lery closed the door behind us. He stood in the middle of the room, looking first at us, then at the scant furniture. "I... I don't get visitors... in my room. Only guards." He brought his one chair from the crude wooden table and set it by his bed. "Guards... never sit down." Next, he rummaged around until he found three empty buckets, which he turned upside down and arranged next to the chair. He surveyed the arrangement, then indicated the solitary chair. "Friend Sable." Then he pointed at each of the buckets. "New Friend Books... Friend Mid... Friend Cheff." He smoothed the rumpled blanket over the stained mattress and patted the foot of the bed. "Friend Mellabee-who-likes-to-be-called-Mel."

We took our assigned seats, but Lery remained standing, deep in thought. Finally, he retrieved his dilapidated pillow from the head of the bed and arranged it carefully next to Buttons. "Friend... Starry and... Friend Moka."

Buttons took the ponies from her backpack and settled them on the pillow facing the rest of the group.

Lery, satisfied with the arrangements, took the large tin box from the table near the bed. He sat down gently at the head of the bed, carefully opened the box, then handed each one of us a large biscuit-like loaf. "All safe." He took a huge bite to demonstrate. "Safe… no jexan." He took another bite. "I make them… late at night in the… the kitchen… while I clean there. No jexan… all safe."

Buttons took a bite, made a sour face, then forced a smile. "Thank you, Friend Lery. It's delicious."

Lery laughed, spraying a cloud of crumbs. "Funny girl. Tastes bad… I know. But no… no jexan. Better than… Bounty. Even better than… regular food."

"What do you mean, better than regular food?" Cheff asked.

"*Lots* of jexan in… in the Bounty," Lery replied, "but all food… has a… a *little* jexan."

"All food?" Mid asked. "But how is that possible?"

"I heard the… the jexan men… talking. It's in… something. Flour? Sugar?" He shook his head sadly. "I'm sorry… Friend Cheff… I just don't… don't know."

I said, "Sugar… sugar… that's it! That's who acted like Tocette!"

"Who?" Buttons asked.

"Mr. Rishten," I said. "He puts heaps of sugar in his felmoss tea, starting early in the morning."

Cheff added, "And he gets more and more intense as the day goes on. Good job, Books! I think we'll have to avoid sugar as much as we can from now on."

Buttons consulted with the ponies, then reported, "The ponies think that's a Bad Idea. They like sugar."

"I'm sure they do, Sis," Cheff said. "But until we find some sugar that isn't contaminated, I'm afraid you'll have to make your cookies without. And anything else made with sugar, too."

Buttons looked disappointed. "I sure hope we can find some uncontaminated sugar sometime soon."

We nibbled the biscuits in silence for a while, then Sable put the remainder of hers in her pocket and slid her chair close to Lery.

Lery set his biscuit aside, folded his hands in his lap, and looked up at Sable.

"Lery, the man with the green eyes—can you take me to him?"

Lery's face fell. "I'm… sorry, Friend Sable, but he's gone… long… long time ago. I told you."

"Gone where?"

"Just… gone."

"Are you sure you never talked to him?" Cheff asked.

"They… they don't let anyone talk to… to the prisoners. Anyway… they… they *can't* talk… after."

"After what, Lery?" Mid asked.

"After… after they give them the… the jexan."

"They give the *prisoners* jexan?" Cheff asked. "What for?"

"To make them happy… before they…"

"Before they what, Lery?" Cheff put his hand on Lery's shoulder. "Please, Lery, it's important."

But Lery shook off Cheff's hand, folded his arms across his chest, and started rocking back and forth. "No… don't… can't…" His eyes glazed over.

Buttons scooted across the bed and set Moka in his lap, then put her arm around Lery's broad shoulders. "It's okay, Lery, don't worry—we're your friends now."

After a while, Lery stopped rocking and cradled the little brown pony in his giant hands. "Nice pony."

"I'm sorry, Lery." Cheff reached over and patted Lery on the knee. "I didn't mean to upset you. The thing is, I think my Uncle Karf is here."

"Uncle… Karf?"

"He was arrested the day before yesterday, and a soldier told me they were taking him to the Fortress. He's a Coastal Lora, with brown markings like me, only a little taller."

"Yes… he's… he's here."

"Here? Can you take me to him?"

Lery looked desolate. "No… Friend Cheff. I'm sorry. It's too… dangerous. Too many… guards." He wrang his hands. "Anyway… it's too… too late… He can't talk now. They already gave… gave him the jexan."

Cheff sighed. "To make him happy?"

"Yes, Friend Cheff. They… they all get jexan to… to make them happy before they…"

"Before they…?"

"Yes."

"Before what?" Mid asked. "Before they execute them?"

"No… Friend Mid. They never… execute them."

"Before being transported?"

"Transported? Not transported… No one ever… ever leaves here."

"My father," Sable asked, "still here?"

"No… not here."

"Then before *what?*" Cheff said. "Please, Lery, what's going to happen to my uncle?"

"I can't…" Lery hung his head, then picked Moka up and held her to his chest. "I can't… can't tell you… I'm sorry… New Friends." A huge tear ran down his cheek.

Buttons put her arm around him again. "It's okay, Lery, don't worry. We know you'd help if you could."

Lery nodded, and more tears spilled over.

"Well, then," Cheff asked gently, "can you tell us how long Uncle Karf will be here?"

Lery blinked hard several times and began rocking back and forth again. "Tonight."

"Tonight? What about tonight?" Cheff asked.

"After tonight he… he won't be here."

"I see," Cheff said. "So, if we're going to help him, it has to be tonight."

"Yes… tonight. But you can't… can't help him." He sobbed. "No one can."

"Right, okay, Lery, that's fine." Cheff jumped to his feet. "There's got to be a way—there's *got* to be. We can't leave him here! We have to do something!"

Buttons whispered, "Cheff…"

"*No!* There's got to be something. Let me think. We can't go to where he is. It's too dangerous. We'd all get caught. Even if we could get back here tonight, we'd never even get through the gate, let alone the front door." He paced silently. "But—we know something most people have never even heard of: there's a working back door. Even the old-timer on the bus didn't know about that." He continued pacing. "But we'd never be able to get in. That door is made of solid steel, three inches thick. We might blow it open if we had some explosives, which we don't—"

Mid said, "Well, actually—"

Cheff cut him off with a glare. "—but even if we did, the blast would give us away."

Sable said, "Key."

Cheff stopped pacing. "What did you say?"

"Cheff," Buttons said, "we could get in if we had a key. The right key." She patted Lery on the shoulder. "The right key for the right door. Right, Friend Lery?"

Lery kept rocking, his hands still covering his face, but murmured, "The… the right… key for the right… door. Gotta have the… the right key."

Cheff sat back down. "Lery, if, maybe late tonight, you were to hear a knock on that door, do you think you could find that right key?"

Lery stopped rocking and stared at Cheff.

"A special kind of knock, only for friends," Cheff continued, "like this." Cheff reached down and knocked on the side of the bucket he was sitting on: *knock-knock-knock… knock… knock-knock.*

Lery said nothing, only continued staring at Cheff.

"Cheff!" Sable murmured. "Taking advantage."

"He's our only chance, Sable. Lery? Listen again." *Knock-knock-knock… knock… knock-knock.* "If you heard a knock like that, do you think you might find a key? The right key? No one would ever know except you and your new friends."

Lery asked hesitantly, "The… the right key for… the right door?"

"The right key for the right door," Cheff agreed.

Lery smiled.

Mid shook his head. "Cheff, even if we could get in, how are we going to get upstairs to Uncle Karf?"

Lery said, "Uncle Karf won't… won't be upstairs… tonight… Friend Mid."

"No? Then where will he be?"

"Downstairs."

"By the loading dock? Are they sending him somewhere?"

"Not the… loading dock. All the way down… where the Sephs go."

"*Sephs?* Where the *Sephs* go?" Cheff smacked his forehead. "Just when I thought I had a plan!"

"Oh, this is wonderful, absolutely marvelous," Mid said. "It keeps getting better and better." He took a long, deep breath. "Which Sephs would that be, Lery? Emperor Pallador himself, perhaps?"

"No, Friend Mid. Emperor… Pallador never… comes here… ever. Other Sephs."

"Cheff, this is insane." Mid stood up and began counting on his fingers. "First, we'd have to come by boat, if we had a boat, and we don't have a boat. Second, even if we had a boat, and even if we didn't drown sailing across the bay, we could never get up to that loading dock—it must be thirty feet (9m) above the water."

Buttons said, "Sable could."

Everyone, including Lery, looked at Sable.

Sable thought for a while, then shook her head. "Could. Want to. But can't. Disloyal."

"Maybe," Cheff said, "maybe it's disloyal, but then again, maybe not. That depends on what's going on down there. 'Truth first, then loyalty,' right? Well, there are simply too many things we learned today that don't add up to what we've been told our entire lives: the holes on the Old Bridge where the plaque used to be, to start with."

"Jexan in our food," Buttons said.

"And the prisoners," Mid said. "We're always told that the prisoners in the Iron Fortress are transported to the West for re-education, right? But Lery says that no one ever leaves the Fortress."

Cheff said, "And what's all this about secret meetings in the basement? Who knows what could be going on down there? Not to mention that Lery met your father, and something happened to him so terrible that Lery can't bring himself to speak of it."

Cheff stopped and took a breath. "Anyway, who gets to say what our duty is? There are lots of kinds of duty, and sometimes they conflict. It's all mixed up right here, right now: duty to the Imperium, duty to Pallador, duty to your father, even our duty to each other. It's up to each one of us to decide where our duty lies."

"Truth," Sable said.

"And our duty to the truth. Without truth, the rest of our duties are dust. Unless we fulfill our duty to capital-T Truth, we might as well go home, forget about Uncle Karf, eat our jexan, do as we're told without question, and wait to die."

The silence that followed was deafening. Buttons hugged Starry tight. Lery stared at his lap, absently stroking Moka. Mid looked thoughtful, and I certainly had my own thoughts.

Sable remained motionless for the longest time, eyes closed. At last, without opening her eyes, she said, "Truth first. Then loyalty."

"So you're in?" Cheff asked. "We can't do it without you, Sable."

She looked Cheff in the eye. "I'm in."

Mid looked incredulously at Sable, then at Cheff, then threw up his hands. "Great. She's *in*. *She's* in. That takes care of getting up to the loading dock. *Now* all we have to do is"—he counted on his fingers again—"sneak out of the Labor Compound, steal a boat, sail across the bay in the dead of night without drowning or getting caught by patrols—"

"—or crushed by a freighter—" Sable added.

"—get Sable onto the loading platform, knock our secret knock, hope our new friend Lery opens the door, find Uncle Karf in the basement of the *Iron Fortress*, no less, and steal him out from under the noses of a bunch of Sephs up to who knows what? Is that all? Did I miss anything?"

"No, Old Son," Cheff said, "I think you got it all."

Buttons held Starry Stargazer up to her ear and listened intently for a few seconds. "Starry says, 'Piece of cake.'"

Mid buried his face in his hands. "Great."

Cheff grinned. "Well, then, I guess we'd better get started."

— 36 —

MIND CONTROL

FTER GENTLY RETURNING Moka to Buttons' care, Lery escorted us back through the dark corridor toward the museum, pushing his mop and bucket ahead of him, but this time, instead of going down the slitherway, we crept along the massive inner wall separating the rest of the Fortress from the Museum. The corridor gradually curved to the left. Every few steps Lery had us duck into a doorway or an alcove or behind a pillar, where we held our breath while he listened for any sound of movement.

At one such stop, Cheff whispered to Lery, "What are we listening for? I thought you said that only you come here."

"Yes. Only… only… me… mostly."

Mid grumbled, "There's that word again, 'mostly.' I'm starting to dislike it."

"Me, too," Cheff agreed.

A little farther along, Lery stopped and peered into the Museum hall through a small peephole in the wall. "No one there… now… New Friends. All safe." He pushed a small button on the wall and another hidden door, much like the one we had first followed Lery through, opened with a click. "Okay… New Friends… go fast."

Cheff clasped Lery's hand. "Good work, Lery, thank you. Don't forget to wait for us downstairs tonight."

"Won't… forget… Bye now." He closed the door abruptly and was gone.

We were, as Lery had assured us, the only museum visitors in sight. There were no guards, either. We looked around and got our bearings. We appeared to be in a small side room at the far end of the Museum opposite the entrance.

"Look casual," Cheff said, "like we've been here the whole time. Seem interested in the exhibits. Mill about." We spread out, feigning interest in the various exhibits, gradually migrating toward the Museum entrance.

The exhibits in this room featured Pallador's improvements in transportation, especially as used in warfare. "Mid, look here," I said. "Some of the trucks in this battle scene are carrying the same kind of dish-things we saw on the roof of the Fortress."

"Mind-control devices," Mid explained. "They're electric. Somehow they amplify the effects of the Sephs' mental Ability to control their Facilitators. In battle, Seph commanders use the dishes to project their Ability onto the soldiers. It raises morale, makes them brave and fierce. Or so we're told."

Cheff grimaced. "Supposedly, it's how the Sephs defeated the Torphs and freed us all from Torph domination."

"The official story," Mid added, "is that the Torph Emperor had a counter-device to counteract the Sephs' devices."

"Did it work?" I asked.

"Dunno. If it did, it wasn't a very *good* counter-device, was it?"

"What about the dishes on the roof of the Fortress?" I asked. "What are they for? Are they turned on all the time?"

"No, they're in case the Fortress is attacked, which it hasn't been, for almost a hundred years. I don't know if they even still work. In any case, it takes one Seph per dish, and it takes a lot out of the operator. Wartime use only."

Cheff brightened. "Which explains why they use the jexan in peacetime. It's all coming together."

Sable looked thoughtfully for a while at the little trucks in the display case carrying the mind-control dishes.

We looked at the exhibits for another twenty minutes or so, then Tocette wandered in, looking surprisingly chipper. She clapped Cheff on the back, nearly knocking him over, then put her arm around my neck. "There you are, my li'l Buddy Boy! I've been looking all over for you. Where've you all been? I looked in all the rooms twice or more, and so did that sergeant, but we couldn't find you anywhere!"

"Hi, Tocette!" Cheff smiled innocently at her. "Sorry, we didn't mean to scare you. We've been looking around. The sergeant said it was all right. Since it's Books' first visit, we've been taking our time and reading all the explanations on the exhibit signs. How are you feeling?"

"Much better now." She shook her head a few times, making her stringy hair fly. "I don't know what came over me. The last thing I remember is we finished eating and went into the museum hall. I remember feeling kinda funny, but that's it."

"You yelled," Buttons said, "and threw up. A *lot*."

"Then you got woozy," Mid said, "and the sergeant called the nurse. She thought maybe you had too much of Pallador's Bounty."

"I guess I did. It sure was good, wasn't it? I can't wait until next time! In fact, I'm kinda hungry again right now." She gave my neck a little squeeze. "Well, did you all learn anything, little Booksie Buddy?"

"As it turns out," Mid said, "we certainly did. More than we'd expected."

Cheff said, "I'd say we saw some things that most people never see."

Sable nodded.

Buttons said, "Starry and Moka learned that Emperor Pallador's giant horses helped rebuild Andaran after the Evil Torph Empire fell."

Tocette petted Starry and Moka. "Good ponies." She checked the clock above the golden bust of Pallador near the door. "Uh-oh—I must have slept a long while. It's time we started for home. Come on, let's get going. We only have fifteen minutes to catch the bus." She trotted off toward the museum entrance.

As we followed Tocette, I said quietly to the others, "Wouldn't it be nice if we had some proof?"

"Of what?" Mid asked.

"Of whatever we see tonight—plotting against the Emperor, what they're doing to the prisoners, to Uncle Karf. Whatever we see, no one's going to believe a bunch of kids unless we have proof."

"What kind of proof?" Mid asked.

"My dad's camera," I said. "Remember I told you I brought it with me?"

"Right," Cheff said. "It's a reminder of your dad."

"Does it still work?" Mid asked.

"I don't know. I guess so. It used to. It's not broken or anything, so yes, probably. But I haven't had any film for it for years. Or batteries."

"No good," Cheff said. "It's not going to do us any good without film."

Sable said, "Gift shop."

Cheff snapped his fingers. "Of course! They sell film at the museum's gift shop."

"Fat lot of good that'll do us," Mid said. "We don't have any more money. Do you have any money, Sable?"

She shook her head.

"We need a plan," Cheff said. "Let me think." We walked along in silence through the main exhibit hall. Tocette was far ahead of us. Right before we got to the gift shop, Cheff said, "Okay, I've got it. Sable, you distract Tocette and get her out of the building."

"Right."

"Books, you and Mid distract the clerk, ask a lot of questions."

"What about?" Mid asked.

"Anything, it doesn't matter as long as you keep her busy. Buttons, you and the ponies head over to the film counter. Pretend you're looking at stuff, then when you see my signal, grab some film and put it in your bag."

"Why, Cheff!" Mid clapped his hands to his cheeks in mock horror. "What's happened to you? Putting your little sister up to stealing? And from the Emperor himself, no less!"

Cheff grinned. "Spoils of war. After all, he did poison our food. If anyone asks, tell them that the jexan must have addled my brain. Anyway, we've all been criminals since we went through that door with Lery. They can only execute us once." He took a deep breath. "Besides, we can always pay them back someday."

"Wait, Cheff." Buttons wrinkled her forehead. "What's your signal going to be?"

"I don't know yet, but don't worry—you'll know it when you see it."

"The ponies say, 'Okay.'"

"Everybody ready? Let's do this."

Operation Break Iron

— 37 —

THE GIFT SHOP

S WE APPROACHED the gift shop, Buttons pointed to a large mural over the entrance of the dining hall. "Look! Look at the inscription!"

The inscription, painted in gold letters, read, "Beloved Pallador, great and powerful, all good things come from you." Above the inscription was a colorful composite scene of rural activities: plowing, sowing, reaping, horses pulling wagons full of beautiful vegetables, and a train with a big, black steam engine pulling freight cars across the plains.

"Hey!" Buttons said. "That's what Tocette was saying."

Cheff said, "She must have read it here when she left the cafeteria and it stuck in her mind."

"Seems likely," Mid agreed.

While Sable hurried to catch up with Tocette, Mid and I entered the gift shop. Every imaginable object that could fit a picture of Emperor Pallador on it somewhere, crowded the shelves—drinking glasses, mugs, all manner of kitchen gadgetry, puzzles, games, models, snow globes, science projects, 'Pallador's Guide to Basic Chemistry—You Too Can Become A Scientist.' Posters of the various murals placed around the museum covered an entire wall. Floor-to-ceiling bookshelves covered another. Buttons went straight to a wire bin full of stuffed Grand Graymoore horses, where she introduced the ponies to every single one. Mid and I made a beeline for the counter where a short, thin, middle-aged clerk wearing her hair in a bun on top of her head asked, "May I help you, boys?" Her glasses were secured by a little cord around her neck.

"Yes, ma'am," Mid said. "We have a few questions if you have time."

The clerk smiled a thin, pinched little smile. "Of course, boys. What would you like to know?"

"To start with," Mid said, "we have a few questions about an exhibit in the main hall."

The clerk pulled her spectacles down her long Fessal nose and looked at Mid over them. "Number?"

"Thirty-four, ma'am."

She took a typewritten list of exhibits from beneath the counter and opened it to number thirty-four.

"And what would you like to know, precisely?"

"I have a question about the railroad system," Mid began, but Cheff, near the front of the store, held the largest snow globe on the shelf over his head. He shouted, "Hey, guys, look at this! It's New City!" He shook the snow globe vigorously.

The clerk pushed her spectacles back up her nose and glared at Cheff. "You there! Be careful with that! Put it down at once!"

"Look!" Cheff yelled. "When you shake it, it looks like it's snowing on the Silver Palace!" He shook the snow globe again, even harder this time. "That's silly! It never snows in Fellstone!"

Out of the corner of my eye, I saw Buttons edging toward the film counter, opening her backpack as she went.

The clerk stormed around from behind the register, brushed past Mid and me, and set a course for Cheff. I watched until Buttons reached the film counter, then I gave Cheff a nod. He shook the snow globe once more, but this time he dropped it. It fell to the floor with a resounding crash.

The clerk took Cheff by the ear. "Shame on you! Look what you've done! You've broken it. I told you to put it down. Why didn't you listen to me? Now, you pick up those pieces, this instant. I'm going to stand right here until you've cleaned up this mess!"

I gave Buttons a thumbs-up. She began stuffing film boxes into her pony backpack as fast as she could. Meanwhile, Mid and I ran over to where Cheff knelt on the floor. Mid stumbled and staggered into the clerk. She screamed and yelled, "Watch where you're going! What's the meaning of this? Who are you?"

"Don't worry," I said, "we'll help clean it up, ma'am." Mid and I knelt by Cheff and started scattering the shards of glass and little pools of water all around the floor. "It'll only take a minute, ma'am."

"Stop it!" The clerk stamped her foot. "Stop it right now! You're only making it worse."

But Mid and I kept 'helping' until Buttons slipped out of the store, backpack bulging. She followed Sable and Tocette out to the bus.

The poor clerk was frantic. I almost felt sorry for her. She jerked me and Mid to our feet and screeched, "Stop it right now, I said. Get out of here or I'll call the guards." She kicked at Cheff with the toe of her pointy red shoe. "You, too. You're useless! Get on out of here, you nasty boys!"

Tocette rushed back to see what the fuss was all about, Sable and Buttons right behind her. She stopped in the doorway and stared at the spectacle. The clerk pulled her glasses down her nose again and glared at Tocette, whose uniform still bore traces of Pallador's Bounty. "Are you in charge of these hooligans?"

"Yes, ma'am." Tocette hung her head. "I'm sorry. I'm sure they didn't mean—"

"I don't care!" The clerk's voice was shrill, almost hysterical. "Get. Them. Out. Of. Here. *Now!*"

"Yes, ma'am. Sorry, ma'am." Tocette grabbed me and Mid in one hand, and Cheff's collar in the other, and dragged us out of the Museum. She screamed, "This is why I didn't want to take you in the first place! I *knew* something like this was gonna happen. Now get outside and get on the bus. Move!" She shoved the three of us roughly out the doorway toward the waiting bus. "Boys! I hate them! You can't take them *anywhere!*"

"Yeah," Buttons echoed, "boys. Can't take 'em anywhere!" Behind Tocette's back, she shot Cheff an angelic smile.

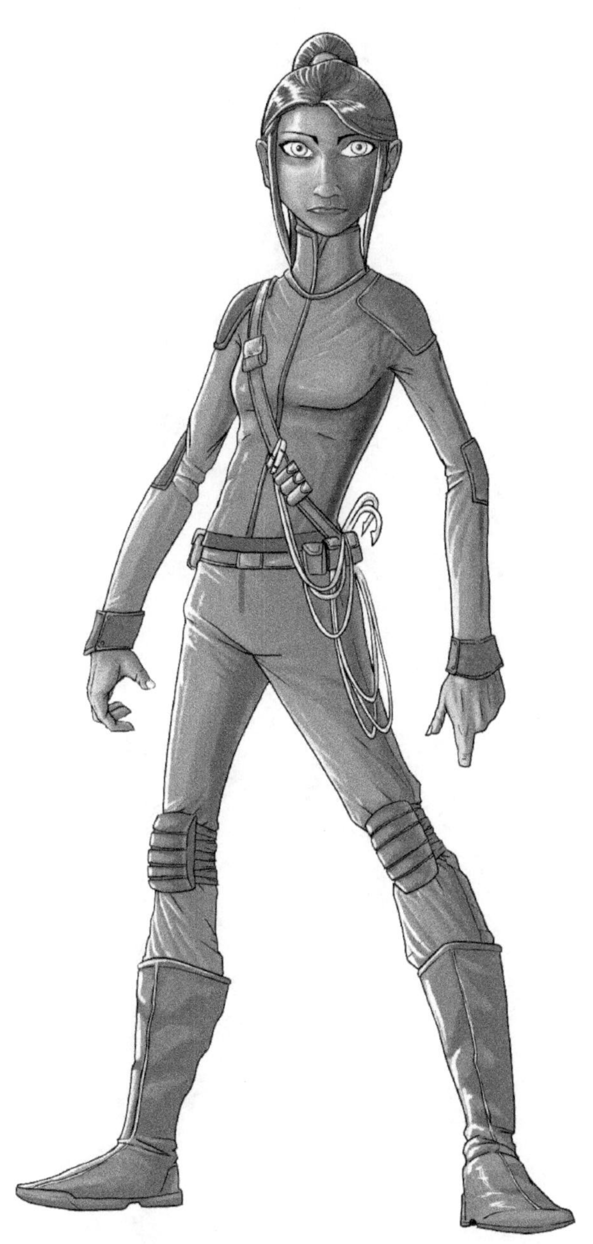

Sable in Her Mission Outfit

— 38 —

THE COMMODORE

ABOUT AN HOUR before midnight, that same night, we crested a little hill to the north of the Labor Compound. "There it is," Cheff said, "Fel Village. See? Down the hill by the edge of the bay."

A couple of miles (3 km) or so to the north, the lights of the little fishing village shimmered on the glassy water of Fellstone Bay. The pleasant, midnight breeze rising from the bay cooled us after our long hike through the storm drains and up this hill.

Cheff studied the village. In the faint illumination from the Great Fisherman Nebula, we made out the outlines of the floating docks full of fishing boats. "There, see those boats? That's where we'll find one we can use. Ready? Good. Let's go down as quietly as we can. If one dog barks, the entire neighborhood will wake up."

"Have you been there before?" I asked Cheff.

"One summer, long ago, when I first started hunting, the game was scarce, and I needed to find new hunting grounds. I tried northward, and I found this place. I've been down to the village a few times. There's a fisherman there who trades fish for my 'fence chicken,' if I get there before he goes to bed. It's a long way from the Compound, so I only hunt in this direction when I can't find any game in the usual places." He stretched and yawned. "Let's get moving. It's a good hour's walk down to that village."

So far, tonight's excursion was much like the one we took to Meltern's place, except this time we *knew* Buttons was with us. Sable was with us, too, wearing what she called her 'mission outfit,' which consisted of a snug, black, long-sleeved turtleneck shirt, black trousers, black boots, and a tool belt with several coils of rope and other mysterious-looking gear. She had pulled her hair back into a ponytail. It was the first time I'd seen her entire face.

We threaded our way down the hill through some ruins, avoiding the outskirts of the village. We circled around by the bay until we came to several dozen small, open fishing boats lined up on the beach.

A dog barked in the distance. Cheff signaled us to stop. We crouched behind one of the boats.

Buttons whispered, "Is it barking at us?"

"I don't know, maybe," Cheff said. "I hope not." After a few seconds, the dog stopped. "Okay, let's go!"

A little farther on, some larger boats were tied to the fingers of the floating docks. Cheff led us past the line of boats onto one of the docks. We went all the way to the end, where a small, white wooden steam launch with red stripes along its sides bobbed in the soft swells. "This will do quite nicely, I think. Get in!" He hopped aboard.

No one moved.

Mid asked, "Are you out of your mind?"

"Probably." The dog barked again, much closer this time. "Get in! Hurry!"

"But, Cheff," Mid insisted, "what about the fisherman who owns this tub? Isn't he going to notice that his boat's missing?"

"We'll be back long before morning. He won't even know it was gone. Or we'll all die tonight and it won't matter. But enough worrying. Let's see if we can—"

"Uh-oh," Buttons said, pointing. "Here it comes!"

A huge yellow dog, snarling viciously, charged down the dock toward us. The clicking sound of his toenails against the wood of the dock seemed far too loud in the silent town. We piled into the boat. Sable cast off, then grabbed an oar and used it to push our boat away from the dock out into the black water.

The dog barked furiously on the end of the dock. A light went on in the village, then another. Cheff said, "Let's get out of here, fast!"

We kept bumping into each other, trying to find our seats and stow our gear. The little boat rocked perilously. After a long minute of confusion, Sable moved to the front of the boat and stood up in the bow, her silhouette dark against the night sky. "Cheff, rowing seat. Oars. Move!" Cheff blinked a few times, then quickly took the center seat. "Mid, engine. Books, rear seat. Buttons, with me. Everyone stow your gear."

In a heartbeat, we were seated, and our gear secured. Mid muttered under his breath, "I'll bet that monster dog will still be waiting right there on the dock when we get back."

"Quiet, please," Sable ordered. "Mid, steam. Cheff, take us out."

Cheff saluted. "Aye, aye, Commodore."

Sable glared at Cheff, but he kept grinning, placed the long, wooden oars into the oarlocks, and began rowing. We soon left the dock behind and were out on the open water. The dog remained snarling and barking on the dock. A voice called out from somewhere in the village, "Porgo! Shut up! Go lie down!" The yellow dog quit barking, sniffed the air a few times, then turned and trotted back to the village.

In the center of the launch stood a small steam engine made of black iron and trimmed in gleaming nickel. A pair of gauges were mounted on one side, along with some shiny brass valves. On the other side, high up, was a brass steam whistle.

I helped Mid get the little engine fired up by bringing him several buckets of coal from the coal bin in the back. Soon it was puffing clouds of smoke from its stack. "It'll take a while to heat all the way up," Mid said. "Keep that coal coming."

Sable was in the bow, facing forward, one foot on the gunwale, shading her eyes with her hand and peering into the darkness ahead.

I said to Mid, "Sable's so dark I can hardly see her."

"She's pretty dark, all right." He grinned at me and lowered his voice. "I shone my flashdark on her once. You know what happened?"

"What?"

"Nothing." We both laughed, then Mid added, "I wish I were that dark—it would make sneaking around at night a lot easier."

"Even if you were as black as Sable," Cheff said over his shoulder, "you still wouldn't be as pretty."

Mid sniffled, wiped an imaginary tear from his eye, and flicked it out into the bay. "Aw, you sure know how to hurt a guy, Cheff." He handed me the empty coal bucket. "One more bucketful will do it, I think."

Cheff had been rowing for only fifteen minutes or so when Mid tapped on the face of a gauge and took a reading. He called softly to Sable, "Ready, I think."

Sable gave Mid a brief nod. "Cheff, ship oars!"

He looked puzzled, then got it. He pulled the oars inside the boat and set them down along the sides.

"Cheff, take the wheel!"

Cheff moved to the stern of the boat and took hold of the spoked wooden wheel. "Ready, Commodore!"

"Mid, ahead slow!"

Mid cracked open the steam valve, which hissed softly. The engine chuffed cheerfully, and waves splashed on the bow as the launch gained speed.

"Where to, Commodore?" Cheff asked. He pointed at a well-lit area across the bay. "I'm pretty sure that's the Iron Fortress over there."

Buttons raised her eyebrows. "*Pretty* sure?"

"Yeah, *pretty* sure, Sis. We'll be able to tell when we get closer. Anyway, it's not like it's hidden somewhere. The Fortress sticks right out into the water. And it's well-lit at night. We shouldn't have any trouble."

Sable pointed at the bright spot. "Full speed ahead."

Mid answered, "Aye, aye, Commodore!" He opened the steam valve all the way, and the launch lurched, then gained speed. Shortly, we were making respectable progress across the bay.

Cheff said, "It's about three or four miles (6 km) to the Fortress, I think. At this speed, we should be there in a half hour or so." He winced as he rubbed his arms. "That was quite a workout. My arms aren't used to it. I haven't rowed a boat since I was a little boy. My father took us on picnics to a little lake up in the hills. I'd sit on his lap while he rowed. He'd let me hold onto the oars, and help him. That was a lifetime ago." He stared off into the darkness.

It was beautiful, wonderful, being out on the bay. The Great Fisherman Nebula outshone the stars in the northern sky. The full moon shone brightly on the bay to the south. A sleepy seagull roused from his perch on one of the harbor buoys and squawked away. From time to time, a school of sea fliers jumped up high, flapped through the air hunting for flying insects, then splashed back down.

Buttons let her fingers drag in the water, making a ripple that glistened in the moonlight.

Cheff shook off his melancholy. "I wish we'd had more time to get some gear together."

Mid checked his tech bag. "Me, too. I grabbed a few things I had in my room. I hope it'll be enough."

"Enough for what?" I asked.

"Well, that's the big question, isn't it?" Mid said. "We don't have a clue about what we might need tonight. Anyway, even if we did know, we didn't have much time for proper planning.

Lery said Uncle Karf would be gone after tonight. Do you think Lery knows what he's talking about? He seems a little slow."

"Maybe," Cheff said. "He's hard to figure, but I have a feeling there's more to Lery than he lets on. Maybe he's a different *kind* of smart."

"Could be," Mid said. "It can't be nice, stuck in that place with all those Sephs, doing their dirty work. I wish there was something we could do for him."

"Me, too," I said, "but I can't imagine what that might be."

"In any case," Cheff said, "there's one thing we know for sure — people who are taken to the Iron Fortress are never seen or heard from again. If we want to save Uncle Karf, and if Lery knows what he's talking about, tonight's the only chance we're going to get, prepared or not."

We were making good time. As we neared the halfway point, Sable said, "Shipping lanes. Watch for ships."

A patchy fog limited visibility, an eerie purplish-gray in the mixture of yellow-white moonlight and the indigo glow of the nebula.

Cheff said, "We'd better keep a sharp eye out for them — they're certainly not going to see us."

I scanned the foggy darkness in vain. Then I saw a flash of light to the north, far above the waterline. I pointed and tugged at Cheff's sleeve. "See there? Is that a ship, or is it the Fellstone Lighthouse?"

Cheff compared the positions of the Great Fisherman, the Fortress, and the moon. "It must be a ship. It's in the wrong place to be the lighthouse. But I can't tell how far away it is. Can you?"

We strained to see, but another patch of purple mist drifted by. Sable ordered, "Stop engines. Listen."

Mid closed the steam valve, and we drifted almost silently.

Cheff cupped his hands around his ears, faced north, then turned his head from side to side a few times. "I think maybe I hear its engines rumbling." He pointed into the fog. "That way.

They sound like they're a long way off. Should we wait, Sable? Go back? Try to cross in front of them? Do we have time?"

Sable shrugged. "Can't tell."

The rumbling seemed louder now, but it was impossible to gauge the distance. Cheff mounted the oars again and rowed gently to keep the boat pointed westward.

Suddenly, a mere twenty yards (18m) away, the prow of an enormous freighter burst from the fog, as big as a mountain and bearing straight down on us!

Sable shouted, "Go!"

Cheff rowed furiously. Mid cranked the steam valve open as far as it would go. Buttons and I leaned over the side and paddled frantically with our hands. The freighter was moving much faster than I would have thought possible. They must have spotted us, because a searchlight from the freighter scanned the water, found us, and lit us up. Men yelled at us from the deck of the ship.

Of course, a freighter that size was too big to stop, or even change course. Disaster was imminent—our little steam launch picked up more speed, but not nearly enough. We were doomed! Cheff yelled, "Hang on!" With one of the oars, he pushed against the hull of the freighter with all his might. I held on to his belt to keep him from falling out.

Our boat surged forward, only a foot (30 cm) or so, but enough to get us out of the freighter's path. The freighter slipped by, missing the stern of our boat by inches, so close that I could count the rivets in the hull.

When our hearts stopped pounding and we caught our breath, I asked, "Do you think they'll report us when they get to shore?"

"They might," Cheff answered. "But what did they see, exactly? It's too dark and too foggy for them to see any details, I'm sure. I couldn't see anyone above us. I heard them yelling, though."

Mid said, "I couldn't quite make out what they were saying, could you?"

"Nooo," Cheff replied pensively, "but if I had to guess, I'd say it was something along the lines of—"

"Yes?" Buttons asked. "What did they say, Cheff?"

"—'I say, would you fellows kindly remove yourselves and your small craft from the path of our ship?'"

"Right," Buttons said. "We all know how polite frightened sailors can be, don't we, Starry?" Starry did. "Starry says, if it's all the same to you, she'd prefer we didn't get that close to a ship again. *Ever.*"

Sable echoed, "Ever."

We made the rest of the crossing in silence. Soon, the Fortress loomed ahead, only a few hundred yards (228m) away, blacking out the western sky.

Sable called, "All stop."

Mid closed the steam valve and released the pressure.

Cheff rowed us silently to our destination. We tied our boat to the little floating dock Lery had pointed out earlier that afternoon. The ironwork of the loading platform gleamed high above us.

"Now what?" Mid said. "That platform's twenty feet (6m) up, maybe closer to thirty (9m)."

"Now," Cheff said, "it's up to the Commodore."

Sable allowed herself the smallest hint of a smile. As she remained standing in the bow of the boat, keeping her balance so perfectly that the boat barely rocked, she unhooked a metal device from her belt, which she unfolded into a three-pronged grappling hook. "Everyone, move to the stern."

Sable unclipped a coil of climbing rope from her belt and tied it through the eye of the grappling hook. After making sure we were all out of the way, she swung the hook a few times, then let it fly upward. It grappled onto the railing of the platform with a satisfying clang. Sable shinnied up the rope and vanished into the darkness above.

"Rock-smooth," Cheff murmured.

The rope disappeared upwards. After a few metallic clicks, the rope came back down. But now there were three ropes, and at the bend, there was a pulley with a loop on the bottom. Sable called down softly, "Cheff, foot."

Cheff went forward to the bow, grasped the ropes with both hands, then put one foot into the loop. "Ready!"

Sable called down, "Pull." Cheff fumbled for the right strand of rope, then helped Sable pull. He, too, rose rapidly out of sight.

Sable repeated this procedure with Mid, Buttons, and then with me. When we were all at the top, Cheff said, "Nice work, Commodore!"

Sable nodded tersely, untied the rope from the railing, then removed her pulleys and clipped them to her belt next to the grappling hook. She tied the rope onto the railing with a strange-looking knot.

Mid walked over and examined the knot.

Sable said, "Quick exit."

"Right," Mid said, then asked Cheff, "What now?"

"It was beautiful, wonderful, being out on the bay."

— 39 —

THE BASEMENT

"**N**ow, we knock." Cheff rapped softly on the door: *knock-knock-knock… knock… knock-knock.*

Nothing happened.

Cheff knocked again, louder: *KNOCK-KNOCK-KNOCK… KNOCK… KNOCK-KNOCK.*

The sound shattered the stillness of the night. I imagined they could hear us all the way across the bay to the Labor Compound.

An eternity passed while we held our breath.

Then came the sound of a key in a lock, much too loud in the quiet night. The door opened, and Lery stuck his head out and grinned. "The right… right key for the… right door. Hello… New Friends. You'd… you'd better come in… quick."

We stepped into the Fortress and the musky stench of Sephs assaulted us again, much stronger than before.

Cheff put his arm around Lery's shoulder and gave him a half-hug. "Good work, Lery! Glad to see you!"

Lery hung his head and blushed. "Right key…"

"It sure was, and we're grateful. So… where's Uncle Karf? You mentioned downstairs, earlier."

"Yes… he's downstairs at… at the… the lowest level, at the… the… the…" He took a breath to calm himself. "The banquet."

"Banquet?" Cheff asked.

"Yes."

"They're feeding him? A last meal or something?"

"No. We must… must hurry… Friend Cheff. They've already… begun. It's late."

Cheff shook his head. "I'm sorry, Lery, I don't understand. Maybe it would be best if you took us to him now."

Lery double-checked that the outer door was secure.

Mid asked, "What about the guards?"

"No guards… downstairs."

Cheff prompted, "Because?"

"Prisoners don't… don't try to… leave. Not… after jexan."

"I see. Where *are* the guards, then?"

"Guards are all… all upstairs guarding… the front door. They only come… downstairs if… called."

Cheff turned to the rest of us. "Well, that's a break, anyway. If we're sneaky enough, we might not have to deal with the guards at all. Excellent! Everybody ready? Okay, Lery, lead on, as quietly as you can, but quickly."

Lery led us across the room into the same smelly corridor we'd used during our afternoon visit. However, instead of heading back up toward Lery's room, he led us in the opposite direction until we came to a broad slitherway leading downward. Lery pointed into the dark shadows below. "To the… the basement… New Friends."

"They used the layout of the Fortress as an example in my architecture and engineering class," Mid said. "It was built in two sections, first the inner tower, called the keep, then, much later, the outer ring. At the bottom, there's a sort of basement that contains all the foundation blocks and the heavy pillars that bear most of the keep's weight. According to the diagram, the basement isn't as big as the other floors. To get there we'll have to go through the keep toward the center of the Fortress."

"Yes… Friend Mid," Lery said, "that's exactly… right. The keep."

At the bottom of the first slitherway, Lery opened a sturdy iron door on the inside of the corridor, and we passed through. Lery rapped softly on the thick walls. "This is… the keep."

Inside the keep, the air was fetid, heavy with Seph musk. As we descended another smaller slitherway, the air rapidly grew hotter and more humid, making the horrible smell of Sephs nearly unbearable. We stepped softly to avoid making noise on the steel decking.

When we reached the bottom of the smaller slitherway, Lery led us along the corridor to yet another slitherway leading down. In total, we descended three long slitherways. At the bottom, Cheff gestured for us to stop. The stench of Seph musk was nearly too intense to bear. We stood motionless in the dim light and listened. The only sound we heard was the drip, drip, dripping of water oozing from a myriad of chinks in the walls. "Lery, is this the basement, or do we have to go down farther?"

"This is the… the bottom." Lery stuck his finger in a steady trickle of water running down the thick steel wall of the corridor. "Sea water."

Mid grinned. "Sure, I see water. There's a trickle of it running down the wall."

Lery clapped his hand over his mouth to keep from laughing out loud. "No… *sea* water. From… the ocean. We're under… under water. Way under."

"Oh," Mid said. "I *see*."

Lery stared at him, then snorted. "Mid sees the sea."

"I see the sea," Mid said, "but does the sea see me?"

Lery giggled.

Buttons said, "That fish sees you!" She wiped the condensation from a large, round window in the outside wall. A blue and green fish with bulging eyes peered in at us, then swam on its way. "We really *are* underwater! How do you like that, Starry?" She held Starry up to the thick glass for a better view.

"But if we're underwater," I asked, "and the Fortress is leaking, why doesn't the Fortress fill up? The basement, anyway."

Lery explained, "There's a… a place… a pit… in the… the middle. All the sea water… runs into the… pit. Gets… pumped out again."

"Now, that's interesting," Cheff said to Mid. "Can we use that for anything?"

"I don't know. Maybe. Anyway, it's good to know."

"This way," Lery said.

We continued through the dimly lit corridor until we arrived at a large, open area, maybe forty feet (12m) across, punctuated by thick stone columns reaching from floor to ceiling.

Mid ran his hand across the stone face of a column. "These must be the original foundation, the first step of the construction of the Fortress. They support the weight of the keep. This entire basement seems to be carved out of bedrock."

An eerie glow illuminated the center of this large open room, but we couldn't make out any details. Lery said, "That's the… the banquet… room." He shuddered.

"That's where Uncle Karf is?" Cheff asked him.

Lery nodded. Beads of sweat formed on his forehead.

"Then that's where we have to go," Cheff said. "Let's circle around the outer edge and find a vantage point."

We cautiously crept from pillar to pillar clockwise around the big room. Buttons wiped the condensation off another large window with her sleeve, then pressed her face to the glass. "There are pillars outside, too. What for?"

Mid joined her at the window. "How strange! It looks like the outer ring of the upper floors doesn't go all the way down to the ocean floor. Interesting." Mid stroked his chin. "I wonder why they built it that way. They must have had some reason—maybe it had to do with the sea bottom or something."

"Figure it out later," Cheff said. "We have to keep moving."

We continued clockwise around the edge of the outer wall until we passed a third window, then came to a large steel door set into the outer wall. Mid whispered to Lery, "Where does that door lead—or where *did* it lead? I mean, what good is a door that leads underwater?"

"Old… old door. Very old. No good… now. Was used when… for when… the Fortress was…"

"When the Fortress was being built?" Mid asked.

"That's… exactly right."

"Of course!" Mid said. "I learned about this in class, too. To build a structure underwater, like, say, the foundations of a bridge—"

"—or a fortress—" Cheff added.

"—right, or a fortress, you first build something called a caisson. It's a temporary wall, made of metal or wood, that makes a dam all around where you're going to build. Then, you pump the water out of the inside of the caisson. That way, you can build your foundation on dry ground. That door must have been used when the caisson was still in place. Of course, the caissons were removed when the construction was over, so there's nothing but water on the other side of that door now. It's too far below sea level—it won't do us any good." Mid squatted against the wall, closed his eyes, and tilted his head back. "Or would it?"

"You have an idea?" Cheff asked.

"Maybe. I'd need a little time to examine the door."

Cheff said, "We don't *have* time. We need to get to Uncle Karf."

Lery stiffened and backed up a few steps.

"What's the matter, Lery?" Cheff asked kindly.

"Can't… can't… go there. Banquet." He started rocking back and forth anxiously.

"Okay," Cheff said, "you don't have to go. Tell you what—while we're figuring out what to do about Uncle Karf, how about you stay here and help Mid examine this door, see if anything comes to mind?"

"Okay… Friend Cheff." He relaxed slightly.

"I'll see what we can come up with," Mid said. "Go ahead."

"The rest of you come with me," Cheff said. Crouching low, we left the outer wall and made our way through the shadows toward the brightly lit center, moving from giant pillar to giant pillar. When we'd covered half the distance, Cheff stopped us. "Okay, Books, your big moment is coming up. Let's you and me see if we can get some proof of whatever's going on down here. Is your camera ready? Did Buttons get the right film?"

"She certainly did. She got all the film, and all the batteries, too."

"*All* the film?"

"Every last roll!" Buttons beamed. "I grabbed everything I could get my adorable little hands on."

"Why batteries?" Cheff asked.

"The camera needs batteries to work the flashbulbs," I said.

Cheff smacked his forehead. "Flashbulbs? I forgot the flash-bulbs!"

Buttons laughed. "I got some flashbulbs, too, Cheff."

"Of course you did. Good work, Sis." Cheff tousled her hair. "You'll be a great Master Thief when you grow up." He stood up. "Sable, Buttons, wait here. Books and I will sneak up and see if we can get a picture."

Buttons jumped to her feet and hissed furiously, "No way, Cheff. I'm not staying here in the dark, not even with Sable. Who knows what could be down here? I'm going with you."

Sable also stood up. "'D.B.U.T.T. Don't Break Up The Team.'"

"Says who?" Cheff asked her.

"Admiral Pitr Karlsin."

"Who's he?"

"Naval Officers' Manual."

"What about it?"

"Wrote it."

"I see. Well, it looks to me like between you, Buttons, and the Admiral, I'm outnumbered." Cheff sighed. "Okay, fair enough, I guess." He narrowed his eyes and pointed a finger at each of us in turn. "But slowly and quietly. We're in the heart of enemy territory, now. This isn't a game. One mistake and we're dead, and so is Uncle Karf. And maybe our new friend, Lery, too."

Sable, Buttons, and I nodded solemnly.

"Follow me." Cheff scanned the big room. When he was satisfied that the room was clear, we crouched and moved toward the lighted area until Cheff stopped abruptly. "Get down!"

"What is it?" I asked.

"Fessals. Lots of them."

"Soldiers?"

"No, I don't think so. Facilitators, maybe. They're wearing uniforms, but not army uniforms. Some other kind of thing."

"Let me see." I crept up beside him and spied around the edge of the pillar. Buttons and Sable peeked around the other edge.

We were close enough to see the lighted area quite clearly. It was an octagonal pavilion built on a raised platform in the exact center of the keep's basement. Its walls, for the first three feet from the floor, were made of sheet iron, like the rest of the Fortress. Above the iron wall, the pavilion was made of glass, including a glass roof. The glass panels were connected by ornate wrought-iron struts and girders, all painted stark white. Condensation fogged the windows. We needed to get closer to see what was happening inside. The reek of Seph musk was overpowering. Electric lights mounted on the struts bathed the entire scene in a creepy greenish-yellow glow.

Outside the glass pavilion stood a dozen or more Fessals dressed in a uniform I didn't recognize: spotless dark-green pants, light-green jackets trimmed in dark green, to match the pants, and shiny black shoes. A silver stripe ran down the outside of each pant leg. The jackets featured white epaulets and a row of silver buttons that ran from collar to beltline. These Fessals went back and forth between the pavilion and a door in a nearby interior wall, carrying large, round trays filled with something too far away to identify and returned with the empty trays tucked under their arms.

"They're Facilitators, all right," Cheff whispered. "They're all Fessals and probably mind-controlled, from which we can conclude that the glass pavilion is full of Sephs. Listen!"

The sound of many Sephs emanated from the Pavilion. We couldn't tell if they were talking, chanting, singing, or something else, but whatever it was, it raised the hair on the backs of our necks.

Cheff said, "If we want to see what's going on in there, we're going to have to get right up to the glass. If we stay in the shadows, I don't think those Fessals will be able to see us." He put his hand on my shoulder. "Let's do it!"

— 40 —

THE BANQUET

THE FOUR OF US, Cheff, Sable, Buttons, and I, crept through the shadows to the wall of the pavilion and crouched below the window line so the Facilitators couldn't see us, nor could the Sephs inside.

I double-checked my camera to make sure that the film was in place, then slowly raised it above the iron wall and peered through the viewfinder. Eight Sephs sat in a circle in the center of the pavilion on giant red cushions with gold embroidery. The Sephs swayed from side to side, chanting softly in a coarse, harsh language I didn't understand. Behind each Seph, a Facilitator stood at attention, his face expressionless. In the center of the circle, a ninth Seph, much larger than the others, occupied a gold dais. His massive serpent jaw dripped with slime, unhinged and wide open.

"Andaran's bones!" I said. "That's Uncle Karf!"

Uncle Karf's head and torso dangled from the serpent's gaping mouth. His lower half was already inside the Seph. Did Uncle Karf twitch a little? It was hard to tell. The Seph whipped his head from side to side, then pointed his ugly nose straight upward. A few more inches of Uncle Karf disappeared into that gaping maw. Then he moaned. At first, I thought he was in pain, but then I saw he was smiling. He was moaning in ecstasy, a look of rapture on his face!

I froze and my blood ran cold. I dropped the camera, sprang to my feet, and pointed through the glass. I tried to speak, but my mouth refused to work.

Cheff grabbed me and pulled me back down below the window line. "Get down! What's the matter with you?"

"They… they're… Uncle Karf… he's… they…" My stomach heaved. I turned away from Cheff and vomited onto the basement floor.

Cheff shook me by the shoulders. "Snap out of it! There's no time for this!" He got up on his knees and peered into the Pavilion. He froze, then demanded in a completely flat voice, "Give me the camera."

I handed him the camera and choked out, "Wait! You have to turn off the fla—"

Like a lightning bolt on the darkest night, the flashbulb illuminated not merely the pavilion, but the entire basement. Cheff dropped back to the deck. "Why didn't you tell me—"

"I tried to, but—"

"You should've—"

Sable stood up and pulled Cheff to his feet next to her. "Stop. Look."

The four of us stood and looked inside. All nine of the Sephs stared at us through the foggy glass. We stared back, motionless.

Slowly, Buttons raised Starry and Moka above the windowsill and made each of them wave to the Sephs. She smiled sweetly and waved, too.

One Facilitator grinned foolishly and waved back, but the Facilitator standing next to him smacked him on the back of the head. There was only one thing to do—the rest of us smiled and waved, right along with Buttons and the ponies, while the Sephs and Facilitators stared, dumbfounded.

The Seph closest to the door of the pavilion collected his wits and bellowed a command at the Facilitators, who sprinted in our direction. Then, with his nose, he hit an intercom switch on the wall behind him, and yelled into it, "Intrudersss in the basssement! Intrudersss in the basssement!" His voice boomed throughout the entire fortress.

Cheff yelled, "Run!" quite unnecessarily, as we were already moving.

As we raced toward the sea door where we'd left Mid and Lery, I shouted, "Wait! What about Uncle Karf?"

"I don't know," Cheff yelled back. "We'll have to retreat and regroup!"

"He's half-eaten already!" I screamed. "There's not going to *be* any regrouping. It's now or never!"

"If you have any good ideas, now's the time!"

A sharp explosion stopped us dead in our tracks. Across the room, Mid and Lery were holding their ears, coughing, and vainly attempting to wave away a cloud of acrid white smoke. A trickle of seawater sprayed through a small crack along the edge of the iron sea door. Mid yelled, "It wasn't strong enough. Lery, hand me another one!"

Cheff looked back at the rapidly closing Facilitators. "Hurry!"

Lery handed Mid a small bundle from Mid's tech bag.

Mid stuck it to the old door, then turned aside and put his fingers in his ears. Another explosion roared louder than the first and the trickle of seawater became a flood.

The Fessals chasing us skidded to a halt, turned around, and scrambled away from the gushing torrent, back toward the pavilion, stumbling and bumping into each other.

Mid yelled, "One more time!" and reached for his tech bag.

Lery pulled Mid gently away from the door. "Gotta have… the right… right tool for… the right job." He swung his giant pipe wrench high above his head with both hands, then shattered the ancient, rusted locking mechanism into a dozen pieces.

The ancient sea door swung partway open and jammed. With a roar like thunder, a furious, raging wall of water nearly three feet high surged across the room and around the massive pillars, with Mid and Lery at the forefront, tumbling over and over in the churning, foaming brine. It swept the rest of us off our feet and barreled all six of us together into the Fessals who had chased us, bowling them over and sweeping them along with us. To our horror, the flood was propelling us straight back into the pavilion!

"Very slowly, Buttons raised Starry and Moka above the window sill, and made each of them wave to the Sephs."

Operation Break Iron

— 41 —

MAELSTROM

I NSTANTLY, THE PAVILION became a swirling maelstrom of floundering, panicking Sephs snapping and biting, and uniformed Facilitators thrashing and trying to keep out of the Sephs' way. In the middle of it all, Uncle Karf still dangled from the giant Seph's jaws.

All six of us washed into the maelstrom. Submerged beneath the surge of icy seawater, I thrashed about blindly until I found a handhold along the wall, a vertical iron strut. I pulled myself to my feet and stepped up onto the narrow stone ledge that formed the base of the pavilion's walls. Even standing on the little ledge, the water was already above my waist. I looked up just in time to see the current spin Cheff toward me, so I grabbed him, pulled him to me, and helped him get a grip on my strut.

The Facilitators frantically tried to catch the Sephs, but the Sephs were too big and too slippery. So around and around they went, bouncing off the glass walls as the water rose higher. Once, we spotted Uncle Karf as he swirled past, barely out of reach, still in the huge Seph's mouth, still smiling, still moaning, eyes closed.

Sable had found her own strut several panels from us. She plucked Buttons from the water, tucked her under one arm, then threw her grappling hook right through the glass ceiling and hooked it onto an iron rafter. She swung herself and Buttons over to Cheff and me, pointed at Uncle Karf in the swirling confusion, and called out above the roiling waters, "Get him!"

While I helped Buttons secure a firm hold on the strut, Sable flipped the grappling hook down from the ceiling and returned it to her belt. Next, she attached a set of pulleys to her rope, fastened one end to the strut, and tied the other end around Cheff's waist. "Ready?"

"Ready."

As Sable gradually let the rope out, Cheff waded a few feet into the foaming mess, carefully avoiding both the frantic Fessals and the thrashing, panicking Sephs. But Mid came by before Uncle Karf came around again, so Cheff caught him just in time to pull him out of the reach of a floundering Seph's snapping frenzy. Sable pulled Cheff and Mid back in. Mid climbed up onto the ledge with us, coughing and spitting.

Cheff waded right back into the maelstrom, not even stopping to catch his breath. Lery was next. Cheff reached out. "Lery! Grab on!" As Lery swooshed by, he grabbed Cheff by the vest. Cheff wrapped his arms around him, and again Sable pulled them both back. Cheff gasped for air, exhausted.

Sable pointed at Lery. "Switch."

Cheff, breathing hard, untied the rope from his waist. "Lery? If I tie this around you, can you save Uncle Karf?"

"Yes… Friend Cheff."

Cheff tied the rope around Lery's waist, and Sable eased him out into the dark, churning waters. The water was rising fast. It was already up to my chest. "Hurry, Lery," I said, "we don't have much time."

Lery grinned. "Quality work takes… takes time." As the enormous Seph swallowing Uncle Karf approached, Lery grabbed Uncle Karf's arm, which caused the Seph to spin around in the flood. Lery raised his mighty pipe wrench and bashed the Seph on the end of his scaly snout. The ugly Seph sneezed and coughed, and Uncle Karf was free.

"The right tool…" Lery tossed Uncle Karf over his shoulder, then Sable and Cheff strained together to pull them both back to the strut.

The water was almost up to my shoulders. Buttons could barely keep her head out of the water.

Cheff said, "We'd better get out of here. Sable?"

Sable tied a loop of rope around each of us, then attached the grappling hook to the other end of the pulley rig. She threw the grappling hook across the room, where it crashed through another window and caught on an iron rafter, then she and Cheff pulled us against the current. Across the basement, the old sea door creaked and groaned. Cheff said, "Hurry, Sable, I think it's going to blow."

The water was up to our necks now. Lery shifted Uncle Karf to his other shoulder. Sable reset the pulley rig and threw the hook again. She and Cheff reeled us in, and we were more than halfway across the basement. After we passed the sea door, the current was on our side. We half-waded, half-swam to the bottom of the slitherway, then dashed to the top. From the basement, there came a final screeching and rending of tired metal, and that old sea door exploded off its hinges.

"We're still below sea level," Mid shouted. "We have to keep going up!"

Cheff yelled, "Go!" and go we did, with an angry tsunami of cold sea water thundering up the slitherway behind us. "Next level up! Let's go, *let's go*, LET'S GO!" He swooped Buttons off her feet and slung her on his back, where she clung desperately to his neck, hitting him with Starry and yelling, "Faster, faster, faster!"

Lery, with his long legs, passed us all as we cleared the first landing. Mid's stubby little legs were barely keeping up, so Sable grabbed him by the hand and dragged him along. The water came crashing up the slitherway behind us as we reached the second landing.

Cheff shouted, "Move! One more to go!"

We turned the corner and raced up the third slitherway, barely ahead of the pursuing tide. As we reached the top, the wild wave surged up behind us and shot us into the air. We flew, briefly, then landed hard on the dry iron deck. The surge of seawater broke in a shower of foam, then retreated to sea level, somewhere in the darkness below us.

We caught our breath and picked ourselves up. Cheff made sure we were all there, then checked us over. "Everyone okay?"

Mid said, "We seem to be, but I couldn't tell you how we managed it."

"How's Uncle Karf?" Cheff asked.

Lery gently laid Uncle Karf on the deck. His skin was stained purple where it had been in contact with Seph digestive fluids. Sable knelt over him and put her ear to his chest. "Still breathing."

Uncle Karf turned his head and moaned softly, but remained unconscious.

"Good." Cheff heaved a sigh of relief. "Okay, let's get up to the loading dock before something else bad happens."

We started up the last slitherway, but stopped dead as we heard a commotion coming our way from above. Cheff asked quietly, "What's that?"

Lery said, "Guards…"

"A lot of guards," Cheff said, "by the sound of it."

"Of course," Mid said. "What else?"

Sable pointed to the dark recesses beneath the slitherway. "Hide."

Lery shouldered Uncle Karf again, and we ducked down the corridor into some shadows and made ourselves small. The guards' boots clattered on the slitherway over our heads. They paused, briefly, then continued down the next slitherway toward the deck below us. They didn't get far before they were stopped by the new inland sea, so they returned to our deck and searched there. The leader was saying something too low to hear. Once, he glanced our way. Another time, he aimed his flashlight in our direction.

Cheff said, "We'd better get out of here! Let's split up—they can't follow all of us. We'll meet up at the loading dock. Don't get caught!"

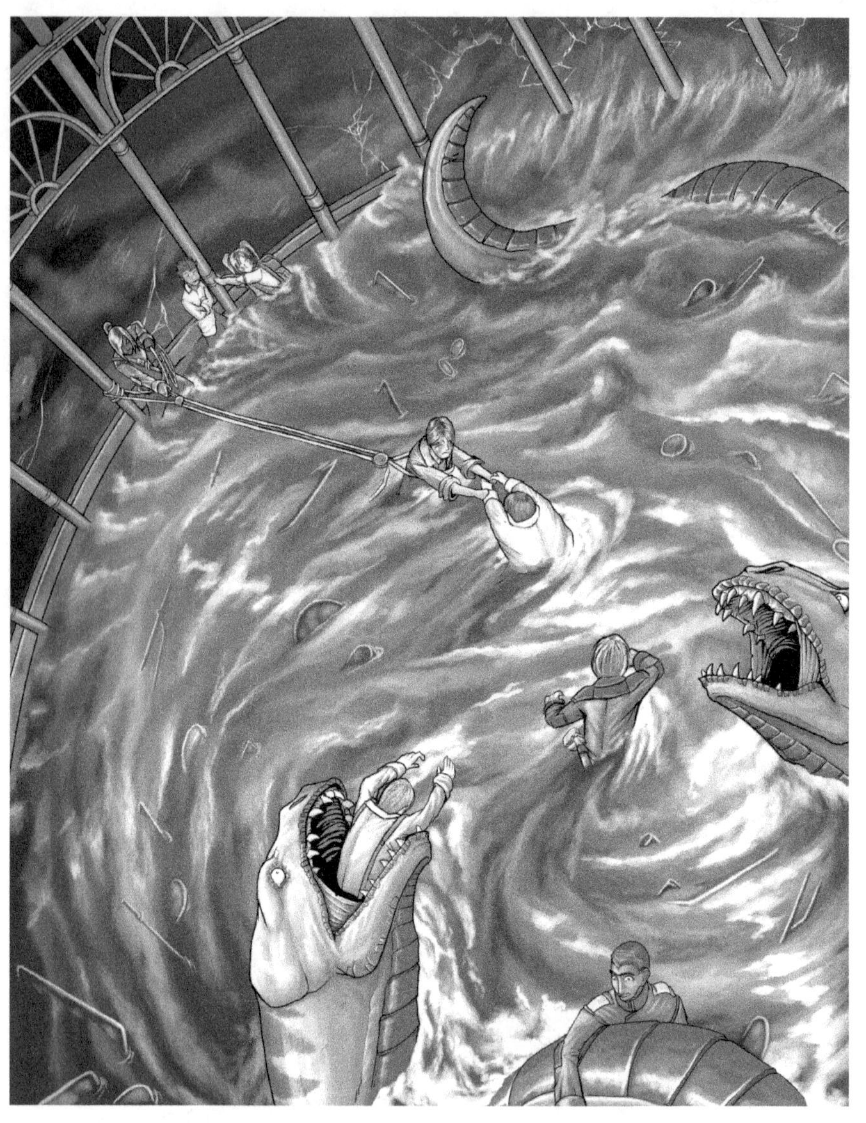

"...the pavilion became a swirling maelstrom..."

— **42** —

STARRY WEIGHS IN

SABLE VANISHED INTO the shadows. Lery, still carrying Uncle Karf, trotted down the corridor a short way, followed by Mid, pulled out his keys and opened one of the side doors. He waved Mid through, then ducked in after him. The door closed behind them, and they were gone, too.

Cheff said to Buttons and me, "Squeeze the water out of your clothes as best you can, so we don't leave a wet trail." When we had done this, he put his finger to his lips, beckoned to us, and whispered, "Follow me!" The three of us sneaked along the right-hand side of the octagonal corridor, crouching low in the shadows. Cheff tried every door we passed, but they were all locked. The guards clattered about in the corridor behind us, trying the same handles we had tried. From time to time, we huddled against the wall as beams from their flashlights illuminated the shadowy areas.

Cheff drew us behind a stack of wooden crates piled high against the corridor wall. "Let's rest a few moments." He wiped the sweat from his forehead with the tail of his shirt. "If we keep going along this corridor, we'll circle all the way back to the slitherway. I'm pretty sure that some of the guards are circling around in the other direction, toward us. If we can find someplace to duck into until the guards meet in the middle, maybe they'll decide that we aren't down here after all."

"What if we don't find an open door?" Buttons asked.

"We end up like Uncle Karf. Don't worry, Sis, we'll find something. We're bound to, right?"

Buttons said, "Right, sure, of course we will." Starry and Moka nodded in agreement, but they didn't look convinced either.

Cheff peered around the edge of the crates. "All clear, let's get moving." He pointed across the corridor to the inside wall. "You take that side, Books. We'll double our chances of finding one open."

I looked both ways, and dashed across to the left-hand side of the corridor, where I ducked into the shadows. Cheff and Buttons crept further along the right side. I paced him, checking all the doors on my side as I went along, but they were all locked. After a few minutes, I heard footsteps in front of us. I saw flashlight beams in the shadows ahead—the other set of guards! When those guards turned that next corner, the three of us would be in plain view.

I tried the next handle, and it turned! I waved at Cheff. "Pssst! Over here!" I held the door open. Cheff grabbed Buttons by the arm, ran across the corridor, and shoved me through the doorway ahead of him.

Cheff locked the door. "Don't make a sound!"

We waited silently in the darkness. The footsteps of the guards approached and stopped outside our door. A gruff voice said, "I'm sure I saw them. They must have gone in here." He tried the handle. "It's locked."

A second voice growled, "It's locked *now*, maybe. But how do you know they didn't go in and lock it behind them?" A flashlight beam flickered through the door's small window and searched the room. "I don't see anything, but you never know."

Our hearts pounded, our breath came in gasps.

The first voice grunted. "Okay, okay, I suppose you could be right." He sighed deeply, his keys jingling, followed by the rasp of a key being inserted into the lock. We froze. The handle jiggled back and forth a few times, then the key was withdrawn. He grunted again. "Wrong key." The keys jingled, another key was inserted into the lock, the handle jiggled, and the key was withdrawn. This was repeated a third time and a fourth.

A loud smack, then the jangle of a ring of keys hitting the floor. The second voice growled, "Forget it, you moron. If you can't get it open, they sure didn't. Even if they did, they're long gone by now. Andaran's bones! Here come the others! Be cool."

More footsteps approached and two men argued loudly about how we could have slipped past both search parties. Cheff gave me and Buttons a gentle tug. We followed him silently across the dark room, which was filled with crates stacked from floor to ceiling. We came to a door on the far side of the room. Cheff tried it. It was open. He peeked through the dark doorway, then motioned for us to follow.

In the dim light, this room seemed much like the other, jammed full of crates and barrels. On the opposite side, we passed through yet another connecting door. We were deep inside the oldest part of the keep. When we were halfway through this third room, the far door burst open with a crash. A fat guard waddled in, shining his light all around.

Cheff and I ducked out of sight behind some barrels. Buttons scrambled up a stack of crates faster than a red-flyer monkey. The guard's flashlight beam probed the top of the stack, but there was nothing there, so the guard started exploring the room, getting closer and closer to our hiding place.

Just as the guard was about to discover Cheff and me, a squeaky voice came from the top of the stack of crates. "Hey, Fatso! I'm up here!"

The guard aimed his light at the top of the crates and again saw nothing. He resumed his search of the room.

The squeaky voice called out again, "Whoa, Sergeant Tubbalard! What are you looking for? There's no one down there. I told you, I'm up here!"

The guard again pointed his light at the top of the stack, but there was still nothing to be seen. He waddled over and struggled to haul his enormous bulk up the tower of crates.

Cheff leaped to his feet. He hissed, "Buttons! What are you thinking? Get down from there!"

The guard stopped climbing and looked around but couldn't determine where Cheff's voice had come from. He sighed, then began laboriously climbing back down the stack of crates.

When he was about halfway down, the squeaky voice spoke again. "Where are you going? I said *up here,* you idiot! Don't you know which way is up?"

The guard turned his flashlight toward the top of the stack again, but a loose crate shifted under him. He dropped the flashlight on the top of a crate as he flailed about, grasping for a handhold. When he regained his balance, he looked around for the flashlight, but it had disappeared.

Cheff clapped his hand to his forehead. "Buttons! Get down here at once!"

The guard stopped and looked up at the top of the crates, then peered back down into the darkness in the direction of Cheff's voice. He pondered, started climbing down, stopped and looked up again, and nearly jumped out of his skin.

At the top of the stack was the valiant Starry Stargazer, illuminated from below with the guard's missing flashlight, giving her a creepy look. Starry's voice was low and spooky. "Bwahahahahaaa! Did you lose something, Mr. Stupid Fat Fessal Guard? I have it right here!" She waved the flashlight back and forth. "Too bad for you, Porkbelly! Finders keepers!"

The light blinked off. In the dark, the guard lost his tenuous hold on the crates and came crashing to the floor. He cried out as one of the crates landed on his head. The light came on again, a mere foot from the guard's eyes. The guard squinted and shaded his eyes with his hand. "What? Who?" His other hand shot out and caught Buttons by the ankle. The guard struggled to his knees. "I've got you now, you filthy brat! Give me that flashlight!"

"Okay, if you say so." She made as if to hand him the flashlight. Instead, with a resounding smack, Buttons lashed the guard across the jaw with her little pony. The guard slumped back to the floor like a sack of potatoes, twitched, then lay still. Buttons smiled sweetly and said, "It's not nice to grab innocent little girls, you nasty, smelly man." She held Starry up to her face. "Is it, Starry? No, it's not!" She turned Starry to look at the inert guard, then said in a baby voice, "Nasty fat man taking a wittle nap. Him's not so gwabby, now, is hims?"

Cheff ran to Buttons. "Are you okay, Sis? How'd you do that?"

"I'm fine. I didn't do anything. Starry did."

Cheff took a deep breath, held it, then let it out slowly. "Of course she did." He faced the pony. "Good work, Starry! You're amazing. How'd you manage it, anyway?"

Buttons handed Starry to Cheff, who nearly dropped her. "She's heavy! What's that about?"

"You know those ball bearings Mid brought home from the factory last week? The ones for his school project? Well, Starry was looking a little thin after her adventure with Mister Snuggles, and I couldn't find any more stuffing, so I filled Starry up with the ball bearings. She really likes the shiny metal balls."

Cheff said flatly, "You packed Starry full of ball bearings."

"Well, mostly. There weren't enough bearings, actually, so I had to add some scrap metal. And some sand." She looked up at Cheff and batted her eyes. "I didn't know they'd come in so handy."

"Riiight, of course you didn't." He mussed her hair. "Good thinking, my dear, sweet, innocent, little *Mellabee*. I'm sure glad you're on our side."

Buttons stuck out her tongue and made a little curtsy.

Cheff hefted the little pony a few times. "She's heavy. I'll bet Starry made him see *stars*!" They both laughed.

I tugged on Cheff's sleeve. "If you two are done, we'd better get moving." I nudged the snoozing guard with the toe of my shoe.

"Books is right," Cheff said. "It's only a matter of time before Fat-and-Ugly here wakes up." He tiptoed to the door leading to the corridor and listened, then opened it a crack and looked out. "We can't go that way—the corridor's full of guards. We'll have to find another way."

Buttons clicked the guard's flashlight on. "At least we won't have to look in the dark anymore. Give me a sec." She swung the flashlight viciously against the guard's temple. "That ought to keep him sound asleep while we get away." She pointed the flashlight toward the far wall. "I think I see a door over there."

As she bounced away, Cheff turned to me. "I worry about her, sometimes. Still…"

"Yeah," I said.

"Yeah," Cheff said.

We followed Buttons across the room.

— 43 —

CAUGHT

THE FLASHLIGHT MADE navigating the Fortress much easier. We wound our way through a seemingly endless maze of storerooms, offices, workshops, and empty rooms until we came back out to the main corridor. Cheff opened the door a crack. "We're almost all the way around to the slitherway again! Look!"

Buttons and I crowded around the door and looked out. Lery stood at the foot of the slitherway with a mop in his hand, talking with a pair of guards. He made a few casual swipes with the mop, then swished it up and down in the mop bucket, put it in the wringer, and pulled the handle. One of the guards jumped back to avoid being splashed, then snatched the mop out of Lery's hand. "Stop that, you imbecile! I'm trying to ask you a question. Did you or did you not see anyone go up this slitherway?"

"I... I didn't see... anyone... sir. I've just been mopping this cor... corri... hallway... like I was told. For the ban... banquet you know. Gotta have... gotta be... all clean for... the banquet. Sephs get... mad if the... floor is dirty. I don't... like it when... when Sephs get mad."

"Yes, yes, all right, nobody's mad at you. We need to know if you saw someone where they shouldn't have been."

"Someone where... no... I..." He stopped and looked up and down the corridor. "I don't see... anybody... sirs. Just me... down here mopping like... I was told. Gotta... gotta have..."

"Yes, yes, we know, you gotta have clean floors." He pointed at the seawater sloshing against the slitherway. "What happened down there? Where did all this water come from?"

"I don't... I'm just... gotta clean..." Lery shuffled to the edge of the slitherway and stared at the seawater below. "That... that's... a lot of... water." He took off his hat and scratched his head thoughtfully. "I'm gonna... need a bigger... bucket." He turned and looked straight at us and winked. "Yup. This bucket's... gonna be too... way too small for... all that water. I'm gonna go... find a bigger... bucket."

"You stay right here!" the guard snapped. "I'm warning you—"

The second guard broke in, "Forget it, Sarge, this dummy's not gonna tell us nothin' 'cause there's nothing to tell. There ain't nobody down here. Anyway, it's lunchtime. I'm starving." He took a small packet of crackers from his pocket, popped one into his mouth, and offered them to the sergeant, who ignored them.

"Yeah, I guess you're right, Farmul. Let's go eat."

Lery froze in his tracks, then slowly turned around. "Hey... that... that's not nice. I'm not... a dummy. I'm... mopping. Gotta have clean... clean floors... for the..."

Farmul dismissed him with a wave of his hand. "Ahhh, go get your bucket, *dummy*," he said, spraying cracker crumbs onto Lery's coveralls and all over the clean floor. The two guards turned and strolled down the corridor, laughing.

Lery stared at the crumbs on the floor. "Filthy... Fessals," he muttered.

When the guards had disappeared around the bend, Lery beckoned to us. We crept slowly out of the doorway, Cheff in the lead, then Buttons, then me. We stayed close to the wall as we edged our way toward Lery and the bottom of the slitherway.

Lery signaled us to stop. We froze. The two guards were coming back. Lery picked up his mop and began mopping vigorously, staring intently at the floor. The guards walked right up to him, but turned their backs toward us. We held our position around the corner nearest the slitherway, barely out of sight. Our hearts thumped, and we struggled to breathe without being heard.

Lery looked up. "Yes… sirs?"

"I was thinking," the sergeant said, "that if any intruders escaped from down there"—he pointed at the churning seawater below the slitherway—"without drowning, which, I admit, is highly unlikely, they would have had to come right past you. It's the only way." He took a few steps toward the bottom of the slitherway and looked up toward the loading-dock level. "If they were attempting to escape, they'd have had to go that way."

He came back and went a few paces down the corridor. "On the other hand, if they were hiding, they might have gone this way." He took off his hat and scratched his head. "Say, Farmul, didn't Gorgol go this way? How long has it been since we heard from him, anyway? You don't suppose he ran into the intruders, do you? If he did, we would have heard something, right? I didn't hear anything. Did you hear anything, Farmul? Me neither." He laughed. "On the other hand, if the intruders did whack him, he'd be too fat to fall down." Both guards laughed. "Anyway, he's most likely taking a nap. *Another* nap." He thought it over. "No, I don't think the intruders went this way. And there's no one on the loading dock, or we would have met them coming down. I'm pretty sure they must have gone *that* way." He pointed directly at our hiding place. "C'mon, Farmul, let's go find 'em."

The two guards drew their pistols, marched resolutely three steps in our direction, and spotted us. They leveled their weapons. With a look of supreme satisfaction, the sergeant said, "What did I tell you, Farmul? It's exactly as I predicted. Never underestimate the power of deduc… dedac… well, reasoning. *Thinking,* you know. Yeah. Brain power wins again. All right, you three, get up and get over here."

The three of us stood up and approached the guards. Buttons cradled Starry and Moka in her hands. Out of the corner of my eye, I saw a dark figure, high above in the shadows of the ceiling, silently making its way from light fixture to light fixture, to a position directly above the guards.

The sergeant tried to pat me on the head, but I ducked. "Well, will you look at that, Farmul—it's only some kids. A couple of Loras, and a Lildur brat. They can't possibly be the intruders, can they?" He turned to us and got down on one knee. "Where did you kids come from, anyway? What are you doing way down here in the basement? Are you lost?"

"Yes, sir," Cheff said. "We were here visiting the museum. Our escort got sick and had to go to the nurse's office, and we got lost. It was hours ago, sir, and we've been trying to find our way out ever since."

Buttons made Starry nod her head at the guard, and said in Starry's voice, "That's right, sir. It's been hours and hours. I'm sooo hungry."

The guard smiled kindly and patted Starry on the head. "Of course you are, sweetie. Look at this, Farmul—she looks about the age of your little Derry. And she's hungry. Give her your crackers."

Farmul quickly crammed the rest of his crackers into his mouth and said around them, "I dunno, Sarge. How do we know these ain't the intruders? We din't find no one else down here, and it has to be someone, dunnit?"

The sergeant frowned. "That's a good point, Farmul." He squinted at me, then at Cheff. "You might be right. Maybe the best thing is to take them upstairs for questioning."

"Right." Farmul gagged down the huge wad of dry crackers and grabbed Cheff, while the sergeant took Buttons and me by the hair. "All right, you brats. Come with me. Best you come peacefully."

"What's that?" Farmul pointed past Lery. "Over there! I heard a door close. There's somebody in there!"

The Sergeant yelled, "Get them!"

Mid stepped out of the doorway and activated his flashdark right into Farmul's eyes. Farmul screamed, "Aaaaah! My eyes! I can't see anything! I'm blind!"

A streak of black fell from the ceiling directly onto the Sergeant who screamed like a little girl and frantically waved his arms about his head in a futile attempt to rid himself of the phantom attacker. Sable wrapped her legs around the sergeant's neck, locked her ankles, and squeezed until he blacked out and collapsed onto the floor.

Mid clicked off the flashdark. Farmul wiped his eyes then stared at his unconscious superior. "What happened to him?"

Lery laughed. "I'd say the… the sergeant has been… *dis-Sabled*!"

Sable flashed Lery a quick grin.

Lery took the pipe wrench from his belt and dealt Farmul a savage blow upside the head. Farmul collapsed in a heap overtop the sergeant. Lery bent over him and said, *"And don't call me dummy."* He returned the pipe wrench to its belt holster.

Cheff clapped Lery on the back. "Atta boy, New Friend Lery. You know, you're a real menace with that pipe wrench."

Lery smiled. "The right tool…"

"And good work with the flashdark, Mid, Old Son. Your timing was perfect, as always! You too, Sable. That was rock-smooth!"

Sable nodded. "Three."

"Say, what?" Cheff asked.

"That's the third time she saved your bacon today," Buttons said.

"So it is. Thank you, Sable." He bowed deeply to her.

Buttons searched Farmul's pockets. "There's still another packet of crackers in here. Anybody want some? No?" She nibbled at a cracker. "You sure? It's pretty yummy." She smacked her lips a few times. "Tasty! Here, Starry, try this." She held the cracker to the little pony's mouth. "Yum! Starry likes it." Buttons put the rest of the crackers in her backpack.

Cheff looked around. "Where's Uncle Karf?"

Mid pointed back toward the door he'd stepped out of. "He's fine. Still out of it, I think."

"Lery," Cheff said, "I think you should get Uncle Karf now. It's time to go. When they"—he pointed at the two inert figures on the floor—"don't report in, more guards are bound to follow."

Lery returned with Uncle Karf over his shoulder. "Ready… New Friend Cheff."

"Excellent! Let's go!" Cheff said. "Listen!" Footsteps echoed down the corridor. "And none too soon, either."

We bolted up the slitherway to the loading-dock level and made for the door to the outside. Another party of guards, descending the slitherway from above, spotted us and yelled as they dashed our way.

Mid said, "Quick, Lery, the door."

Lery pulled out his keys and unlocked the door to the loading dock.

Mid said to Cheff, "Go, quick! Lery and I will lock up."

"The right key…"

"Not this time, Lery. This time, we need the wrong key."

Lery frowned.

"Any key will do," Mid said. "Quick!"

Lery handed Mid his key ring. Mid grabbed the most unlikely-looking key, then jammed it into the keyhole. "Lery? Pipe wrench."

Bang! Lery hit the key with the enormous tool.

"Harder. Break it off. Hurry!"

Lery swung his mighty pipe wrench once again, and the key broke off flush with the keyhole. He and Mid stepped outside and pulled the door shut behind them.

"That ought to hold them for a while," Mid said. A ferocious pounding commenced from inside the door. Mid chuckled. "Long enough, anyway."

Lery's smile spread across his face. "Gotta… gotta have the… the wrong key for the… wrong lock."

The pounding on the door stopped. A moment later, the metal around the lock glowed red.

"Not as long as I thought," Mid said.

"Time to go," Sable said, readying her escape ropes.

"Well, New Friend Lery," Cheff said, "How would you like to come with us? It appears that there's no future for you here."

"Okay."

Cheff swung his legs over the railing and slid down the exit rope to the little boat waiting for us below. He stood in the bow of the boat, holding the line steady.

Sable helped the rest of us over the railing and down the rope, first Buttons, then me, then Mid, and finally Lery, who went down with one hand on the rope, the other still holding Uncle Karf securely over his shoulder. Lery laid Uncle Karf gently on the bottom of the boat, then took a seat.

Sable slid down and did something magical with her special quick-release knot. The rope came free from the railing and landed in a heap by her feet. She took her seat in the prow. "Mid, engines."

The boiler was still hot. Mid opened the steam valve, and the little engine chuffed earnestly.

"Full speed ahead!"

"Aye, aye, Commodore!"

The Iron Fortress faded into a massive, grim specter behind us.

— 44 —

MELTERN

IT WAS STILL long before dawn when Cheff knocked on the back door of Meltern's Guest House. We had seen no sign of Buttons' 'cute little puppy,' Mister Snuggles, in the deserted streets.

Cheff had been right—we left the little fishing boat tied to the dock where we'd found it, with no one the wiser, except that the fisherman, whoever he was, might wonder what happened to some of his coal, but that couldn't be helped. There was still plenty in the coal bin, so he wouldn't run out in the bay.

It had taken us another long hour to hike up from the fishing village to Meltern's back door. Lery carried Uncle Karf the entire way without a single word of complaint and without appearing to tire.

At Meltern's back door, Cheff stationed Lery, still carrying Uncle Karf, out of sight of the door in a clump of shrubbery, then knocked softly.

We waited in the cold morning air, shivering, until Meltern opened the door, rubbing the sleep out of his eyes. He looked us over. "Are you kids back again? I told you, there's nothing I can do for you." He stuck his head out of the door and looked both ways up and down the alley. "Did anyone see you? Are you sure no one's following you?" He took another look around, then waved us inside and steered us into a small side room. "Crazy kids! You must be out of your minds, to be out of the Labor Compound, after curfew, tonight of all nights."

"Why, what *about* tonight?" Cheff asked innocently.

"Didn't you hear? All the guards in the city are on alert. The IID and their Blueband snoops are everywhere. Fellstone City is locked down tight. There's been a raid on the Iron Fortress. Our reports say that fifty to a hundred armed men broke into the Fortress, killed dozens of Sephs and their Facilitators, and escaped with one of the prisoners. Might even be your uncle, for all I know." He shook his head in wonder. "I can hardly believe it—there's never been an escape from the Iron Fortress."

Cheff said casually, "As it happens, we did hear something about that. In fact, it's why we're here." He hesitated, then continued, "Mr. Meltern, we're not alone. Don't worry, we weren't followed, but we did bring a friend with us. Two friends, actually. They're waiting outside. It seemed prudent to speak with you first."

Meltern stared. "You brought friends… Listen, boy, what kind of place do you think I'm running here? This isn't a—" He took a deep breath. "Okay, fine, you brought friends. Who are they?"

"I think it would be best to show you, sir. May I call them in?"

Meltern threw up his hands. "Sure, why not? I always invite strangers into my house in the middle of the night because some crazy kid asks me to. Makes perfect sense. In any case, it won't do to leave them outside. If the guards or the Bluebands stumble upon them, it'll come down on me, anyway. Go ahead, go get them."

Cheff went to the back door, opened it softly, checked the area as Meltern had, then whispered, "All clear, Lery, come on in."

Lery, crouching, carried Uncle Karf inside, and gently laid him face-down on the floor, then took a seat next to Mid and stared at the wall, rubbing his left shoulder muscles with his right hand.

Meltern's jaw dropped, and he kept looking from Lery to Uncle Karf, then back again. "I don't understand. Who is this?" He stabbed his forefinger at Lery. "That's an Army uniform! You brought a soldier here? Are you trying to get me killed? And who's that on the floor? What's the matter with him? Is he dead? And why is he half purple?" Meltern grabbed Cheff by the front of his shirt. "You'd better start explaining, boy, and make it quick!"

Cheff pulled loose, knelt by Uncle Karf, and gently turned him over so that Meltern could see his face.

Meltern gasped. "Is that… is that Karf? How could that be?"

Cheff grinned. "It's Uncle Karf, all right. He's not dead, he's drugged, something called jexan. Our new friend, Lery, here, carried him all the way from the Iron Fortress."

Lery glanced up and smiled vaguely at Meltern.

Meltern stared at Lery. "Carried him from—" He collapsed into a chair. "Then you… you kids… how did you…? How could…?" He collected himself. "The raid… that was *you*?"

Cheff's grin broadened. "Yeah, all fifty of us. Or was it a hundred?"

Meltern looked at Cheff curiously, then called, "Hern! Bring a stretcher, quickly!" He asked Cheff, "Why is Karf's skin purple."

"We think it's from the Seph's digestive juices, sir. He was half swallowed when we found him."

Meltern said, "We've heard rumors of Seph cannabalism. I didn't believe them until now." He looked like he might vomit.

Hern and another man, both Loras, entered and carefully eased Uncle Karf onto a stretcher and covered him with a blanket.

"Get him downstairs, right away!" Meltern commanded, "Get those wet clothes off him, and see to it that he gets warmed up. If he wakes, give him some hot broth."

They took Uncle Karf away.

Buttons watched them go, anxiously.

"Don't worry," Meltern said, "they'll take good care of him. Meanwhile, maybe you can fill me in on just what you've been up to."

Cheff briefly related the highlights of our escapade. When he got to the part about the banquet, Meltern's eyes widened, but he didn't interrupt Cheff's story.

When Cheff finished, Meltern looked at each one of us. "It's almost impossible to believe, but here you are, and here's Karf." He shook his head again. "Why'd you do it, boy? You could've been killed, you and your sister, and your friends."

"I know, sir, but, well, he's my uncle. I've already lost my father and mother. I just couldn't stand the idea of losing him, too. Also, I kept asking myself, 'Who would I be if I *didn't* try.'"

Meltern's voice was gentler now. "And your friends? Why would they go along with such a crazy stunt?"

Mid said quietly, "Cheff's my friend, sir." The rest of us, including Lery, nodded in agreement.

Meltern's face softened. "I see. I guess I see." He turned to Cheff. "You're a most fortunate young fellow."

"Yes, sir, I know that's true."

"But tell me this: why did you bring Karf *here*?"

"It's like I told you on our first visit, sir. When he was taken, he told me to contact you. He didn't say why, but I can guess." Cheff lowered his voice. "You *are* FRM, aren't you?"

Sable raised her eyebrows.

Meltern growled, "The FRM is a myth, understand? I told you before!"

Cheff said nothing, only looked Meltern in the eye.

Meltern glared back, then dropped his gaze. "Okay, I guess you deserve to know that much. Yes, I'm FRM, and so is your uncle. And your father was, too. And yes, that's why they used to come here when you were a boy. And now that you know that, I may have to kill all of you. We'll see what headquarters says."

Buttons giggled and raised Starry to her face. "Hear that, Starry? The big, bad FRM man is going to kill us. Oooh, I'm scared! Aren't you, Starry?" Starry nodded. "Okay, Mr. Meltern, sir. We're ready to go." She scrunched her eyes shut. "Make it quick, sir, if you don't mind."

"Quiet, Mel," Cheff said, and put a hand on her shoulder. "I think he means it." He asked, "Seriously, sir? *Do* you mean it?"

"Probably. The FRM has to protect its secrets. There might be a chance that I could swear you all to secrecy. But how do I know I can trust you to keep quiet?" He pointed at Lery. "He *is* Army, after all, and the dark one here has an Academy mission outfit. Looks to me like I'm dealing with the enemy. What do you say about that?"

Cheff stood up. "Well, sir, to start with, I think we've demonstrated beyond doubt where we stand." He gestured toward Lery. "*All* of us. It should be obvious that we're not the Emperor's good little boys and girls."

"Go on," Meltern prompted.

"Besides the fact that they stuck us in that stinking Labor Compound, all of us have a more personal stake in this, don't we, Sis?"

"They killed our parents," Buttons said. "And they were going to *eat* Uncle Karf." She held Starry up to her face. "It's not nice to eat people, is it, Starry?" Starry shook her head. "No, it's not. Starry says that eating people must stop."

"They shot my father right in front of my mother and me," I said. "And they burned my history books, and that stupid museum is full of lies!"

"They kidnapped my baby sister," Mid said, "and sold her to a fat Fessal woman for a servant girl. My poor mother hasn't been right in the head since."

Sable looked up from behind her dark hair. "They *ate* my father."

"And a lot of other people, too, it seems," Cheff said. "Lery says that no prisoner has ever left the Fortress since he's been there."

Meltern said to Lery, "You there, soldier boy. What's your name? Lery? What about you? You're a Fessal and a soldier. Why should we trust you?"

"Don't… don't call me Fessal. I don't… like Fessals. Fessals are mean. They hurt me. They call me 'dummy.' I'm not… not a dummy." He took his army cap off and flung it to the floor. "I… I never wanted to be a… a soldier. They made me. I hate soldiers! *And* Fessals." He gathered his thoughts. "And Sephs. Sephs smell bad." He looked up. "I'm Mid's friend… new friend… now." He swept his arm around the room. "Everybody's new friend. *Not* a Fessal. *Not* a soldier. *Not a dummy.*" He looked down and plucked at his army uniform. "I gotta… gotta get some new… clothes."

"Okay, Lery." Meltern patted Lery on the shoulder. "I think I get the picture. But there's something you should know. It's okay to be a Fessal—not all Fessals are mean and hurtful. Some Fessals are good and kind." Lery looked doubtful, but Meltern continued, "There are even some Fessals in the FRM. If you like, someday I'll introduce you to some Fessals who are my friends. Would you like that?"

Lery stared at the floor. "I… I don't know. Fessals are… mean… but… maybe."

"Okay," Meltern said, "I guess you all do have reason enough to hate the Emperor." He sighed. "We all do. That's one reason we joined the FRM. As I mentioned, we've been hearing rumors of cannibalism for years, the so-called 'dark food' or 'night meat,' but we've never found any conclusive evidence. Even if what you kids say is true, and I, for one, believe you, there's still no proof. And without proof, there's nothing anyone can do about it."

"But there is, sir." I stepped forward and handed Meltern the camera. "We, well, Cheff, took a photograph of the Sephs eating Uncle Karf. We kept the camera dry, so the picture should be good."

"You did? How did you take a picture? I thought you said it was dark in that basement?"

Cheff hung his head. "It was, sir. I, um, didn't turn the flash off before I took the picture. That's what gave us away."

Meltern stared at Cheff, then started to laugh. He laughed until the tears ran down. "You forgot to turn off the flash." He held his sides and gasped for air. "Oh, my. That's amazing. What I would give to have seen the looks on the Sephs' faces!"

"Well, sir," Mid suggested, "if you have any way to develop the film in that camera, you still might."

Meltern wiped his face. "We do, we do indeed." He opened the door and called out, "Hern! Hern, come here, I need you."

Shortly, there were footsteps in the corridor, and Hern stepped into the room again, alone this time. Meltern said, "I guess it's time for a proper introduction. Children, this is Hern. He's my chief assistant. He'll stay with you for a few minutes while I notify headquarters about what happened tonight. You kids stay put. I'll have someone bring in sandwiches."

"Before you go, sir," Cheff said, "there's one other thing you should know. We told you the part about the jexan in the cafeteria food, but there's more to the story. From what Lery told us, the Sephs have been giving small amounts of jexan to everyone in Fellstone City. We're not sure how, but it's likely in the food, maybe the flour or sugar, and maybe in the water supply, too. It's how they keep people happy, or at least placated. Lery doesn't know how it works, but he's been avoiding it by not eating his army rations and cooking his own food in the kitchen at night when no one's around. He's not even sure what it does, but from what we saw of our friend, Tocette, it seemed to make her love Emperor Pallador, willing to believe what the museum said about him. And Uncle Karf when…" He swallowed hard.

"Go on, Cheff," Meltern encouraged gently.

Cheff took a deep breath, held it, then let it out slowly. "Uncle Karf, when he was being eaten, he looked happy. Too happy. There's a word…?"

"Ecstatic?" I offered. "Rapturous?"

"Yeah, that," Cheff said. "He wasn't struggling or trying to get away. He didn't seem to be in pain. He seemed to be enjoying it." Cheff stopped and swallowed again. "Lery said that they give the prisoners large amounts of jexan to keep them from running away. He doesn't know what small amounts of jexan do over a period of time."

Meltern ran his hand through the white Fruen stripe in his hair. "That's new information. We know about jexan, but we didn't know that everyone was getting it. In the food or water, you say? That might explain why getting anyone to care about anything has been so hard. Good work, son. That's valuable information. Perhaps, in time, we can find an antidote or some other way to counteract it. I'll let headquarters know about that, too." He turned and went out the door.

Hern sat down next to Cheff but said nothing. We waited in awkward silence until a woman came to the door and handed in a tray of sandwiches, a pitcher of cider, and some glasses. We ate and drank in silence, then put our glasses on the tray, which Hern set by the door. Then we waited for another long while, our silence broken only by the occasional cough or the scuff of a shoe on the wooden floor.

At long last, Meltern returned, his face set like stone. "I've contacted headquarters and advised them of the situation. I'm sorry, kids." He turned to Hern. "Take these kids out back and shoot them."

Hern stood up, eyes wide. "But, sir—"

"You heard me. Get moving!"

We leaped to our feet, our hearts pounding their way out of our chests. But before we could speak, Meltern's face softened and he chuckled. "Aww, siddown, kids. I'm fooling with you. Actually, I've got some good news."

Cheff's face flushed. "With all due respect, Mr. Meltern, *sir*, that wasn't funny!"

Meltern lifted his eyebrows. "You didn't think we were actually going to…?" He examined our faces. "Ah, I see you did. I apologize, children. I'm sorry. I guess my wife is right—sometimes my sense of humor is a bit misplaced."

Hern scowled, "A bit, sir? A *little* bit?"

Meltern blushed. "Maybe more than a bit."

Hern added, "I'm going to go with 'not one tiny little bit funny.' Especially for them. *Sir*."

"Okay, okay. Kids, I apologize again." He brightened. "The truth is, I've got some good news. Somewhat unusual, perhaps, but good."

Buttons held Starry up and said, her voice quivering, "See, Starry? I told you he didn't mean it."

Our hearts had stopped pounding, mostly. Cheff glared at Meltern. Through clenched teeth, he inquired, "And what might the good news be, Mr. Meltern, sir?"

Before he could answer, Lery snickered, which turned into laughter, then outright guffawing. "Take… take us out and… and shoot us!" He slapped his thigh. "That's… *funny!*"

All of us, including Meltern and Hern, stopped and stared at Lery. Finally, we couldn't help ourselves, and one by one we laughed, too, until, finally, Cheff allowed himself to smile a little. "Yes, fine, whatever. Very hilarious. Andaran's bones!"

I said quietly, "I'll bet Captain Utaliak would have thought it was funny, Cheff."

Cheff stared at me, then grinned and clapped me on the shoulder. "He would, he would at that! Okay, I guess the joke is on me this time." He turned to Meltern. "You were saying something about *good* news, sir?"

Meltern nodded. "I contacted headquarters and gave a brief report about you kids and what you did tonight, including the jexan and the 'dark food.' I was told to wait, and in a few minutes, Madame Entigy herself came on the line. She's the chairman, the head of the FRM. She's rarely heard from directly. Usually, we only hear from her second in command, an Altaar named—well you don't need to know his name. She asked me to personally convey her appreciation for what you did tonight, and to commend you for your bold and courageous spirit."

Cheff smiled, and we slapped each other on the back. Even Sable looked pleased.

— 45 —

THE FRM

"**T**HERE'S MORE," MELTERN continued, "and I have to tell you, children, that I've never heard of anything like this in my thirty-five years with the FRM. Madame Entigy pointed out that had you been adults, you could not have done what you did tonight. She says that there will likely arise many situations that only kids can handle. So far, the Imperium has suspected adults, not children, of complicity in the FRM. For that reason, Madam Entigy has invited you to become part of the FRM. What do you think of that?"

We sat in stunned silence, until Cheff asked, "You mean, officially? Like my dad and Uncle Karf?"

"I mean officially."

We gave a nod of assent, first Mid, then Buttons, then me. Last was Sable, who gazed at Cheff. Finally, she gave the slightest nod.

Meltern turned to Lery. "What about you, son?"

"Me? You… you want *me* to… to be in the FRM… too?"

"Madame Entigy said *all* of you. Besides, I don't think the rest of the gang could have done it without you."

"But I don't even… know what FRM… stands for."

"It's a secret!" Meltern whispered, then he smiled. "But I guess you ought to know before you join, eh? Come close." We scooted our chairs together in a circle. Meltern continued, "It's not really a secret. It stands for Fellstone Resistance Movement. It started right here in Fellstone City more than a hundred years ago, before the fall of the Sixth Kingdom, then spread throughout Andaran. We're dedicated to opposing Emperor Pallador and finding the true heir to the Maghorn dynasty and the Sixth Kingdom."

"Opposing the Emperor is good," Mid said.

Sable asked, "Heir?"

Meltern said, "FRM history says that when Pallador defeated the Sixth Kingdom, the Prince and the very pregnant Princess escaped the destruction, aided by FRM agents. However, no one knows where they went. It was over a hundred years ago, and at the time their destination was a closely guarded secret. All Andaran was in chaos, and if there ever were any records, they've been lost. However, the FRM believes, and there is evidence to support it, that the true heir survived and went into hiding somewhere. There are FRM agents all over Andaran searching for his or her descendants."

"Her?" Buttons asked. "The heir was a girl?"

"She might have been. The heir could have been a prince or a princess."

Buttons batted her eyes. "Hear that, Starry? The heir could be a princess, and not even know who she is. Maybe it's me! I'd be a good princess, wouldn't I?"

Starry looked doubtful.

Meltern laughed. "I'm sure you would be, but there's one little problem with that—the true heir is of the Torph People."

"Andaran's Bones!" Cheff smacked his forehead. "I hope it isn't Brex!"

We all laughed, then I said, "Mr. Meltern is right. One of my books says that all the rulers as far back as anyone can remember were Torphs."

"Exactly right," Meltern said. "'When Torphs rule, Andaran prospers.' So, children, are you sure about joining the FRM?"

"Yes, sir," Cheff said, "we're sure."

"Before I swear you in, you must agree to some conditions. First, you must promise to say nothing about either the jexan or the 'dark food' to anyone."

"But, sir," Cheff broke in, "don't you think the people need to know?"

"Yes, of course they do. But the FRM has learned over time, the hard way, how dangerous such knowledge can be. If the people find out too soon or in the wrong way, it could cause panic or even riots and many lives could be lost. The FRM's strategy committee will review the information, investigate further, and come up with a plan designed to do the maximum good. That's not your problem, nor mine. Understand?"

We nodded.

"That brings me to the second condition: you must promise to carry out all orders given to you by the FRM to the best of your ability, even if you don't understand or agree with them. The FRM keeps a lot of information secret, on a need-to-know basis. Only Madame Entigy knows everything, and we're told she's hidden away in a safe place. Do you agree?"

We nodded again.

"Third, and this one should be obvious, you are to speak of the FRM to no one, not even your parents or relatives. That's for their safety as much as yours. And you're never to speak of the FRM where anyone can overhear you. Never indoors or in school—Pallador's intelligence division has microphones planted everywhere."

We agreed.

"Finally, you must swear the FRM oath. Are you ready?"

Cheff said, "I am. Buttons?"

"Me too."

"Mid?"

"I'm in."

"Books?"

"Ready."

"Sable?"

"Yes."

Cheff said, "Sable, are you sure? It's… well, it's a big change for you."

"Truth first. I'm sure."

"Good enough. Lery?"

"Yes, New Friends."

"Very well," said Meltern. "Stand up, please, and face me."

We did so.

"Do you swear to search for the true heir to the Sixth Kingdom and restore to Andaran its rightful ruler?"

"I do," we all answered.

"Do you swear to fight evil and resist corruption in all forms?"

"I do."

"Do you swear to help bring about a world in which every man, woman, and child shall be free to think their own thoughts, without control or influence?"

"I do."

"Do you swear to execute loyally and faithfully all orders given to you by the FRM to the best of your ability, and to protect and preserve the FRM and its secrets, unto death if necessary?"

We considered this seriously, and Buttons looked somber, but we all answered again, "I do."

"Then I, Horcho Meltern, with the authority given to me by the FRM and at the direction of Madame Entigy, do hereby name you official members of the FRM." He shook each of our hands and said, "Congratulations."

— 46 —

THE BSI

W E SAT BACK down, and Meltern continued, "There's one other item. Madam Entigy has issued your group a code name: BSI. It stands for Bayside Insurgents."

"Because the Labor Compound is by Fellstone Bay?" Buttons asked.

"Yes, that, and also in honor of your first mission which was to cross the bay to the Iron Fortress, which is also on Fellstone Bay. See? It works three ways."

Cheff said, "I think I speak for all of us when I say that BSI seems appropriate. What's our next mission, sir?"

"There's no specific mission yet, Cheff. But there are a few general orders. One: see if you can find a suitable location for your group to meet that is safe from prying eyes and ears. Two: be on the lookout for other prospective members in the Labor Compound. Young people, not adults. But don't approach them until they've been cleared through headquarters. Three: you and I are to set up a method for regular, safe communication. I'll have more for you on that later. Think you can handle that?"

"Yes, sir." Cheff stood up straight. "We'll get on it right away."

Mid added, "I have a couple of ideas about a base of operations. We'll look into it."

"What about our individual assignments?" Buttons asked, "Do I get a job of my own?"

Meltern thought about that. "Madame Entigy didn't give any specific work assignments or titles, but from what you've told me, I think I could make some recommendations. Would you like that?"

We nodded.

"Every group needs a leader, or a captain, someone to make the final decisions. It seems to me that Cheff has been the one in that position. It would work this way: before Cheff makes a decision, it's everyone's job to advise him, argue with him, present alternatives, and so on. But once Cheff makes the final decision, the rest of you need to support him, even if you don't agree with him. *Especially* if you don't agree with him. For your part, Cheff, the complement is true: before you make a decision, you must carefully listen to all your advisers and make the best decision you can. You must never abuse your authority and become arrogant or pushy. Got it?"

"Yes, sir, I understand."

"Are you all willing to accept Cheff as your leader?"

We were.

"You'll need a second-in-command, too, for times when Cheff isn't with you. I think that should be Sable. Sable should also be in charge of tactical planning. Her military training will come in handy for that.

"Mid seems to have some talent with inventions. Perhaps he should lead your technical department. He'll make sure you all have the equipment and gadgets you need to accomplish your missions. Speaking of which, I'm sure the FRM's technical department would like to have a word with you regarding your—what did you call it?—your *flashdark* sometime soon."

Mid glowed.

"Books, with his talent for remembering, could be the official BSI historian, keep all the records, that sort of thing. Later on, I'll show you how to keep your records safe from prying eyes and ears."

"Thank you, sir," I said. "I'd enjoy that."

"Lery, how would you like to have two jobs? You can be Mid's assistant in the tech department, but you'll also be Sergeant-at-Arms. Do you know what that means?"

"I… I know what… helping Mid… means… but what's… Sergeant-at-Arms?"

"It means that you'll be in charge of keeping order in the BSI. That will be important as you get more members. It also means you'll be in charge of the weapons, as you get them, and make sure that everyone has the weapons they need. Understand?"

"Yes." Lery took his enormous pipe wrench from his belt and held it up for Meltern to inspect. "The right… right tools for the… right job."

We laughed.

"Exactly!" Meltern clapped Lery on the shoulder. "Perfect. I see that you are, indeed, the right choice. The right man for the right job, eh?"

Lery blushed, and we laughed again.

Mid asked, "But where's Lery going to live? How can he be my assistant? We can't simply sneak him back into the Labor Compound."

"I asked Madame Entigy about that. She has some connections inside the Labor Compound administration office. Lery will have to stay here with me, but only for a few days, maybe a week or two. He'll be my new employee, perhaps a kitchen helper. You mentioned that he knows his way around a kitchen, right?"

"I… I can cook… a little."

"Good. There's an empty room on the top floor with a skylight. You can stay in that as long as you're here."

"A sky… skylight?"

"It's a window in the roof. You can see the sky all day long, and when you go to sleep at night, you'll fall asleep with the moon and stars and the Great Fisherman shining down on you. Sound good?"

"Sounds… good. I don't… get to… to see… the sky… very often in… in the… the Fortress. Yes."

"Excellent. Meanwhile, Madame Entigy will do her magic and, in due course, a new resident of the Labor Compound will arrive at the front gate. He'll be an orphaned Fessal youth, whose most convincing papers say he's about the same age as Cheff and Mid. I think that will be okay, Lery. You do look young for your age, don't you? He'll need a place to live, and it will just so happen that Mid and his mother—you two live alone, right?—that Lery will be assigned to live with you. He'll get a work assignment in some likely place and be assigned to a school class."

Lery smiled. "I'd like to… live with… New Friend Mid."

"Mid, will that be all right with your mother, do you think?"

"I think so, sir. We aren't using one of the upstairs bedrooms. Anyway, she's not been herself since they took Losari, my sister, away. I don't think she'll mind at all. In fact, I think she'll be glad to have someone else to fuss over. So will I, for that matter—I could use the break."

"What about Lery being a Fessal? Will she be okay with that?"

"Yes, sir, I'm sure she will. She doesn't pay too much attention to species. Even when that *stinking* fat Fessal sergeant sold Losari to that *stinking* Fessal rich woman, she wouldn't let me badmouth the *stinking* Fessal species. Stupid Fessals. No offense, Lery."

"Stupid Fessals," Lery agreed.

"Very well, then, that's settled. Besides, it'll get your family some extra ration points and privilege points, too. And, if you like, I can have someone look into what happened to Losari."

"That would be wonderful, sir," Mid said, his eyes brimming with tears.

"Wait—what about *my* job?" Buttons asked. "You said I'd have a job of my own!"

"Actually, I didn't say that—you said that. Now, hang on! Hold that chin quiver! I didn't forget about you," Meltern said, and chuckled. "To the contrary, I saved the best for last!"

Buttons instantly brightened, then held Starry and Moka up. "Hear that, ponies? We get the best job! Aren't you excited?" They were. She turned them around to face Meltern. "Listen carefully, now, ponies." The ponies listened attentively.

"Yes, all three of you listen," Meltern said. "This job is for all three of you." The ponies exchanged a glance. "Since you've demonstrated your talent for shoplifting, diversionary tactics, sneaking, curfew violation, and quick thinking under fire, I think we should make you the official BSI Criminal Mastermind."

Buttons looked enormously pleased with herself, as did Starry and Moka, but Cheff moaned and covered his face with his hands.

"Criminals, I mean," Meltern continued. "The three of you are to be the Criminals of Cuteness. There are a lot of things a cute, innocent, little girl can get away with that a teenage boy can't. I have to warn you: this is *not* a license for bad behavior. You can only use your... what did Cheff call it?—your Cuteness Super-power—you can only use it for officially sanctioned FRM missions, never for your own advantage."

Cheff snorted and Starry kicked him in the ribs with her fuzzy foot.

Buttons batted her eyes at Meltern. "Yes, sir, Mr. Meltern. We'd never dream of such a thing, would we, ponies?" The ponies shook their heads solemnly, but Cheff snorted again.

Meltern leaned over and whispered to Cheff, "She's something, isn't she? You'd better keep an eye on her."

"Don't worry," Cheff said. "I always do."

— 47 —

UNCLE KARF

"What's to become of Uncle Karf?" Cheff asked. "Even if his mind is okay, he'll never be able to come home again, will he?"

Meltern shook his head. "No, son, he won't. Don't worry, though, the FRM will take care of him. He can stay here until he gets well. We have a… um… a place in the basement. You don't need to know more about that."

"But what about Aunt Dee?"

"Tell her nothing."

"Can't we even tell her he's alive and well?"

"No, son, I'm sorry. You can't tell her a single thing. It would be dangerous for you and her both. And for the FRM. I thought I made that clear."

"Yes, sir, you did. Do you think she knows that Uncle Karf is with the FRM?"

"She probably suspects, but she never asked, and he never told her. She's a wise woman, and a good one, too. Your uncle was—*is*—also a fine man. Karf and your father decided, when they joined the FRM, that their wives should not join, so that you kids would have one parent who wouldn't be likely to be caught and killed. Sadly, that didn't work for your mother—they had no proof, but the brutes took her anyway. But not knowing that Karf was FRM is what kept your Aunt Dee alive. And that's how it has to be, for now."

Cheff stared at the floor. "I understand, sir, but it seems so sad. Will she never find out what happened to him?"

Meltern considered the matter. "If I had to guess, I'd say things *might* work out like this: Karf will stay here until he gets better. *If* he gets better, I should say. We've never had anyone that had been given this much jexan, not to mention being partially digested by a Seph. We don't know what it will do to his brain. But, assuming he recovers to the point that he can function reasonably well, he'll be given a new identity and relocated to another city, probably far away in the West, and he'll resume his FRM duties as much as he's able. Then, in a couple of years, after you've received your work assignment and have left the Labor Compound, Dee will be called away, or get a new work assignment through official channels, or she'll get 'sick,' or her death will be faked somehow—the FRM has ways of dealing with such things—and she, too, will get a new identity and rejoin Karf. That's about the best we can do, I'm afraid, but I'll promise you this: I'll make getting her to Karf my personal responsibility when the time comes."

"Thank you, sir. I don't like it, but I see why it has to be this way. At least there's some hope. Can you live with that, Buttons, and keep your mouth shut, no matter how sad Aunt Dee is?"

She held Starry to her ear. "Starry says it's the only way. Better sad than dead. We'll be careful. Moka agrees."

"Fair enough," Meltern said. "I guess you kids had better get moving. It's going to be light in another hour. Would you like to see Karf before you go?"

He led us through a door into a passage and down a set of stairs. In a small room, on a cot next to a warm coal stove, Uncle Karf lay sleeping. We watched him for a short while. As we turned to leave, Uncle Karf groaned loudly and tried to roll over.

Cheff knelt by his side and helped him to turn onto his back. "Uncle Karf, wake up!"

Karf blinked hard a few times and tried to focus on Cheff's face. "Cheff? Is that you? Where am I?" He let Cheff help him up to a sitting position. "I've had the most horrible dream I was being swallowed by a giant Seph"—his face contorted—"and I *liked* it!" He covered his face with his hands.

Meltern stepped in. "Easy does it, Karf. You're safe now, thanks to these kids. Try to rest. Hern! Get him some hot broth right away!"

"Yes, sir! I'll be right back."

Meltern said, "Looks like his brain is going to be fine. Only time will tell for sure. You children had best say your goodbyes now—you won't have another chance. Then it's time for you to get home."

* * *

After we'd said our goodbyes and shed our tears, we left Meltern's place and made our way down the dark alleys toward home. As we went past Mister Snuggles' house, Buttons stopped to give him a pat on the head. Cheff said, "Hurry up, Buttons. We've got to get back in time to sneak in and get ready for school."

"You know," Mid said, "I have a feeling that school's going to seem awfully dull today, don't you think?"

We struggled to keep our laughter quiet as we left Old City and headed for home.

Operation Lockdown

Cheff dropped his pencil onto his drawing table. "Finished!"

I looked up from my Library Management textbook. "What's finished?"

"A map."

"Another map? Of what this time?"

He put his finger to his lips and beckoned me close. We leaned our heads together. "The BSI's new headquarters, possibly," he whispered. "You know, Books, the one Meltern said we should set up."

The BSI is the Bayside Insurgents, a special cell of the FRM, the Fellstone Resistance Movement. We did the jobs that adult agents couldn't do. Meltern was our boss. At the moment, the BSI had six members: Cheff, Mid, Sable, Buttons, Lery, and I. But we had orders to recruit additional agents.

"Right, I remember. Where is it?"

"Down in the old storm drains, a few blocks north of here." He pointed to a location to the northeast of the Fellstone Labor Compound, our home-sweet-home, in the ancient ruins immediately outside the walls. "I found it a few nights ago, when I was, ehem, 'sleepwalking.'"

"Sleepwalking! You mean you've been hunting again? Are you crazy?" All of Fellstone City had been under a strict lockdown since we rescued Cheff's Uncle Karf from the Iron Fortress a few weeks earlier. "The city's swarming with soldiers and Blue-bands!"

"Not down in the storm drains, it isn't. Don't worry, I haven't been hunting outside the borders of the Labor Compound. But there's precious little game in the storm drains, so I figured, why not do some exploring on the side? I've been keeping an eye out for more exits from the storm drains and a suitable location for our new HQ."

"And you found one?"

"Maybe—that's what we have to figure out. There's this one place that looks promising. It's in a tunnel that I think might go a distance outside the Labor Compound. See?" He indicated a tunnel on the map, across the road from the northeast quadrant of the Labor Compound. "Right about here, I ran across an old, rusted access hatch. I tried to pry it open, but it was rusted pretty badly. It would only budge a few inches. I held my miner's lamp up to the crack and peered inside, but I couldn't see much, only what looked like some old furniture. We need to take a crowbar, force that door open, and have a good look inside. I marked the hatch with chalk." He stood and stretched, then sat back down and leaned close again. "I haven't been able to go exploring for a few days. That big storm we had flooded the tunnels. They're probably dry enough by now, though. In fact, I was thinking that you and I might do a little exploring tonight."

"Tonight? Only you and me?"

"You up for it?"

"Well, I, uh… sure, I guess. Why not? I'll tell my mom that we'll be studying late, and I'm going to sleep over."

Cheff grinned. "All true, Old Son, all true."

* * *

We studied until after Cheff's Aunt Dee and his little sister, Buttons, had gone to bed, then Cheff and I crept down and lifted the trapdoor in the floor of the closet under the stairs. Silently, we descended the wooden ladder into our secret underground room and pulled the trapdoor closed behind us. Before Cheff could get his ancient miner's lamp burning, we heard the muffled sound of the trapdoor opening again in the darkness above our heads. We froze, our hearts pounding. Had the Bluebands discovered us? Or the Labor Compound guards? Or worse, Cheff's Aunt Dee? A diminutive figure scrambled down the ladder and thumped onto the dirt floor beside us.

Cheff finished lighting the miner's lamp and held it high. "Buttons! What—?"

Buttons, Cheff's younger sister, smiled.

"Hi, Books! Hi, Cheff!" She held up Starry, her little stuffed tan pony, and made her wave a hoof at me.

I waved back. "Hello, Starry!"

"Where are we going?" Buttons asked.

Cheff narrowed his eyes. "How is it that you always seem to know when I'm going out?"

"Starry tells me."

"Uh-huh. Of course she does. Why do I even ask?" He sighed. "I suppose there's no point in telling you to go back to bed?"

Buttons shook her head, making her twin black ponytails swing. "Not a chance." She grinned up at him and batted her eyelashes.

"Right." Cheff made a sour face. "Okay, then, let's get going." He handed me a stout metal bar about three feet long with a claw at one end. "Here, Books, you carry this. I'll take the lamp. Buttons, you… do whatever it is you always do."

We crawled through the dirt tunnel that led from our secret underground room to the storm-drain system and eased ourselves down to the shiny wet cobblestones. My small, slender Lildur build made it easy for me to navigate the narrow tunnel, but my spiky hair seemed to attract every particle of loose dirt.

Cheff led the way northward, carefully counting the intersecting tunnels. When we got to the fifth junction, he turned right, eastward. "This way."

We splashed after Cheff down the long, dark storm drain. Again, he counted junctions, six this time, turned left, and headed rapidly northward again for several hundred yards. He slowed down and held the mining lamp up to examine the walls. "Look for a chalk mark, an X."

Shortly, Buttons pointed to a small, white X right below the handle of a rusted metal door. "There it is, Cheff! That must be the one."

"Yep, that's the one, all right. Good work, Buttons. Let me have that wrecking bar, Books."

I handed him the bar and he pried at the rusted metal door.

"I should have brought some oil," Cheff said, "but I didn't expect it to be this hard to open." He worked the bar a few more times. The ancient door creaked and groaned. Flakes of rust and dirt fell to the tunnel floor, but the door wouldn't budge. He rested one end of the bar on the floor of the tunnel and wiped the sweat from his forehead. "It's stuck. It opened farther than this before. It's almost as though… as though someone has locked it from the inside."

He raised the bar again, but before he could begin prying, the door crashed open with a loud thunk! We froze where we stood. A bright light from inside blazed into our eyes, blinding us. A deep voice roared, "All right, you kids, don't move a muscle. You're under arrest. I've got you now!" then broke into insane laughter.

ABOUT THE AUTHOR

Liam Kincaid was born to parents of Scottish descent on December 30, 1953, in a boxcar in the high Sierra Nevadas during a raging snowstorm. After graduating from high school, Liam declined a medical scholarship to Stanford University and a musical scholarship to Julliard.

Instead, Liam served for a time in the United States Air Force, then traveled the world working at many jobs, including professional woodworker and stilts maker, maintenance supply specialist for Pacific Southwest Airlines, kelp processor for Kelco, hot-air balloon pilot, cow clipper (for one day), house painter, time-share salesman in Mexico, hospital housekeeper, school bus driver, wrestling-arena peanut vendor, street musician, English teacher in the Dominican Republic, ranch hand, e-zine publisher, bio-diesel manufacturer, carpet cleaner, pig photographer, and computer programmer.

When his roaming days were over, he longed for the wholesome science-fiction adventure stories of his youth, so he decided to try his hand at writing some. Having raised four sons, he was inspired by the powerful, astounding feats a group of intelligent, determined children can accomplish.

Liam welcomes correspondence from his readers and does his best to answer each one personally. E-mail him at: LiamKincaid@WorldHeartEpic.com

About the Artist

Daniel Wood is a freelance artist and illustrator based in Richmond, Virginia.

He honed his skills at Virginia Commonwealth University, where he earned a Bachelor of Fine Arts degree in Communication Arts. Drawing is the love of his life, so much so that he often spends his spare time drawing the day away.

Skilled in many forms of illustration, including concept art, comic art, book illustrations, and game art, both colored and black-and-white, he specializes in fantasy, science-fiction, and all of their more specific subgenres. Every project is a joyful challenge to transform the author's concepts into compelling visual imagery.

Daniel welcomes discussions regarding new projects. See more of his work at DanielWoodArt.com, or e-mail him at woodillustration@gmail.com.

WE NEED YOUR HELP!

Dear Reader,

We depend on your reviews and word-of-mouth.

If you enjoyed this book, please help spread the word through Twitter, Facebook, and other social media, and please consider giving us five stars and writing a brief review on Amazon.com and Goodreads.com, or your favorite book-review venue.

Thank you very much!

Liam Kincaid
North California Coast,
March 2024

To view full-size, full-color maps and illustrations,
and to learn more about Fellstone and its peoples, visit:

https://FellstoneTales.com